NO SECRET LIKE NANTUCKET

A SWEET ISLAND INN NOVEL (BOOK 5)

GRACE PALMER

JOIN MY MAILING LIST!

Click the link below to join my mailing list and receive updates, freebies, release announcements, and more!

JOIN HERE:

https://sendfox.com/lp/19y8p3

ALSO BY GRACE PALMER

Sweet Island Inn

No Home Like Nantucket (Book 1)

No Beach Like Nantucket (Book 2)

No Wedding Like Nantucket (Book 3)

No Love Like Nantucket (Book 4)

No Secret Like Nantucket (Book 5)

No Forever Like Nantucket (Book 6)

No Summer Like Nantucket (Book 7) (coming soon!)

Willow Beach Inn

Just South of Paradise (Book 1)

Just South of Perfect (Book 2)

Just South of Sunrise (Book 3)

Just South of Christmas (Book 4)

NO SECRET LIKE NANTUCKET

A SWEET ISLAND INN NOVEL (BOOK 5)

A secret bundle in a dusty corner sends the Benson family reeling.

It wasn't meant to be uncovered.

But when her son Brent stumbles across something curious hidden in the workshop, innkeeper Mae Benson must relive events she thought she left thirty years in the past.

Her boyfriend Dominic is doing his best to help. But the arrival of a movie crew on Nantucket to film the adaptation of his latest novel has upended everything at the Sweet Island Inn.

And Mae's children are just as preoccupied.

Eliza, eight months pregnant, can't be reached—and Mae is terrified that something is going wrong with the baby.

Holly is dealing with an unexpected houseguest with a grim and mysterious past.

And Sara is struggling to answer a thorny question: who is stealing from her restaurant?

Follow along with the trials, tribulations, and triumphs of the Benson family in this sweet, clean women's fiction novel.

If you haven't already, check out the other books in the series:

No Home Like Nantucket (Book 1)

No Beach Like Nantucket (Book 2)

No Wedding Like Nantucket (Book 3)

No Love Like Nantucket (Book 4)

1

ELIZA

Summer on Nantucket was usually postcard-perfect.

Bronze sun over an azure ocean. Sand dunes, white as pearls, framed by lush beach grasses waving in the sea breeze.

Everything warm. Everything beautiful. Everything glowing with life.

Today was... not that.

Today, even though it was the middle of June, the clouds outside Eliza Patterson's window were gray and thick and her toes felt like ten chips of ice on the end of her feet.

The moment she stepped out of bed—though "rolled out" is more like it, seeing as how she was eight months pregnant and nothing she did was done gracefully anymore—she hissed and pulled her feet back off the frigid hardwood floor.

Getting out of bed was tough enough these days, with the exhaustion and the extra weight around her middle.

But add cold feet to the mix? Nothing had ever seemed more difficult.

Her husband, Oliver, emerged from the bathroom by the time she finally coaxed herself upright. He was still in his pajamas, his dark hair an unruly mass on top of his head.

"You were snoring," he informed her. "Loudly."

"I most certainly was not," Eliza retorted.

Truth be told, he was probably right. If her sisters Holly and Sara were to be believed, she'd snored while pregnant with her first daughter, Winter, too.

But Eliza preferred to believe her sisters and her husband were dirty, rotten liars, the whole lot of them.

Growing a child came with enough embarrassing symptoms. She didn't need people around her pointing them out.

Oliver flopped down on the bed next to her and pulled the blanket up to his chin with a shiver. "Alrighty then. Must've been someone else snoring in our bed."

"Must've been," Eliza agreed.

"Or maybe the neighbors were running their leaf blower all night. Right outside our bedroom window. As they like to do." Oliver rolled over and batted his eyes. "Was that it, dearest?"

"Don't 'dearest' me," she snapped, tossing the comforter over his face.

Eliza's husband had taken to calling her any number of pandering pet names over the course of their eight-month-long marriage— usually when she was annoyed with him. She hated them all equally.

She didn't hate his teasing, though. It was how he expressed love.

Thirty-five years old hardly qualified for a senior citizen discount, but Eliza needed reminding of that from time to time.

Oliver sure didn't.

He still teased and laughed and played games like he lived his life in a sandbox. Everything in his world was a game. To this day, he'd never seen a grocery cart he didn't want to turn into a race car. Clouds weren't clouds to him, they were creatures, a whole menagerie in the sky to be cooed at and admired.

And whenever Oliver roped their eighteen-month-old daughter into his little fantasies, she'd laugh and laugh and laugh. The kind of laughter a mother never forgets.

She felt lighter with Oliver around. Younger.

She felt like she could breathe.

Winter's cries echoed fuzzily through baby monitor speakers. Oliver jumped out of bed before Eliza could budge.

"You take a shower and get ready for your appointment," he said on his way out the door. "I'm on dad duty."

"Aye-aye," Eliza murmured. She threw a salute at his retreating back. Then she turned her attention to the arduous trek from bed to bathroom.

But with the promise of an uninterrupted hot shower, walking across the chilly hardwood floor wasn't such a daunting chore.

Alone time—especially time spent taking care of herself—happened so rarely that Eliza snatched at it when she could. Even before Winter, Eliza hardly had time for herself.

Until a few years ago, she'd been running the rat race as an investment banker in Manhattan. She'd been engaged to a narcissistic drug addict and failing miserably at keeping in contact with her parents.

And then came the changes.

The breakup with her ex-fiancé, Clay Reeves. The unexpected pregnancy. The exodus back home to the island paradise where she was raised.

But it was the death of her father that had done more to make Eliza feel older than almost anything else.

She'd always thought she'd be in her fifties at the very least before she had to consider losing a parent. But Henry Benson had died suddenly. Tragically. Now, even three years later, Eliza had to work hard not to be bitter about the theft her family had endured.

Especially as her daughter—*daughters,* she amended silently in her head; that was still taking some getting-used-to—grew up without their grandfather.

On the flip side, she didn't have to work to be thankful for the family that still surrounded her.

All of her siblings were back in Nantucket, her mother was the most devoted grandmother in existence, and Oliver had stepped up as not only a husband, but a father to Winter in a way Eliza never dared imagine.

For all the heartache, beauty still reigned.

After dressing in maternity jeans and a fluttery, short-sleeved top—one of only four shirts that still fit over her belly—Eliza walked down the hallway to the sounds of Winter giggling and Oliver talking.

"...Attention, passengers, this is your pilot speaking..."

Oliver held a bite of pancake high in the air, his hand cupped over his mouth as he pretended to speak over an airplane intercom.

"...We seem to have encountered an unexpected obstacle in the form of a giant, hungry baby..."

He swirled the spoon through the air, dodging Winter's attempts to catch the pancake. The little girl cackled. Eyes bright, hands reaching.

"...I'm doing my best to reroute. Please remain seated and belted in, and I will update you as—Ahh! Mayday! Mayday!"

He let out a long scream and then crackly static as the bite swooped down into Winter's open mouth.

"A little macabre, don't you think?" Eliza grabbed the coffee Oliver had left on the table for her. "Most parents go for a simple choo-choo train."

"Winter has an extremely advanced sense of humor. It's actually rather dark, I'm afraid."

"She's a year-and-a-half old."

He shrugged. "Hey, you provided half the DNA. I'm just catering to my audience."

Eliza could only laugh and shake her head as she gathered her things for the day's errands.

Behind her, Oliver had switched gears. This new pancake-related catastrophe had something to do with black holes and the spacetime continuum. It too ended in Winter laughing like a loon and chewing up her breakfast greedily, so there wasn't much Eliza could do to object.

As Winter ate, Oliver looked over his shoulder at Eliza. "What time is your appointment this morning?"

"Eight-thirty."

Eliza reached absently for her phone to check the time, but it wasn't in her pocket. She must have left it in the bedroom.

"It's just a check-up, right? I don't need to be there?"

"No. And thank goodness for that. Your plaid pajama shorts aren't exactly suited for a doctor's office."

Oliver frowned. "*You* bought these for me. Anyway, dress code aside, I can hurry and get ready if you want me there."

A few appointments back, the doctor had told Eliza the baby was in a breech position.

"There's still time for the baby to turn, but you should prepare yourself for the possibility of a C-section," Dr. Geiger had warned.

Despite the doctor's assurances that the baby was doing fine, Oliver was deeply concerned. He insisted Eliza keep her feet up and rest as much as possible. That she not lifting anything heavier than their daughter. That she do some horrendously boring stretching routine he'd found on the Internet.

It took weeks for him to relax enough to let Eliza go back to her normal habits.

She didn't want to worry him anymore than he already was. Especially since she felt confident the doctor would have good news for her today.

"It's a standard, boring appointment. We aren't even doing a scan today. I can go alone." Eliza caught a glimpse of the digital clock above the oven and yelped. "I have to leave right now, though."

Eliza swallowed one more sip of coffee while Oliver jogged to the door. He grabbed the car key from the hook next to the wall and held it up in the air, demanding a quick kiss before Eliza could snatch it from his hand and hustle down the porch.

"No running. You don't want to go into labor," he joked, waving from the doorway. "And no speeding!"

"Yes, yes!" She waved him off and hurried away.

Everything was going to be fine. Oliver had no reason to fret at all.

Even if Eliza had wanted to speed, the traffic in Nantucket wouldn't allow it.

There weren't many cars on the road, but Eliza still managed to find herself trapped behind the slowest folks in existence. They puttered over the cobblestones mere inches at a time.

Her haste to get from one place to another was one of the New York habits Eliza had yet to break. She'd grown up in Nantucket, but New York had a way of resetting one's expectation of personal pace for good.

After parking in the lot in front of Dr. Geiger's practice, Eliza jogged inside and gave the receptionist her name through a wheeze.

"Sit down and take a rest," the kind, middle-aged woman said. "The doctor will be with you in just a moment."

Eliza dropped down into her usual spot in the back corner of the waiting room and took long, deep breaths in through her nose and out through her mouth.

A whole slew of magazines were fanned out across the coffee table in front of her. Fishing and boating, cooking and interior decorating. "The Nantucket Special," her brother Brent always called it. "I swear there's a mail order subscription that just sends you all this junk every month. Along with nautical wallpaper and a pair of boat shoes."

Eliza didn't much feel like reading, though. And the small, square television in the corner was tuned to soap operas, which was if anything even less appealing than the latest trends in marlin-luring technology.

So she leaned her head back against the chair, still trying to catch her breath.

As she did, her stomach tightened.

Braxton Hicks contractions were common enough this late in pregnancy, but this clamp-down viciously snatched away what little breath Eliza had left.

She sat forward, hands on her stomach, and bit down a pained groan that wanted badly to force its way out of her.

Two or three or maybe twenty seconds of sharp, unrelenting pain— she wasn't sure how long it lasted—until the contraction passed and she could finally release the breath she'd been holding.

The contraction was just practice, she knew. Her body's way of preparing for delivery.

Still, it unnerved her. Thrilled her, of course, but unnerved her.

Just a few more weeks, little one, she thought, patting her stomach. *You have to stay put for a few more weeks.*

"Eliza Patterson!" a short-haired nurse called, holding the wooden door open with her hip. She held a clipboard in her other hand.

"That's me," she croaked in an odd voice that sounded nothing like her. She stood, still a little light-headed, and tottered along after the nurse.

As they walked, Eliza tried to peek at the clipboard in the woman's hand. The folks who worked here were always scrutinizing those pesky things. Dr. Geiger, especially. After a few months of visits, Eliza was more familiar with the top of his head than with his face.

She never asked to see the clipboard and he never offered to show her. But Eliza wondered what it said all the same.

The nurse led her back to the exam room, took her blood pressure, and asked her the usual questions.

"How have you been feeling?"

"Tired," Eliza admitted. "But good."

"Any discomfort?"

"I've had a few contractions this morning. I suppose that means there's a light at the end of the tunnel."

The nurse smiled, but her mouth was pinched. "Any pain beyond what is considered normal?"

Eliza shook her head, but before she could answer properly, her stomach tightened again. She winced.

"Well, what's normal?" she joked. When the nurse didn't laugh, she sobered and added, "That one kind of hurt, I suppose. But I'm fine."

"Mhmm." The nurse made a hurried note of something on the clipboard. "Dr. Geiger will be with you in just a few minutes."

Then she was gone.

Eliza looked around when she was alone again. She had always loved doctor's offices. A place for everything and everything in its place.

The walls were beige, the floor tiles square and flecked with mottled browns, and the exam table covered in the white, crinkly paper that existed nowhere else on planet Earth.

Without a window to glimpse the sky outside, Eliza could have been in a doctor's office anywhere in the world.

Except for the wall of island babies.

Someone—Eliza presumed it wasn't Dr. Geiger, but you never knew for certain; some people had odd ways of making a space their own— had put up a bulletin board in the room, and it was absolutely dripping with pictures of newborns.

Some of them were dated, almost as old as Eliza was. Others looked brand new, fresh as the dawn.

A rough estimate pegged more than seventy-five percent of the pictures as nauseatingly "Nantuckety."

Babies swaddled in a fisherman's net.

Babies wearing fishermen's bucket hats.

Babies in tiny swim trunks embroidered with whales.

Eliza tried to imagine her daughter's picture up on the wall amongst the others. But for some reason, she couldn't. Which was odd, because when she was pregnant with Winter, she'd had no problem envisioning things. She'd seen her first daughter's life play out before her eyes, long before the girl had ever been born. First words, first steps, first loves, first everything.

Not so with this one.

Odd.

A quick knock on the door interrupted her thoughts. Dr. Geiger came strolling in a beat later, frowning down at the clipboard in his hands as per usual.

"Mrs. Patterson," he said on an exhale, never looking up. "How are you feeling today?"

"Fine. Tired." Eliza laughed again, though Dr. Geiger didn't join her.

She'd long ago given up delving into Dr. Geiger's personality. As one of only a few obstetricians on the island, he had a full slate of patients and barely enough time to see them. But what he lacked in personal rapport, he made up for by being an incredibly well-respected doctor.

The man radiated competency. Eliza of all people could respect that.

"Marcy said you've been having contractions." He dropped the clipboard on the counter and motioned for Eliza to lay back on the table.

"Just a few. Braxton Hicks, I'm sure." She sounded confident, and for the most part, she felt that way.

But there was a niggle of concern, somewhere deep down. A festering doubt.

He nodded and lifted the hem of her shirt, feeling around on her stomach before grabbing the doppler and checking for a heartbeat.

Eliza tried to feel something when she heard the whoosh-whoosh of the doppler, but it eluded her. It didn't sound like a heartbeat. The stormy sound didn't make her own heart jump with delight.

That feeling wouldn't come until the baby was in her arms.

Then Eliza would feel everything.

Abruptly, Dr. Geiger pulled her shirt back over her belly and held out a cold hand to help her sit up. "I'd like to get some images of the baby today. Just a precaution."

"Oh. Okay." She wasn't due for another scan before the baby was born, but surely this was all normal.

Precaution, as Dr. Geiger had said. That was a nice word.

"This way."

Eliza only had to walk two doors down to find herself in the dim sonographer's room. A petite, thin-lipped woman ushered her into place and set to work without a word.

Eliza gazed around the room. A television hung from the ceiling, ostensibly so she could watch as the scan came to life. But today, the screen remained blank.

Not to worry. If there was a problem, they'd point it out to her.

Plus, she could feel her little girl kicking around in her belly, playing bongos on her ribs the way she liked to do.

All was well. All was fine. She had no reason to fret at all.

After only a couple minutes, the sonographer pulled away the wand and handed Eliza a sheet of paper towel to wipe the jelly off her stomach.

"The doctor will be in to talk with you about the results. It should only be a minute or two," she said with another thin smile.

"Thanks," murmured Eliza. The woman nodded and slipped out of the room.

Eliza patted around for her phone. She'd told Oliver this appointment would be quick, so she figured she ought to send him a text to let him know what was happening. She didn't want him to worry.

But it wasn't in her pocket, and when Dr. Geiger swept into the room, she abandoned the hunt.

As expected, the clipboard was in his hand once again.

But this time, his face was lifted. Aimed at her.

He had green eyes, she noticed. Maybe she'd noticed before, but if so, she'd never truly looked at them. They suited him. Piercing, intelligent, frank.

Up until perhaps thirty seconds ago, that would have made her feel better. A doctor should have eyes like that.

But she'd have preferred they not be looking at her so intensely. Because, when Dr. Geiger made direct eye contact with Eliza, her stomach fluttered nervously for the first time all morning.

"What is your pain level right now?" he asked. "On a scale of one to ten."

Right on cue, Eliza's stomach squeezed in another contraction. This one wrapped around to her lower back, a vise grip working on her from the inside.

"Three."

"Okay, good." With deft fingers, Dr. Geiger slid a sonogram photo out from between other papers in his stack and held it in the air. "So you seem to have suffered a placental abruption."

The words meant nothing to Eliza. But they didn't sound good.

Dr. Geiger kept talking. The next pitter-patter of words coming from his mouth made as little sense as the first few. Heavier on the anatomy than a former finance woman would understand.

He pointed at the picture and said more things. Mostly, Eliza just looked at his eyes. They really were a very nice green.

She realized with a start that he was waiting for her to respond. To her embarrassment, she had no idea what the question was.

"I'm sorry, could you repeat that?" she mumbled.

"I asked if you were still with me."

She started to nod like she was with him every step of the way. But then she wilted under those piercing eyes and shook her head instead. "I, uh... no, I apologize. Could you just tell me what that all means?"

He lowered the pictures and sighed. "It means you are going to meet your baby earlier than planned. And since she is still breech, it will be a C-section."

Eliza once again patted the pocket where she usually kept her phone, already drafting a text to Oliver in her mind. *You're not gonna believe this...*

But her pocket was empty. That's when she realized she'd left it at home. Forgot to grab it in her hurry to get out the door.

What a day for that happen.

She'd just have to tell Oliver everything the moment she got home. He'd worry, of course, but as always, there was nothing to worry about. A Caesarean was not such a big deal. It would all be fine.

No reason for anyone to fret.

"Okay," she said, "so, scheduling-wise, my nephew and my mom have a joint birthday party tonight, but beyond that, I've kept my schedule clear because all kinds of craziness happens towards the end of pregnancies, am I right, so anyway I'm glad I did that because really any time this week works for me, or next if that's better, perhaps Monday, or maybe—"

Dr. Geiger blinked and held up his hand. Eliza's words died on her lips.

"Mrs. Patterson, I think you're misunderstanding me. You are not leaving here today. The baby has to come right now."

2

BRENT

114 HOWARD STREET—BRENT & ROSE'S HOUSE

Almost a year into living with Rose and Brent still couldn't get over what it was like waking up next to her.

If they traded places, she would think her hair messy, but he thought it was endearingly gorgeous. He liked the tousled look of her when she first woke. Cheeks pinked by a good night's rest, hair in wild disarray.

Thinking back over the last few years, Brent smiled. He had matured a lot. Perhaps he had been a late-bloomer when it came to fully embracing adulthood, but once the process had begun, it came to fruition fast.

Susanna, Rose's daughter, helped with that. Before her, Brent's biggest responsibility was his dog, Henrietta. Now, he had a full-fledged tiny human to look after.

It was a lot, but he also couldn't think of anything in the world he'd rather be doing.

As he gently brushed the stray lock of hair from Rose's forehead, Brent felt he was well on his way. The alcoholic, depressed mess he had been seemed to lie in the far and distant past. A memory from another life.

He supposed it was, in a way.

Rose stirred and softly groaned in the back of her throat. Her hand stretched across the bed and felt for him, curling into his shirt.

"Well, well, well—look who decided to finally wake up." He kissed her forehead. "Thought you were going to sleep all day."

"What time is it?" Pushing to her elbow, Rose looked toward the window and immediately scowled at him.

"Barely past sunrise," he said.

"You scared me. I thought I was going to be late."

"Impossible," he said. "Your internal clock never fails. I'm not even sure why you set your alarm."

She leaned over and pressed a kiss to his cheek. "Because the one day I don't set it, I'll oversleep. It's the rule of the universe."

Brent grabbed at her nightgown as she slid to the edge of the bed, feet already in her slippers. "You just woke up. Stay in bed."

"Can't." She pried his fingers loose and kissed his knuckles. "I told you yesterday, I have to be into work early today."

"I remember," Brent sighed. "I was hoping you'd forgotten."

"You're handsome, but not 'causing a case of amnesia' handsome."

As the bathroom door closed, Brent chucked a pillow at it. "Gah! My ego!"

Her laugh echoed underneath the door.

Thirty minutes later, Rose came out of the bathroom with her hair artfully arranged into a bun on top of her head and her makeup done. She dressed in a pair of dark gray cigarette pants and a bright blue short-sleeve button-down with a ruffled Peter Pan collar.

Brent had never heard of a Peter Pan collar before Rose came into his life, but now he was intimately familiar. An essential part of The Rose Uniform, as he called it.

He whistled as she slipped on a pair of red ballet flats. "How does a man like me get this lucky? You look amazing."

Rose raised a brow at his bare chest and bedraggled pajama bottoms. "You, too. Very haute couture."

He held his arms out in welcome. "The offer still stands. I'll be here all day if you wanna play hooky."

"You better not be," Rose warned, a twinkle in her eye. "Your mom and Dominic are coming to stay soon."

"So?"

"So I don't want them to think we're slobs!" she said with slightly more alarm in her voice. "We need to clear out a room upstairs for them and make some space in the workshop for their stuff. Your mom said the film crew is making them remove some furniture, and I don't know if you've peeked in that pigsty you call a workshop recently, but there's barely enough room for a house plant, much less a couch."

Brent waved a dismissive hand. "My mom has known me my whole life. She already thinks I'm a slob."

"Some of us don't have the benefit of being related to her," Rose drawled.

"You being related to my mother would not be a benefit for me. It would be illegal."

Rose laughed. "I only mean she has to love you. She doesn't have to love me."

"First, she loves you. And Susanna. Neither of you have to 'earn' her love," Brent said. "Second, I'm only teasing. I am going to take care of all the cleaning and tidying today like I'm Cinderella. Even though, like I said, it's unnecessary. She already loves you."

Rose hurried to the bed and pressed a quick kiss to Brent's lips. "Well, I better keep working at it, just in case. You know me—I'm an over-achiever."

"You mean *I'll* keep working at!" Brent yelled as she threw a wave over her shoulder and disappeared into the hallway. "I'm the one who has to do all the cleaning!"

Almost the moment the door shut behind Rose, Susanna woke up, and Brent had to turn his attention to "The Other Woman," as he called her—a joke that pretty much no one else found funny but that never failed to make him laugh.

The first item on the agenda was getting the little girl dressed.

"I can't wear a flower shirt with flower tights," Susanna said, wrinkling her nose and swinging her pajama-clad legs from the edge of her bed.

"What about a pink shirt with flower tights?" Brent asked hopefully.

"I want to wear my sparkly purple tights. And my light-up shoes!" She jumped off the bed and pushed past Brent to get into the closet.

Ten minutes later, she had on a pair of sparkly purple tights, a yellow- and black-striped bumblebee t-shirt, and pink light-up shoes.

How she could lack faith in Brent's clothing choices, yet come up with this outfit, Brent had no idea. But he was smart enough to know not to question it. The women ruled the roost at 114 Howard Street. Brent Benson was merely along for the ride.

"Runway ready," he said with a big smile and a thumbs up. "Now, waffles and then we're shipping you off to China."

Susanna shoved him in the thigh. "You can't send me to China!" she cackled.

Brent smiled softly, unfazed. "Did I say China? I meant daycare. Come on—I'll race you to the kitchen."

He lost the race due to some questionable delaying tactics on Susanna's part, but that was all well and good.

Everything was, really.

Not a thing in his world out of place.

By the time Brent made it back to the house from daycare drop-off, a paper cup of coffee in hand from Two Birds Coffee downtown, he already felt like he needed a break. But there was no time. He had a to-do list to tackle.

First, Brent cleared out his old bedroom with a vengeance.

Most of the furniture was hand-me-downs from his sisters and covered in dabs of nail polish, perfume bottle stains, and stickers that had been haphazardly scraped off over the years.

Brent moved two bedside tables, a desk, and a fraying wicker disc chair down to a growing pile of trash next to the curb.

He also ripped all of the band posters and swimsuit models off of the walls and wadded them up in the trash. Teenage Brent had never been so betrayed.

Then he started the deep clean. He threw all of the linens in the laundry, swept the floors, dusted what furniture remained.

Lunchtime found Brent sweating and worn, but at least the room looked comfortable. Nothing like the lurid den of teenage boyhood it had been earlier that morning. Mom and Dominic would be just fine in here.

Onto the workshop, then.

The space was perpetually covered in a thin layer of sawdust, even years after his father's death.

Henry Benson had been handy. He made built-in bookshelves for the living room, a bassinet for an infant Grady, and built the deck on the back of the house ten years earlier.

But his main and most beloved hobby was whittling. He could sit all day in the shop with the large door wide open, the breeze swirling wood chips and sawdust around his feet, and turn a solid block of wood into anything. A wooden spoon or a French bulldog or a walking stick covered in flowering vines.

Brent could almost hear the old sounds now as he stepped into the familiar space. As he inhaled the familiar smell.

Life's meant to be enjoyed, isn't it, son? Dad's catchphrase, ringing in Brent's head almost like he was standing right beside him.

Eliza, ever the pragmatist, had suggested selling all of Dad's old tools, but Brent couldn't quite bring himself to do it. Brent had all of his own tools now. But he'd learned everything he knew about wood-working and construction in this workshop. Using these tools. He wasn't ready to part with anything just yet.

But he could certainly tidy up.

Over the course of an hour, Brent played a real-life game of Tetris. He arranged and rearranged a cutting table, various saws and saw horses, large wood scraps and pieces of leftover trim, and seemingly endless bags of small hand tools until it all fit just right.

At the very least, they'd be able to squeeze a couch and a few other large items into the shop. Which seemed like more than enough space to Brent.

He was ready to call it quits. Then his eyes fell on the shelves stuffed fat with half-finished projects that Dad had left behind.

Some of the pieces were misshapen mistakes his dad couldn't let go of. Mom always said Henry was a sentimental pack rat, and it seemed Brent was well on his way to being that way, too.

"You're a hoarder!" Rose had accused more than once. "You and your whole family. Not one of you Bensons can bear to part with a single thing."

He denied it, of course. But she may've had a point.

So, with a sigh, he set upon the shelves, muttering under his breath the whole time, "I am *not* a hoarder. I am *not* a hoarder. I am *not* a hoarder..."

In the end, two of the four shelves was available for anything Mom or Dominic might need to store.

Brent was just about to call it quits for the day when one last item on the top shelf, curiously wrapped in a dusty white trash bag, caught his eye.

The bag was tucked in the corner next to the four mobiles his dad had carved for Brent and his sisters.

Each of the mobiles had the same overall design—a wooden placard with the child's name and then four arms from which hand-carved bobbles hung.

Folks on the island were always after Henry to carve them something or other, and as much as he liked to oblige them, these pieces he kept for himself. For his family.

No one but a Benson child got a mobile like this.

And each Benson child got one uniquely their own. Eliza's, for instance, held planets and shooting stars bobbing from the strings.

Holly's featured a menagerie of farm animals, which she still jokingly complained about. "Eliza got shooting stars and I got a cow," she always grumbled.

Sara's mobile dripped with rainbows and butterflies, a pairing so ironic Brent couldn't help but laugh. Nothing about his sister was as gentle or delicate as a butterfly. Dad didn't call her his "little bull" for nothing.

And Brent's, perhaps the most fitting of all, was the ocean brought to life. A bright blue fishing boat, a sea bass with shimmery rainbow scales, a fishing pole with a pink worm dangling from the hook.

Then, shoved into the back corner, there was the plastic-wrapped bundle.

Brent grabbed the ladder from the wall and climbed up it carefully.

The bag was even dustier than it looked, clearly not touched in years and years. Whatever was inside felt fragile. It shifted and twisted in his hands, and Brent was afraid he'd broken it as he freed it from the jammed-up spot in the far corner.

But when he was back on solid ground, he ripped open the trash bag and realized why it felt so unstable.

It was another mobile.

Brent frowned. His parents had always told him they'd refused to make any other mobiles. That it was for them and them alone. Had

Dad finally relented for a friend or a coworker with a newborn on the way?

Or maybe it was a discarded mistake. A slipped hand, a broken chip. But when he held it up, the bobbles hanging from fishing line yellowed with age, Brent didn't see any obvious mistakes.

This mobile was ocean-themed—or, really, Nantucket-themed. It had seashells, a red-and-white striped lighthouse, a replica of the old mill, and a piece of wood chiseled into the outline of the island.

Then, he saw the name placard at the top.

Christopher.

Brent turned the placard over, and just as he had for each of the other mobiles, his dad had carved a year.

It was a year before his eldest sister Eliza was born.

A flurry of possible explanations rushed through Brent's mind as he held the carefully-crafted mobile in his hands.

But only one made sense.

His father had only made mobiles for his own children. Never anyone else. Which meant... Christopher must have been one of Henry's kids.

Brent had a secret brother.

3

SARA

LITTLE BULL RESTAURANT

Little Bull was alive.

From where she sat inside her office—drowning with order forms, budget templates, and piles of endless business documents she could make neither heads nor tails of—Sara Benson could hear the kitchen bursting with life behind her.

Lunch service wouldn't be for another hour, but her staff was already busy. Perfecting sauces, prepping marinades, running the restaurant like the finely-tuned machine that it was.

And they had to be.

People did not schedule reservations three months in advance to have a mediocre meal. They came for food that made them swoon.

And swoon they did. In droves and in repeats, in ones and twos and tens, they came and they ate and they fell in love with the food on their plates. When they left, they told their friends, and those friends told other friends, and before she knew it, Sara Benson was running one of the most popular fine dining restaurants in Nantucket.

Martin Hogan couldn't kill that if he tried.

He had tried, of course. The notoriously prickish food critic had done has damndest to sever the head from the bull. But to no avail.

Martin wasn't entirely to blame, though. Gavin Crawford was the true culprit.

So far, Sara had refrained from mailing glowing reviews to her former boss and not-quite-ex. That didn't mean she wouldn't do it eventually.

After all, you don't show up to the opening night of someone's restaurant, sneering food critic in tow, in order to extort them into sleeping with you—unless you're overdue for a little karmic revenge.

Sara smiled at the memory.

It never got old, reliving the moment she'd pressed the room key back into Gavin's big, lusty paw and told him to get lost.

Even if it had resulted in one doozy of a bad review. If the Little Bull had been the *Titanic*, Hogan's review was the nearest thing to an iceberg.

But Sara's little restaurant that could had come out the other side unscathed. Unsinkable.

Though the paperwork piling up on her desk might be the death of her after all.

Sara's business manager, Patrick Burton, shuffled a stack of papers together on the other side of the desk. He set them aside pointedly, letting them thwack as they hit the table.

Sara, pulled from her thoughts, looked up to find him staring at her, as humorless as ever.

Quickly, she tried to play back the last couple seconds of potential conversation with zero luck. "Sorry, what was that?"

"You've had these in front of you for ten minutes," Patrick repeated, tapping a stack of files in front of her with the tip of his pen. "Are you done with them?"

Patrick knew the answer to that question. Because he knew Sara.

Their relationship worked because they were a study in opposites. Where Sara was driven by excitement and passion, by the raw drive to succeed and prove everyone else wrong, Patrick was driven by numbers. Facts. Organization.

He placed a large importance on petty little nuisances. Things like the bottom line, making payroll, and paying the bills.

She hated that stuff. But without Patrick, Sara would be lost in a stormy Nantucket sea of paperwork and business jargon. It was why she cherished him so.

"So," she began warily, "hypothetically speaking, if I was to ask you what these papers were *for,* exactly—not that I don't know, because I definitely do; I'm just asking to make sure that *you* know—"

He sighed and cut her off. "Approval on tomorrow's order, signature of approval on the payroll, and I need the register X-outs and Z-outs for the last week," Patrick intoned, tone flat, betraying neither annoyance nor patience.

When he was in business mode, he reminded Sara of a robot. A vitally necessary robot, but a robot nonetheless.

"Roger that. Good job—you nailed it. That's exactly what these are," she mumbled, lowering her head and getting to work.

In the beginning, Sara assumed the business side of being a business owner would begin to come more naturally to her. Maybe that was still true and, one day, she would be a natural.

Until then, however, she had to muddle along under Patrick's guidance.

The one thing she'd taken on in the last few months, however, was the X-outs and Z-outs. Patrick had been handling it for her, but Sara wanted to do more than sign order forms. She wanted to understand, at least on some small level, precisely how her business was running.

Unfortunately, the latest batches of numbers were not behaving so neatly.

Sara had been noticing some discrepancies in the last few weeks. They were minor at first, just a few dollars here or there. But as the weeks passed, the squiggly little numbers that refused to lie in place kept growing and growing. Large enough that it was time for Sara to swallow her pride and admit to Patrick that she might not know what she was doing after all.

Surely it was just a math mistake. Sara's fault, nothing else. Patrick would fix it. Patrick would know what was wrong.

"Okay, so I might have made a mistake."

"Go on." He folded his hands on the table and waited for her to continue.

"With the X-outs and Z-outs," she explained hesitantly, "I've noticed some discrepancies. It could be my mistake, but—"

Patrick held out his hand and Sara slid them across the table without a second glance. It felt like passing off a hot potato. Nothing but blissful relief washed through her.

"How long have you been noticing the discrepancy?"

Sara twisted her mouth to one side. "Three weeks, maybe? Definitely no more than four. Five at the most."

Patrick pushed away from the table and strode out of Sara's office. She twiddled her thumbs and listened to the sounds of the kitchen. *That* was where she belonged. With clacking pots and blaring music and the sizzle of delicious things percolating.

Not here, in this stuffy office that smelled overwhelmingly like lavender disinfectant.

A moment later, Patrick reappeared with a small stack of file folders and sat back in front of her. "I'll check over all the records for the last month. It'll take me a little while, so if there's something you need to tend to in the kitchen…"

He shifted his eyes briefly in the direction of the silver double doors.

"I have prep to do, anyway," Sara said gratefully. "Gimme a yell when you're ready for me."

With that, she slid out of the chair and hurried into the kitchen before Patrick could change his mind.

As she swept into the kitchen, she felt like a kid who'd been told by the principal she could leave detention early. Sometimes she had to remind herself that she was the boss and he was the employee.

Still—no reason to look a gift horse in the mouth, right?

Her seafood supplier had brought in a nice haul of fresh cod that morning that needed to be skinned and deboned. Her sous chef Jose had offered, but Sara asked him to leave it to her.

There was a deep sense of calm that came from the simple act of preparing food. Meditation, in the oddest way. Sara had been doing it long enough that her muscle memory took control. Her mind went blank, and she was able to lose herself in the process. While she worked, time didn't exist. Nothing existed beyond the countertop and the food in front of her.

The cod was stacked in the refrigerator, already rinsed, dried, and wrapped in wax paper. Waiting for her.

"C'mere, you beauties." Sara pulled out the tray and plopped it down at her station.

Some people didn't enjoy the technical, gritty aspects of cooking. When meat needed to be sliced and bones wrenched free.

But Sara loved the physicality of it. It felt like *doing* something. It felt real.

The white fish was popular with her more finicky patrons, the kind of folks who said they didn't like the taste of seafood. Paired with a pop of tomato-lime salsa, though, they devoured it and begged for more.

When she finished with the fish, Sara broiled the bell peppers in the oven. Once the skins were blackened and bubbly, she peeled them and threw the steaming insides into the food processer, along with roughly chopped tomatoes and fresh lime juice. A hearty pinch of Maldon sea salt went in last to finish out the simple salsa and bring it all to life.

Just before Sara cranked on the food processer, Patrick called to her from the doorway. "Chef, I think you should come have a look now."

His voice was low but it carried over the background din of whisks against metal, spatulas against flat tops, dishes and silverware being stacked—the symphony of Sara's life.

But at the sound of him, her kitchen Zen fell like a ruined soufflé.

Patrick's face was an unreadable mask of neutrality most of the time. Now was no different. As she reclaimed her seat across from him in the office, Sara couldn't discern anything from his expression. But she couldn't shake the feeling there was bad news ahead.

Her default belief was that she'd messed up. Not that that was so rare —Sara messed up all the time.

It was the admitting-she-messed-up that didn't happen so often.

Growing up, her siblings had actually cheered the few times Sara had admitted she'd been wrong.

In this case, however, she would've shouted it from the rooftops or bought a Times Square billboard to proclaim her wrongness. That was better than the alternative:

That someone was stealing from Little Bull.

That possibility was bad enough. And it got worse. As much as Sara would like to believe a masked stranger was sneaking in at night and skimming cash from the till, it was most likely one of her thoroughly-interviewed-and-background-checked employees.

Perhaps Sara had to accept her ability to discern people's character was as deficient as her business skills. After all, she'd once been head over heels for Gavin. Now, she knew he was a greasy, smooth-talking playboy.

Who else had she read completely wrong?

"Okay. Lay it on me," Sara said, taking a deep breath.

Pushing a single sheet across the table, Patrick began to explain. "This should be self-explanatory. It's all the discrepancies in a single list."

Patrick's tediously neat handwriting filled two columns. Sara read over both of them carefully. It was a detail of the shortages with the dates and shifts on which they'd happened.

"This has been happening longer than I thought," she noticed.

Patrick nodded. "And the discrepancy is growing each time."

He was right. The first theft was a measly three dollars, but the most recent one totaled over fifty. How could anyone expect that much money would go unnoticed?

She swallowed down the lump of dread that had formed in her throat. Each of her employees flitted through her mind like a spinning wheel on a game show.

Which one will the ticker land on? she wondered.

There wasn't a single employee Sara could imagine stealing from her. She could say without blinking that she trusted each and every one of them.

Or at least, she used to.

Each employee had a personal identification number to enter on the register for each ticket, and the register wouldn't work unless a PIN was entered. The staff had been told not to share their numbers with anyone else, so barring a tech error, the missing money should be easy to track back to a single employee.

Patrick's mind was in the same place. He slid another piece of paper across the table.

"This is the schedule for the last six weeks. With employee PIN numbers."

"Have you already looked?" she asked.

He shook his head. "I didn't think it was my place. They are your employees."

Sara couldn't decide if she was relieved or disappointed.

"Do you want me to do it?" he offered cautiously.

For a moment, Sara considered throwing the papers at Patrick and running back to the kitchen. That's where she felt safe, confident. She could call out someone for over-salting meat or keeping a messy work station.

But theft? Here, Sara was out of her depth.

Patrick was right, though. This person was her employee. It was her responsibility to clean up the mess.

"No, I'll do it." Sara placed the schedule beside the list Patrick had compiled and began to compare times.

By the end of the first column, the culprit was obvious.

Casey Norman.

Still, Sara did her due diligence and checked the other column against the schedule, too. And sure enough, each time money had gone missing, it was Casey's name on the schedule. It was Casey's PIN that opened the register.

"Casey," Sara muttered, flipping the schedule closed and shaking her head. "It's Casey Norman."

Patrick twisted his mouth to the side in disappointment. The most outright expression of emotion Sara had seen from him.

Casey often brought in baked goods and side dishes for family dinner —a meal for the employees to eat together before shift started. Even though Patrick was usually gone by then, Casey always made sure to leave a goody bag on his desk.

He was a nice guy. One of hers. One of theirs.

Or rather, he was—once upon a time.

Now, he was something else entirely.

Why couldn't employees be as easy to manage as vegetables? Sara wondered idly. Vegetables never stole from you. Vegetables never broke your heart. And when a vegetable was rotten, you just threw it out and kept on chopping.

People? Not so easy.

"You need to confront him about this, Sara."

"You're right," she sighed. "I'll call him."

She knew if she didn't do it now, she'd chicken out. So Sara grabbed her phone, cued up her contacts, and hit Casey's name before she could think about it too much.

Casey answered on the second ring. "Hey, Chef! What's up?"

She almost expected to hear more malice in his voice. Something slimy and deceptive she'd never noticed. But Casey sounded chipper as ever.

"Hey, Casey. Something came up, and I wondered if you'd come in today to, uh, chat?"

Don't raise your pitch at the end like that, she counseled herself. *Just say what you mean. Cut out the rotten bits.*

"Do you need me to cover Josh's shift tonight?" he inquired warily.

"No, Josh is fine. Or at least I think he is," Sara said, looking for some wood to knock on. She didn't want to jinx anything going wrong with the rest of her waitstaff. "I just want to talk. Shouldn't take more than a few minutes."

Casey hummed, thinking. "I'm free in a few hours, but that would be in the middle of the dinner rush..."

Sara shuddered. Absolutely not. She had a vivid and horrific memory of being cut from the cast smack dab in the middle of rehearsals for *Les Misérables* in seventh grade. She had no desire to pass that public mortification onto anyone else.

If Casey had to be let go, it didn't need to be witnessed by the rest of the waitstaff. They'd gossip enough as it was.

"I'm on the schedule tomorrow," he continued. "Would you rather talk about it then?"

Yes, she wanted to scream. God, yes, she would.

Better yet, she'd rather talk about it never. She'd rather scrub plates or complete inventory or, hell, do more paperwork than look someone in the eye and ask, *"Did you steal from me?"*

Unfortunately, that wasn't an option.

"I understand if you can't make it, but I'd like to take care of it as soon as possible. If it wasn't important, I wouldn't call you in on your day off."

"Of course, Chef. I have an appointment in an hour, so I can't stay long, but I could be there in twenty minutes?"

"Perfect. It'll be quick," she said. "See you in twenty."

She hung up the phone and dropped down into her chair, suddenly exhausted.

Patrick materialized in the doorway, his shoulder leaning against the frame. "I can sit in on the meeting if you want. In case things go south."

"Thanks, but no thanks. Some things I've gotta do myself."

He nodded. "I'll be in the back if you need me." Then he rapped his knuckles on the door frame as a goodbye and disappeared.

Sara stared at the mountains of paperwork on her desk. This little baby of hers, this Little Bull, was alive, wasn't it? Hadn't she birthed it and nurtured it and raised it this far?

Yes. She had.

But there was something rotten in it now.

Something that needed to be cut out.

And she was the only one who could do it.

4

MAE

THE SWEET ISLAND INN

The inn was completely and totally empty.

Mae Benson had never felt stranger.

The day outside her door was normal enough, though. A break in the clouds sent summer sun slanting through the pane glass windows, breaking up the fearsome cold that had gripped the island since dawn.

Sunshine filled the Sweet Island Inn with golden light and set the leaves of the trees outside aglow.

That was a welcome sight, Mae figured. A good omen for the party she'd be hosting in the backyard later that night. A birthday present of sorts from Mama Nantucket.

Still—even warm summer sun couldn't dispel the odd chill that had set into her bones. An empty inn just wasn't right.

The production company turning Dominic's book into a movie had booked out the Inn for two solid weeks. As such, no one was staying in any of the rooms. Or rather, only the actors would be staying in the rooms, and only then when cameras were rolling.

It should have meant less work for Mae. A well-earned respite. But she felt busier than ever. She'd been cleaning like a madwoman for days, wanting every surface shined and spotless for the cameras.

Now, no mote of dust dared set foot in the house, and Mae was out of tasks that needed doing.

So, with nothing else demanding her attention, Mae found herself making muffins. Lemon poppyseed—a Mae Benson specialty.

It came to her easy as breathing as she moved around the kitchen. She knew the precise weight of the batter in her bowl, exactly how long to whisk to make them fluffy and light. No need for a recipe— she knew it in her bones. A splash of lemon juice here, a fistful of poppy seeds there.

On a normal day, she'd have pans full of the stuff rising in the oven in no time. An army of muffins for her army of guests.

But today, half a pan would do. It would be just her and Dominic eating breakfast, after all.

By the time Dominic came downstairs, the muffins were nearly done.

"Impeccable timing," she drawled with a wink. The man had a knack for showing up right when food was ready to be eaten.

"You lured me out of bed," he accused playfully. "I couldn't possibly resist."

He yawned, lifting his arms over his head in a stretch.

"And," he added, "if I may be so bold as to press my luck... has any coffee materialized?"

Mae grinned despite herself. She was already on her second cup of coffee and buzzing with energy, though she'd keep that secret to herself. Dominic liked when they drank coffee together. It had become a tradition of sorts.

"It really is your lucky day," she remarked. Mae poured him a cup of coffee, black, and slid it across the island to him.

His hands wrapped around the mug like it was a flickering candle he was worried would extinguish. "Every day is my lucky day since I met you."

His face looked somber—much as it always did—but Mae knew where to look to see the flash of mirth in his eyes.

"Laying it on rather thick this morning, are we?"

He took a sip of his coffee and winced at the heat. "I got some good writing done and then slept the best I have in a month. The world is my oyster."

"Does that make me a pearl?" she fired back.

He chuckled quietly. "I suppose it would. No one better for the role."

Dominic didn't like to rise quite as early as Mae. Some of his best novel writing happened late at night, so he operated on a late-to-bed, late-to-rise schedule. But he never missed their morning coffee date.

"I don't even remember you coming to bed," she said.

"I was quiet," he replied with pride. "It took some time, but I've finally mapped out all of the squeaky floorboards."

Mae laughed, imagining him navigating their bedroom like it was a bank vault in the heist movies Brent liked to watch, red laser lines crisscrossing through the air.

Mae's hand-wound timer went off just then. Muffins were ready.

She plated one for Dominic, who murmured his thanks, and then moved directly into cleaning, humming under her breath all the while.

The muffin tin went into the sink to soak. Flour and crumbs were swept from the counter. Measuring cups and her treasured ring of dented metal spoons were rinsed efficiently and set out to dry.

The years had gone by faster than she ever knew they could. But "Hurricane Mae," as her late husband Henry used to call her, had never slowed down.

She finished and stood stock-still in the middle of the kitchen, eyeing a closet door and wondering if she ought to go fetch the stepladder so she could dust the top of it.

Dominic sipped his coffee and patted the bar stool next to him. "Sit down. I'm getting tired just watching you."

"Too much to do," Mae demurred.

"I'm sure there's time to sit and enjoy your coffee, though."

"Oh, I don't know," Mae said, unconvinced. "You haven't seen my plans for this party. It's going to be a rather raucous affair."

She was teasing. Mostly.

Mae loved sharing a birthday with her grandson Grady. His birth had been the best present Mae could have imagined. And every single one of the ten years since then had felt the same.

Celebrating herself had never come naturally to Mae, though, so Grady provided a conduit for her festiveness. She could shower him in desserts and decorations and gifts without a lick of self-consciousness. Aging was fun when you got to do it without all the fuss and bother aimed at you.

Lately, though, the party-planning had become more of an undertaking. All of her kids had significant others and most of them had kids of their own. Slowly but surely, their family had grown from six to eight to fourteen.

It didn't seem to be slowing down anytime soon.

Eliza, Mae's eldest, would be having her second baby any day now. Mae couldn't wait to see if the child would arrive with golden hair like her mom and sister or dark hair like her daddy. The adorableness, though, was guaranteed.

Brent was living with his girlfriend, Rose, and her beautiful little girl, Susanna. Mae already claimed the two girls as her own, but whenever Brent finally got around to proposing, it would make their place in the Benson clan official.

She sank into a barstool next to Dominic at the counter, but she stayed perched on the edge.

"You're making me anxious," Dominic said wryly.

"I'm just sitting here."

"And yet practically vibrating with the effort of it." Dominic reached out and snagged Mae's apron string, undoing it. "One of the reasons I love you is that you radiate life and energy. But even the sun has to set once a day."

"I slept a full seven hours, Dom," Mae argued, swatting at his hand and reclaiming her apron string.

He let loose a languished sigh. "Coffee or no, I haven't the energy to keep up."

Mae's late husband used to call her his hummingbird. He always teased that she flitted around constantly from here to there, rarely relaxing or resting.

Henry would be happy to know she had someone here to remind her to take it easy.

Though she had no intention of listening to Dominic.

"You better have a second cup, then," Mae teased. "You're going to need it today."

Before she could hurry off to find a broom and sweep the kitchen floors, Dominic stood up and wrapped his arms around her.

He wasn't a big man, but he stood almost a head taller than Mae. His long limbs folded around her easily. Even with the extra weight she'd put on in her later years.

"Happy birthday," he whispered, nuzzling his stubbly face against her temple.

Warmth zipped down Mae's spine, and suddenly, she felt like she had enough time for a little break.

She sighed. "Fine. I'll sit." She spun and wagged a finger at him. "But only while you drink your coffee. Then I'm putting you to work."

Dominic smiled and held his hand in the air, palm out in a kind of oath. "Anything for the birthday queen."

She rolled her eyes but couldn't help but smile. "Silly man."

He laughed before sitting back down on his stool. "I've been called many things in my life, but few more accurate than that."

They sat together in an easy silence for ten minutes, speaking only to point out the ruby-throated hummingbirds gathering at the feeders just outside the dining room windows.

As soon as Dominic finished his coffee, he rinsed his mug, put it in the dishwasher, and hurried up the stairs to change.

Five minutes later, he came down with water-dampened hair, khaki shorts, and a plain white pocket t-shirt.

"Put me to work, Miss Mae."

And Mae did.

First, they worked together to pull the six-foot-long folding tables out from the storage shed and set them up in the grass. The inn's previous owner, Mae's sister-in-law, Toni, had used them many times over the years for weddings, parties, fundraisers, and other events the inn hosted, but the tables were still in great shape.

They dragged them into a horseshoe shape on the grass. That way, everyone could sit along the outside and see everyone else. The party was, at its heart, a family dinner, after all. She wanted it to feel intimate.

As soon as the last table was in place, Dominic clapped and placed his hands on his hips. "Look at that. Fifteen minutes of work and done already. I told you we'd have plenty of time."

Mae laughed. "Oh, if only. We've just begun, dear."

Dominic followed Mae into the house and to her office. The room had been chaos before Mae had taken over the inn. Toni kept great records, but finding those records was another question entirely.

Upon finalizing ownership, Mae had opened this room up and been confronted with sheer horror. Toni had receipts from a week ago stuffed haphazardly into a stack amongst invoices older than Grady. Her tax returns had been shoved in an old shoe box along with an X-ray of a broken arm. Whose arm it was, Mae didn't know, and she wasn't sure she wanted to find out.

Things were different now. Mae had bought two filing cabinets to go along the side wall, a bookshelf on the back wall for guest records, business expenses, and other miscellany, and an important document box she kept locked in the closet for all of the sensitive information to do with bank accounts and security codes.

Still, even with her honed-in system of organization, nothing could keep the room from looking chaotic today.

That was largely thanks to the seventy-four silver and gold helium balloons bobbing close to the ceiling. Their shimmering ribbon tails scratched lightly over the wooden floor.

"Goodness. How many balloons does one party need?" Dominic asked from behind her.

"This party needs seventy-four."

Dominic whistled. "That's a lot."

"Careful, buster," Mae warned him, eyes narrowed. "It's a balloon for every year Grady and I have been alive."

"Oh! Then it's hardly any balloons at all," Dominic amended with a wink. "Spring chickens, the both of you."

"That's what I thought you said," Mae laughed. "Anyhow, the tablecloths are there. And the balloons are... everywhere, as you can see. The tie-down weights are on the table by the window, the tablecloths need to be unfolded and Velcro'd to the undersides of the tables so they don't blow away, and the chairs still need to be carried outside. Which do you want to tackle first?"

Dominic twisted his lips in thought. "Would you find it incredibly attractive if I carried all of those chairs outside by myself?"

"Only if you carried them all in one trip," she joked.

He snapped his fingers and grabbed two or three chairs under each arm. "Then stand back and marvel."

Mae laughed and moved to help him. She didn't have anything to prove and today was not the day to throw her back out, so she carried only one chair under each arm.

When they finished, Dominic was sweating, his brow glistening.

"Tired already?" Mae asked, breathing a little heavily herself.

"Me? Never. What's next?"

Ninety minutes later, they stood in the thick grass, admiring their hard work.

The white linens let the metallic balloons shine while still adding a touch of class. Streamers and string lights hanging from the back door to the tree branches upped the ante even more.

Mae had secured everything with weights and ties to make sure the party wouldn't take off in the wind off the water. But the balloons still bobbed in the breeze and the tablecloths flapped happily against the metal legs of the tables.

The garden Mae had shaped over the last few years wouldn't be winning awards anytime soon—that was more her best friend Lola's department—but she was proud of it nonetheless. Something about nurturing a fragile young flower to bloom made her dizzy with happiness every spring.

A wooden trellis rested against the side of the guest house Brent had remodeled a few years earlier. Sweet pea now climbed up the slats.

The black-and-white oak tree was ringed with a bed of perennials— echinacea, liatris, and buddleia. The proper names escaped her most of the time, but she liked the hardy little fellows. They didn't require much in the way of TLC.

"I think I'm too old for this kind of work," Dominic said, fanning his shirt out from his chest. "This is why I write books. Very little physical exertion involved."

"I'm just glad Sara agreed to bring all the food. I can't imagine going to cook now," Mae admitted.

Dominic wrapped an arm around her waist and nudged her hip. "Well, since you find yourself with some free time, can I interest you in a walk down to the beach?"

The hummingbird inside of Mae wanted to rush inside and hurry into a shower and get dressed before anyone arrived. But the look of hope in Dom's eyes made the decision for her.

"Of course."

"Great. Stay put. I'll only be a second." Dominic walked into the house at a fast clip and returned holding a box.

Mae narrowed her eyes. "What's that?"

He shrugged, his smile devious. "Nothing for you to worry about. Come on."

Dominic led Mae down a well-worn dirt path through the trees. Over the winter, some of the branches had become unruly, dipping across the path. With summer approaching, Mae would need to get someone out to trim them back for her. But for now, Dominic held them out of the way so Mae could safely pass.

The beach behind the inn was a huge selling point with the guests. She could guarantee private beach access to every guest who stayed with her.

Mae didn't mind it one bit, either.

Living in the inn had been an escape for her immediately after Henry's passing. But in the years since, the house and the land surrounding had become her home. The thought of leaving this slice of solace—even for just a couple of weeks—made her stomach turn.

Every time she closed her eyes, she saw that night again. The night of the accident.

Opening the front door of 114 Howard Street.

Brent standing there, framed by the pouring rain.

The gray distance in his eyes.

Mae couldn't imagine going back there. The memory was too sharp, prickling against her like a rock in her shoe.

But "there" wasn't "there" anymore, now was it?

114 Howard Street was no longer the home of Mae and Henry Benson. It was Brent's home now. Brent's and Rose's and Susanna's. They'd taken it and reshaped it and made it their own and now it was a whole different thing, a new thing, a fresh thing, and surely that was good for everyone involved.

She liked that story. A story of clean beginnings. She'd told it to herself often since she'd finally agreed to vacate the inn for the movie crew.

Perhaps a shred of her was even starting to believe it.

"There's nothing quite like this place," Dominic said as the branches parted and they stepped onto the sand. "Even temporarily, I'll miss it."

"I'll miss it, too."

It was the closest she'd come to sharing her mixed-up feelings about the temporary transition with Dominic. She didn't know how to share these fears with him, these anxieties. So she just kept them to herself. Buzzing in her stomach like a swarm of bees.

They walked past native grasses poking out of the ground and paused for a moment on a patch of soft sand. The ocean lapped at the shore a safe distance away, leaving white foam behind.

Throughout the day, the air had warmed and the clouds had dissipated, giving way to clear blue skies. Party weather.

"Shall we sit?" Dominic dropped the box in the sand and held out a hand, helping Mae to the ground. "The move will only be temporary, though, you know."

"It's just been a long time since I've been anywhere else," Mae murmured.

"Well, we'll still be on the island. We'll still be together," Dominic said. "It will be like a staycation."

"What do you know about staycations?" Mae asked, one brow arched in surprise.

"Eliza told me about them," he said with a chuckle. "She was working on marketing that would bring more locals to the inn. Apparently, 'staycations are all the rage.' Her words, not mine."

"I'm sure she's right, but I don't think I'd care much for a staycation. I like my own bed."

"Is that why you seem so worried about leaving?"

Mae sighed. "Am I that transparent?"

"Only to me, I think," he said thoughtfully. "To everyone else, you look as cool and collected as ever."

It was silly of her to think she could keep anything from Dominic. He'd been in her life for three years now, but it seemed as if they'd known each other much longer. He had a way of seeing right to the heart of her.

"I haven't gone back to the house very often since Henry passed," she admitted in a hushed voice. "It makes me miss him too much."

"That makes sense."

"I'm sure that isn't nice for you to hear," Mae added. "But It isn't as though I do not enjoy our life here. I do. Very much."

He laid a hand over Mae's and squeezed. "I never doubted for a second. People can be two things at once. You can miss Henry and still love me."

Mae's throat tightened. She didn't know what to say.

Thankfully, she didn't have to figure it out. Dominic turned and picked up the box he'd carried down to the beach. Mae had almost forgotten about it.

"I have a gift for you," he said, "and I think you should open it."

"I thought I told you no gifts!" she crowed. "That is a very strict rule in my household."

He winked. "Sue me."

Chuckling in dismay, Mae took it from him and carefully opened the cardboard lid. After sifting through a bundle of tissue paper, she saw a neatly folded square of fabric—the white backside of what looked to be a quilt.

Pulling it out, she stood up and let it unfold in the air in front of her. When she saw the care and detail, she gasped.

A family tree took up the center of the blanket. Mae's name was stitched into the topmost branch. The other branches filtered downward and outward, the embroidered names of each member of her family set into delicate green leaves. There was space enough to add grandchildren further down, and lying beneath the tree like roots was a nautical map of Nantucket and the surrounding sea.

It was hand-quilted and personalized. Likely commissioned months ahead of time. The thoughtfulness was enough to bring tears to Mae's eyes.

Then she caught the name stitched into the top right of the quilt, and the tears spilled over.

Dominic ran his hand over Henry's stitched name and laid his other hand on Mae's shoulder.

"Henry is a part of this family, Mae. A part of your family and your life. I don't want you to ever have to apologize for missing him or loving him."

Mae was too busy wiping away tears to respond, but Dominic understood how touched she was. He pulled her close and pressed a kiss to her forehead.

"He helped you raise a wonderful family full of people I'm beyond grateful I get to know. Including you. And if you don't want to go back to the house you shared with him, we can stay somewhere else." Dominic shrugged. "I've never been much of one for camping, but surely between the two of us we can operate a tent."

Mae sniffled with teary laughter and folded the blanket over her arm. "Thank you."

Dominic nodded. "Just know: you don't need to hide your feelings from me."

"It seems I can't," she sniffled. "Even when I try."

"If being in your old house upsets you, be upset. Feel what you need to feel. Believe me, I know grief isn't always linear."

Dominic had lost a loved one, too. His young daughter, decades earlier. He understood where Mae was coming from.

"Thank you," Mae said again. The words seemed insignificant in the face of his beautiful gift and even more beautiful words, but it was all Mae could manage to say.

Dominic kissed her forehead again. "You're welcome."

They sat there for a moment, curled against each other, as the day broke open wide and hot and delightful around them. Seagulls swirled in the distance, cawing for scraps. Little crabs scurried across the scarred face of the sand.

And the waves—endless, roiling, perfect—kept on coming, one after the next after the next.

It was hers.

It was home.

It was Nantucket.

5

HOLLY

MIDDAY—PETE & HOLLY'S HOUSE

"Cufflinks?" Pete asked, turning from the closet with a black case in his hands.

Holly laughed. "I was just about to ask about the diamond earrings. Too much?"

Pete's eyes pinched together in concern. "Maybe we should call Eliza."

Holly would be lying if she said she hadn't considered it. But no. They did not need her older sister telling them how to be sophisticated adults.

Just because Holly spent most of her time up to her elbows in grass stains and macaroni noodle crafts didn't mean she couldn't be classy when the situation called for it.

"It's an outdoor luncheon. Skip the cufflinks and roll the sleeves of your shirt," she said confidently. "If you're underdressed when we get there, you can roll the sleeves down. Otherwise, you'll look collected and casual."

"This is why I keep you around," he teased.

Holly and Pete were going to the inaugural awards luncheon at his law firm. His maritime and property firm had humble beginnings, but Pete and his partner, Billy, had come a long way. From starting out in a microscopic back room borrowed from a friend, they'd upgraded into a new office in a gleaming, remodeled firehouse. Pete had insisted they keep the fireman's pole—because of course he had —but almost everything else had been revamped, redone, and refurbished. It looked fabulous.

And it wasn't just the two of them anymore. Pete and Billy had brought on enough employees to warrant an awards luncheon. They wouldn't fill a stadium anytime soon, but the courtyard behind the firehouse would be full to bursting, Holly guessed.

Pete rolled his sleeves and checked his appearance in the full-length mirror, tilting his chin this way and that, admiring himself. When he spun back around, his smile was bright, eyes hooded. "Are you swooning? Because I look amazing."

"And not lacking for confidence."

"How could I, when I'll have the prettiest woman in attendance on my arm?" He stepped forward and twirled Holly into a graceless dance move. She tripped over her feet, but Pete caught her before she could fall.

"Smooth," she chuckled, both to herself and her husband.

She liked seeing him like this. Cheerful. Optimistic. Playful.

Living in Plymouth, Pete's job had nearly swallowed him whole. All of the things Holly had always loved about him had faded. He'd been a diminished version of himself. Overworked and overextended. He'd barely had enough energy to make it through the door at the end of the day and drop down onto the couch, let alone play with the kids or help Holly run the house. The stress of it all had nearly torn them in two.

Now, living in Nantucket with Pete running his own business, their life had balance again. An effortless harmony that filled Holly with hope.

There were still late nights. Running your own business was a big task for anyone to undertake. But Pete managed his hours well. Rather than coming home at the end of the day worn down and numb, he came home invigorated. Excited to be with his family. Excited to be a father and husband.

Pete wrapped his arm around Holly's lower back and curled the other hand around her jaw. His finger brushed her earlobe.

"Wear the diamond earrings."

"Are you sure?" Holly asked, standing up and taking Pete's place in front of the mirror. "I don't want to be too showy."

He waved his hand dismissively. "Believe me—whatever you choose will be tame compared to Cecilia."

Holly bit back a groan. She and the wife of Pete's business partner, Cecilia, had mostly buried the hatchet. But Holly still found herself reluctant to embrace the woman with open arms.

On one hand, Cecilia's mean-spirited comments and haughty attitude stemmed from insecurity. She was jealous of Holly's ability to have children. But still, that was hardly an excuse to be a witch.

Plus, despite it all, Holly still found herself jealous of Cecilia from time to time. The woman exuded an air of effortless chicness. Never a hair out of place, never an eyelash uncurled.

Holly wanted to exude the same air as Cecilia today. To impress the other employees and clients, yes, of course. But also to make Pete proud. She wanted his compliment to be true. For today, she wanted to feel like the prettiest woman in the room. No matter how shallow that made her sound.

"I'm still not sure about the dress," she admitted, pinching the lacy material between her fingers and pulling it away from her body.

The white, floral dress gathered at the waist and then flared down to just above her knees. It had cost her a small fortune at Dahlia's Dress Barn and toed the line between garden party and cocktail dress.

The problem was less about the dress and more about the lack of it. Especially up top.

"This neckline is too low, I think," she said, leaning forward and back, eyes trained on the flappy bit of fabric just above her chest. "I'm afraid it's going to flop open."

"I think you look amazing," Pete said, leaning over her shoulder to kiss her cheek. "But you'll do whatever you think is best in the end."

Pete wasn't wrong. They'd been together long enough that her husband knew he had no ability to change Holly's mind when it came to her clothes. He could tell her she looked great until he was blue in the face, but Holly would still change three more times before they left the house.

Not for the first time, Holly was jealous of Pete. Of men in general, really. She'd spent four hours at the Dress Barn trying on anything that fit.

Pete was wearing the same suit pants and white button-down shirt he wore to his cousin's wedding the year before.

He looked good, though. Holly had thought that since the first time she'd ever seen him in a tux. Pete had arrived for Senior Prom photos in his freshly washed and waxed two-seater car wearing a white tuxedo with a ruffled baby blue shirt underneath.

The pictures made her laugh until she cried now. But oh, back then, how Holly had swooned! And, even though she hadn't admitted it to Pete, she was swooning now, too.

"You wait downstairs and I'll be down in ten, no matter what," she promised.

Pete eyed her dubiously before saluting her farewell and marching down the stairs. She heard the click of the television and the babble of daytime sports chatter emerge.

Meanwhile, Holly turned to her closet, determined.

After considering her options, Holly decided a jacket was too bulky, a shrug blouse made the dress look out of proportion, and nothing else even came close to matching besides a scarf she'd worn only once since returning to Nantucket. It being June, though, a scarf was out of the question.

"I just won't bend over," she muttered to herself, grabbing her white clutch and a large sunhat.

Pete was sitting on the couch in his spot, as relaxed as could be. He was visibly shocked when Holly came down the stairs.

"This might be a record," he said, looking at his watch. "If we leave now, we'll actually be ten minutes *early*. Billy won't know what to do with himself."

"I wouldn't dream of making us late to your big day, hot shot."

"Perfect. As the host of the evening, I oughta be the first smiling face everyone sees as they arrive. 'Best Handshaker in the Northeast'— that's what they used to call me in law school."

"Pete, honey, I knew you back then, remember? No one in history has ever called you that."

He winked and laughed. "Oh, how wrong you are, sunshine." He grabbed the car keys off the coffee table and extended his elbow to her. "Ready?"

Holly smiled and began to nod before she caught something out of the corner of her eye. On the corner of the kitchen island sat a box of fruit punch juice pouches.

She winced. "Oh no! I forgot to take the juice."

"What?"

"The juice. To go with the cupcakes." When Pete's face was still blank, Holly's eyes widened. "For Grady's birthday. I took snacks with him to share with the other kids."

"Oh, darn," Pete said with a shrug. "That's okay. It's a summer camp. I'm sure they'll have something for the young'uns to drink."

"I don't know. This place is a stickler. Do you not remember the handbook they gave us with all the rules?" Holly chewed on her lip. "Should we swing by and drop these off?"

Pete looked panicked. "No. No, we shouldn't," he said, shaking his head. "We are going to arrive at the luncheon at the perfect time as it is."

"But it's his birthday," Holly protested.

"And we'll make it up to him tonight at his party. He can drink all the juice pouches by himself if he wants."

"That would make him sick." She dragged her finger along the colorful cardboard box, guilt settling in her core. "He didn't even want to go this morning. Did you hear him? He asked if he could stay home. But I convinced him to go because he'd have a party."

Pete grabbed Holly's shoulders gently and pulled her towards the door, coaxing her along with gentle words. "And cupcakes are still a great party. The kids will mainline their sugar and drink their water and it will be fine. I promise."

"I just don't want anyone teasing him about it."

"Who on Earth would do that?" Pete asked, opening the garage door and stepping backwards down the steps.

It didn't escape her notice that he was trying to coax her to the car. "I don't know. One of the counselors mentioned yesterday that there had been a little something going on. Not quite bullying, I don't think, but in that realm. She wasn't very specific."

"I'm sure it has nothing to do with Grady," Pete dismissed, unlocking the car doors with the fob. A mechanical *thunk* echoed around the garage. "He's a good kid. Confident. He won't let himself be bullied."

Pete pulled open the passenger door and held Holly's hand as he helped her into the car.

"Believe me, hon, everything will be fine. Grady will have a great time today and we'll have a fun birthday party for the little rascal tonight. But for now, you and I are going out on the town."

Holly still felt guilty about sending Grady away on his birthday, but Pete was right. The kids were having fun at nature camp, Holly and Pete were going to have their first adult outing in far too long, and at the end of the day, they'd all reconvene and celebrate together at the inn with Mom.

Aside from the juice pouches, everything had gone perfectly so far. Holly didn't want to jinx it by worrying.

She smiled and Pete gave her a wink before he shut her door.

The luncheon was held in the courtyard behind the old firehouse—now Pete's offices.

Holly had taken lead on buying the furniture and decorations for the inside of the building, which had gone well after some initial bumps and bruises. But a professional landscaper had worked on the courtyard—and goodness, how it showed!

The center of the space was a simple square of grass, but bundles of wildflowers grew in the flower beds along the fence. They'd exploded into blooms of every color imaginable since Holly had seen them last. And the white stone pavers set into the grass to create a square path around the perimeter gave it a royal garden vibe.

For celebratory purposes, a large white tent stood proudly in the center, draped with tulle and a crystal chandelier hanging from the center point.

"Pete, this looks amazing." Holly knew Pete wanted it to be a lavish affair, but this was more than she'd ever imagined. "Do you have the budget for this?"

Pete tossed his head back and laughed. "Ha-ha. Do you think I bother myself with the matter of money?"

"Yes," Holly said flatly.

"Once you reach a certain level of success, such petty things don't matter, Hollyday."

Holly raised a brow, not buying his rich man persona. She did the budget with him once per month and knew money was no petty thing at all. At least, not in their household.

He grinned at his own joke and leaned down to whisper in her ear. "Only joking. The owner of Soiree Floral is a client and offered to help with the decorating for a reduced rate."

That explained the centerpieces. Blue and white vases sat in the center of each table with soft pink peonies, red roses, white carnations, and green poms for filler. The perfect snapshot of a Nantucket summer.

"And the food?" Holly asked, tipping her head towards the tables of food with servers in white coats bustling around them.

"I happen to know the owner of Little Bull," Pete said.

"Sara helped you?"

"I paid her full price," he said as a matter of pride. "She is booked solid, but managed to make some things ahead of time."

"That was nice of her," Holly murmured.

If she'd known Pete was going to ask Sara for help, she would have done it. Her youngest sister could certainly handle her own, but she never seemed to know when to say "no" to helping family out. Holly hoped Sara hadn't overextended herself.

"Sara actually offered to make the food. I didn't even have to ask," Pete continued. "She heard about the luncheon and figured it would be good exposure. There are a lot of bigwigs at this thing, and a newer restaurant can always use the publicity, I suppose."

Holly was touched Pete thought of her sister—on his own, without so much as a suggestion from her—but she was also impressed.

She'd never been the kind of person who found success all that attractive. It wasn't a selling point for her, at least. She always knew there was a possibility she and Pete would amount to nothing, but so long as they had each other and their family, they could weather any storm.

Which is why she'd been surprised to found how attractive success was on her husband. Pete had gained a newfound confidence this last year, and it looked very good on him indeed.

The ruffled blue shirt might belong firmly in their high school days, but Holly felt a little swoony again nonetheless.

"What kind of bigwigs?" Holly asked, sipping on her champagne. "Any movie stars?"

"Brad Pitt RSVP'd as a maybe," he teased.

"Classic Brad. You can't get him to commit to anything."

"But the Honorary Mayor, Myra Gambol, and District Attorney Matthew Galliert are coming," Pete added. "That's something."

Holly looped her arm through his and patted his arm. "That's a very big something, Pete. You should be proud of what you've built."

Her husband looked down at her with pure pride and love shining in his eyes, and suddenly, Holly wasn't self-conscious about her dress or worried about her hat.

She may not be the prettiest woman in the room.

But with this man on her arm, she was darn sure the luckiest.

By the time they got back to the car after the party, Holly was buzzing with champagne and pride in Pete's achievements. A belly full of lobster cakes helped matters.

"You were right about Cecilia," Holly said as soon as they were safely in the car and away from prying eyes and ears. "I can't believe she had on a full-length formal gown."

"I can. That cruise they're taking next week is being catered by a Michelin-starred chef."

"And stopping at four different islands."

"Oh, right. How could I forget? She only mentioned it to everyone who would listen."

They both laughed and then fell into an easy silence. Holly looked out the window at the familiar roads and neighborhoods they'd both grown up in.

It felt good to be back on the island. More than that, though, it felt good to see Pete doing so well. To actually witness how respected he was by his employees and his clients.

"Today was really fun," she said, leaning back against the headrest with a sigh. "I knew you were doing well, but seeing you in action like that was..."

Pete turned to her and wagged his eyebrows. "Irresistible?"

Holly laughed but then shrugged, bobbing her head back and forth. "Something like that, actually. You looked like a boss out there. It was fun to see."

Pete whistled. "Well, the kids are gone the rest of the afternoon, you know. We'll have the house to ourselves."

The car rolled to a stop at a stop sign. Rather than answer her husband with words, Holly took the opportunity to lean across the console, grab his face, and kiss him.

Pete murmured in surprise and then kissed her back, looping his hand around her neck.

For a second, Holly could forget they were stopped at an intersection in the middle of the day. It felt like they were teenagers again, kissing clumsily in the back of Pete's car in the dark.

When they pulled apart, Pete smacked the steering wheel. "Giddy up!"

Holly laughed.

She was still laughing when they rounded the corner of their block and pulled into the driveway.

Then, at the sight of her front door, her smile died on her lips.

"Who is that?"

It was broad daylight, but their porch was shrouded in shadow from the large oak in their front yard.

In that shadow, a dark silhouette separated from the wall.

It appeared to be a large man, dressed all in black. Holding a suitcase and leaning against the house casually.

Almost as if he was waiting for them.

Pete shoved the car into park and squinted towards the porch. "I have no idea. I'm not expecting anyone."

"Me either," Holly said, fear fluttering in her chest. Her champagne buzz had dissipated like fog under a hot sun. She felt stone cold sober. "Should I call the police?"

She wouldn't request a squad car be sent out right away—though, given the kind of activity the Nantucket Police Department dealt with, they probably had a squad car or two to spare. But it would be nice to have an operator on the phone just in case something wasn't right.

"No, no. He has a suitcase."

Holly snorted. "What does that have to do with anything?"

"What kind of criminal carries a suitcase?"

"The kind of criminal who wants somewhere to stash the bodies!"

Pete turned off the ignition and grabbed the key. The man on the porch seemed to notice them now. Holly could feel his eyes on them even if she couldn't see them.

"A body couldn't fit in that suitcase."

But a gun could. Or a knife. Or a bomb. *Or, or, or...*

Holly's imagination was running wild with possibilities. She was so distracted that she didn't realize Pete had opened his car door until he was swinging his legs out, dress shoes clacking against the pavement.

"Are you crazy? Don't get out!"

Pete turned back, shoulders raised. "Am I just supposed to sit here and wait?"

"Yes!" Holly knew it wasn't much of a plan, but it had to be better than confronting the stranger. "We have no idea who this person is."

"That's why I'm going to go talk to him." Pete said it like it was the easiest thing in the world to understand, but Holly couldn't have disagreed more.

Before she could say anything else, Pete shut his door and walked towards the front porch.

Pete and Billy had refrained from giving themselves any awards at the luncheon. It made sense. The bosses clapping themselves on the back would have felt bizarrely self-congratulatory. Still, Holly knew which award she'd hand to Pete if she could: *"Most Stubborn Man Alive."*

Holly grabbed her phone and punched 9-1-1. Just in case.

If something went wrong, she'd hit the Call button. Someone could be here in a flash.

But just as she finished entering the numbers, she heard the men laugh.

It didn't sound like an ominous noise, but Holly wasn't taking any chances. She eased out of the passenger seat, phone still clutched in her hand.

Outside the car, she could now hear conversation. Animated conversation.

Friendly, animated conversation.

Pete turned around and waved Holly onto the porch. "Holly, come on up here. Meet Rob."

Rob?

Who was Rob?

As she got closer to the porch and her eyes adjusted to the gloom, Holly was shocked to see Pete was hugging the man. With both arms!

If Pete was hugging a man he'd just met, Holly expected *Rob* to be with Publishers Clearing House, here to announce they'd won some kind of sweepstakes. His suitcase better be full of cash.

The man was tall, maybe six-foot-two, with broad shoulders, black hair, eyes so brown they seemed black, and a week's growth of scruff on his face and top lip. His hair flopped to one side and hung to mid-cheek in a careless tumble that might have been cute if he had been, oh, say fifteen or sixteen.

But this man was at least forty, maybe even forty-five by her estimation. He had deep lines around his mouth and creases across his forehead. His skin looked tanned and dry.

"I can't believe you're here," Pete said, shaking his head.

So Pete *did* know him.

Holly tried to wrack her brain for a mention of a Rob, but nothing came immediately to mind.

Maybe he was someone Pete knew from his old job? Though that wouldn't make sense. He'd hated his old job. He hadn't kept in touch with anyone, as far as Holly knew.

"Doing a little traveling," Rob replied, lifting his suitcase with one arm.

"And decided to drop in on your favorite cousin?" Pete asked, smile wide. "About time. It has been ages."

Cousin?

Holly wanted to be surprised she hadn't recognized Rob's name, but she wasn't. It made sense, actually.

When Pete and Holly were dating in high school, they spent most of their time with Holly's family. Pete's parents didn't go out of their way to visit family members off the island, and even when they did, they didn't have many holiday traditions. Not the same way the Bensons did.

Come to think of it, Holly had still hardly met anyone outside of Pete's most immediate relatives. If she strained her mind, Holly could vaguely, maybe-maybe-not remember a few old tales Pete had shared that she thought might've had something to do with a cousin. Most of them involved playing Ding Dong Ditch or taking the air out of other kids' bikes. Harmless, delinquent stuff.

"That's actually what I'm here to talk to you about, Petey. I've been out of circulation for a bit." Rob winced. "I was sort of... Well, no easy way to say this: I was in prison."

"*Sort of?*" Holly bleated, speaking her first words since she'd joined the group.

Rob turned to her and shrugged. Pete shot her a warning look.

"Oh no, man. I'm sorry," Pete said. "But you're out now?"

He better be, Holly thought. Otherwise, they might be on the hook for harboring a fugitive.

"Yeah. All clear," Rob confirmed. "Free man."

"That's great. Awesome." Pete looked genuinely pleased for Rob, and Holly wondered if Pete had ever even stepped foot in a prison.

This whole day had shifted from delightful to bizarre so quickly. Holly felt like she was in a dream.

"Unfortunately, I'm a bit too free. I don't even have a roof over my head right now. I'm couch-surfing, you could say. Trying to find what's next for me."

Oh no.

Oh no, no, no, no, no.

Holly barely resisted the urge to violently shake her head.

Absolutely not. This ex-con could not stay with her family. With her *children.*

Pete nodded sympathetically. "Of course. That's a tough transition, I'm sure."

As if Pete would know anything about the transition from prison to normal life. He'd never even gotten a speeding ticket before.

"It is," Rob agreed. "I'm hoping to line some work up on the mainland soon, but until then, I was wondering if I might take advantage of your kindness and spend a little time with you and the ocean."

How many different ways could a person say no? *No, non, nein...*

Holly braced herself for the awkward conversation to come. The one where Pete would inform Rob that unfortunately, he couldn't stay with them and would have to hop back on the ferry. *But we of course wish you the best of luck and know that you'll land on your feet wherever you do go next; it's just that there's no vacancy here because of this and that and the other...*

Instead, Pete's next words stunned Holly into awed silence.

"Of course, you can, Rob! Anything for family. Stay as long as you need."

Before Holly could formulate words or even breathe, Pete unlocked the front door and let his cousin and his suspicious suitcase over the threshold. Into their home.

Looks like they wouldn't have the house to themselves anymore.

Cousin Rob was coming for a visit.

6

SARA
LITTLE BULL RESTAURANT

Sara's outward layer of cool, calm professionalism cracked as soon as she heard the back door to the kitchen open.

"Smells good in here!" Casey called to the staff on duty. "Like always."

"What are you doing here, chief?" Jose asked. "You pick up a shift?"

"Talking to the boss. I'll be in tomorrow, though."

"Well, before I forget, Gabby wanted me to tell you thanks for the card and gift you sent over," Jose said.

Casey dismissed him with a *pfft*. "It was just a gift card. The least I can do now that you have a new baby at home."

"Gift cards are gold, man," Jose said. "So much better than another ridiculous outfit she'll never wear. We're going to buy diapers."

Casey laughed. "Happy to help. And congratulations again!"

Sara wanted to bang her forehead against her desk. He had gotten Jose a gift card to celebrate his new baby? And a card? Sara hadn't even done that, and Jose was her right-hand man. Her go-to kitchen partner. Mr. Dependable.

There was no way Casey could be the thief.

Except that Sara had gone over and over the read-outs and the list Patrick had compiled. She'd hoped to find some huge mistake she and Patrick had both made in the comparisons. Some form of exoneration or an alibi in the data. Anything that would keep her from having to confront her employee with a crime.

But the evidence was damning from top to bottom.

When Casey knocked on her office door, Sara did not feel like a little bull at all. She felt like a little mouse, scared of the smallest noise.

She flinched and then straightened quickly. "Come in."

The door opened. Casey stood there with his usual cheerfulness. He sauntered into the room and gave her a friendly wave.

"Good afternoon, Chef."

Was it a good afternoon? Sara didn't think so. It felt like the walls of her office were slowly closing in on her.

"Have a seat, Casey," she said in lieu of a greeting. "I know you're in a hurry, so let's get started. I'm sure we'll have this cleared up in no time."

She'd looked online for some kind of script to follow. A way to navigate this situation that wouldn't dissolve into a screaming match. But there hadn't been anything helpful.

All of the advice felt too cold. Too stiff.

Sara *knew* Casey. She'd been working with him for over a year. She couldn't lead with the bad news and then shut down any of his attempts to explain himself.

More than her employee, Casey felt like a friend. Her entire staff did.

He frowned for the first time since entering the room. Maybe for the first time since she hired him, actually, come to think of it. "There's something to clear up?"

Was that guilt in his eyes? Sara searched his face for any sign that he knew what she was about to say, but she no longer trusted herself. Her people-reading skills were on the fritz, apparently.

"Casey, there have been some ..." she sighed, looked at the papers for a moment to gin up her courage again, and continued, "some discrepancies in the register read-outs and the deposits. I called you in to see if you'd know anything about them."

Nice delivery, Sara. Direct and to the point. Like ripping off a bandage. Just like the internet had said.

And when was the internet ever wrong?

Casey's eyes narrowed further, brow furrowing. "What kind of discrepancies? I don't know what you mean."

Okay, maybe she'd ripped off the bandage too quickly.

As a kid, her mom had always run warm water over their bandages and then worked the edges loose with a cotton Q-tip and baby oil. Within five minutes, the bandage fell off on its own.

So forget the rip-it-off method. Backtrack. Try again, with a Q-tip and baby oil. Ripping off bandages was overrated.

"Patrick and I were going over reports today. While doing the Z-outs, I noticed some money went missing from the register."

"And you think I have something to do with it?" Casey looked awestruck. And not in a pleasant way.

"Patrick looked at the reports, too. He found the same thing," Sara explained. "It has been going on for a few weeks."

Casey leaned back in his chair, arms folded over his chest. "And you're asking everyone on staff about this?"

Sara blinked. Unsure what to say.

She didn't want to answer and admit he was the only suspect. But she didn't want to lie, either. That would be an easy fib to catch her in. As soon as Casey texted Josh or Haylie or anyone else on staff, he'd know he was the only other person who'd been interrogated about the missing money.

She didn't have to answer for him to put the pieces together.

"Just me, then." Casey's shoulders sagged and he shook his head. "Unbelievable."

Sara sighed. "I called you in today because every time the money went missing, you were on shift."

"Because I pick up more shifts than anyone else," he retorted.

"Your PIN was used to open the register."

"Because I'm always helping everyone else out when they're closing tabs."

"That still puts you behind the register," Sara said softly. "I'm just following the trail of technology."

"I can't believe this." Casey flopped back in his chair.

"I'm sorry."

Sara really was sorry. She hated this.

He snorted. "Sure doesn't seem like it. You're treating me like a criminal."

"That's not what I'm... I'm not trying to do that. I'm just trying to figure out what's going on."

"And I'm trying to tell you," Casey said, leaning forward, eyes wide, "that I have no idea what is going on here. But it isn't me."

Sara looked at the stack of papers in front of her. At the list Patrick had made. At the clear evidence that something strange was going on.

"I don't know what to tell you. All I have to go on is the reports and—"

"And the reports don't know me like you do," Casey said. "C'mon, Sara, are you serious? You have to know this isn't me."

Sara's stomach flipped.

She'd expected Casey to be upset. Maybe even angry.

But she hadn't expected him to appeal to her better judgement. To fight for his job. She should have, but she hadn't.

And now, she didn't know what to do.

The guy was likable. He was organized. Prompt. Consistent. Dependable. The last person she'd suspect of this.

And yet, all the evidence pointed to him.

"All the waitstaff have PINs and yours pops up way more than anyone else's." Sara flipped over one of the reports and runs her finger down the line of PINs. "With Josh, Augustine, Bonita, and Serena all serving with you last Friday, you couldn't have waited on seventy-two tables."

"I didn't! Of course I didn't."

"Then how do you explain—"

"I help them out because they're slow as molasses!" Casey practically shouted. "If customers had to wait for the others to ring them out, you'd be getting a pile of complaints every night."

"Well..."

"Augustine would rather stand up at the hostess stand and flirt with Margaret," Casey accused. "And everyone else looks for any excuse to pull out their phones and take a break. Serena spends half of dinner service in the bathroom."

Sure, Augustine could be a flirt and Serena's bathroom breaks sometimes ran long. But they were nice and mostly good at their jobs.

"Then you should come to me if there's a problem," she said lamely. "If people aren't pulling their weight, you should talk to them. Or to me. Tell me, and I'll—"

"Make sure everyone knows I'm a snitch. Yeah, that would be great for morale." Casey rolled his eyes.

He had a point.

"The fact is," Casey said, "I do more on accident than the rest of the staff does on purpose. I just can't believe I'm being punished for it. Augustine gets an incentive raise and I get accused of being a thief. How nice."

She wanted to protest. But he was right.

Just say something despicable! she wanted to scream. *Say something nasty so I can fire you and sleep well tonight.*

But Casey sat there across her messy desk looking up at her like she was a monster.

Did I get this wrong? Doubts began to creep in. *Did I misread something? Maybe I jumped to a conclusion too quickly.*

"Casey, I'm not trying to accuse you of anything. I just want to—"

"This is you *not* accusing me?" he scoffed. "Boy, I'd hate to see what an accusation would look like."

"Hey, I'm sorry this is awkward, but—"

"It's unbelievable." He cut her off again. "I've worked my tail off for you. I've only called in sick one time. I covered in the back when a dishwasher got a cold last week. And this is the thanks I get."

Maybe Sara should have sat on this for a bit longer. Observed the waitstaff more closely. Found some hard evidence before calling anyone into her office.

After all, no numbers were perfect, right? People went to jail all the time on faulty evidence. Could Sara really trust the PIN system over her own gut?

"Listen, I'm as shocked as you that the evidence pointed here," Sara started.

Casey sat up, brows raised. "So you don't think it's me?"

"Well, I mean... I don't really know what to think. The PIN system is there, and you were logged in. But you help out." Sara was rambling, all of her confused thoughts leaking out at once. She sighed. "I don't know who did it."

"What does that mean?"

Sara had no idea. Her thoughts roiled and collided with one another until she couldn't think straight.

If working in a kitchen gave Sara complete clarity, this situation gave her the exact opposite. She felt lost at sea.

"I wanted to ask you if you knew anything about the missing money, and you're saying you don't. So that's it," she said. "Thanks for coming in."

Casey ran a hand through his dark hair and blinked. "That's it."

"That's it."

Sara needed that to be it. At least for now. She couldn't make any decision. She wasn't in the right headspace.

"I'm not being fired?"

Sara shook her head. "No."

Not yet. Maybe not ever. She didn't know.

"And you're not going to tell anyone else about this?" he asked. "About the accusation? Because I'm not coming in tomorrow if I'm going to be humiliated in front of everyone. I don't want everyone here thinking I'm some sort of thief. Because I'm not. I would never."

"I won't tell anyone else," Sara said. "You aren't being fired. I'll question the people who need to be questioned, but I want to keep this under wraps, as well. It isn't exactly a good look for me."

What kind of boss was she that she couldn't even manage a waitstaff without wilting under the pressure?

When she'd worked for Gavin Crawford, walking into his office had been terrifying. Partly because she'd had a crush on him. But also because she'd respected him. She'd valued his opinion.

How could her staff possibly feel that way about her?

"You do great work here," Sara said in an attempt to wrap this disastrous meeting up.

"Thanks. Just... maybe look at some of the others more closely before jumping to conclusions."

Sara wanted to melt into the group of her tile office floor. "Right. Yeah."

"See you tomorrow, Chef," Casey said, leaving with much less enthusiasm than he'd entered with.

Sara could relate. She felt deflated, and the day wasn't even half over.

At this point in the restaurant's lifespan, Sara trusted her staff to serve dinner without her being present.

And tonight, that's what needed to happen.

Sara's head wasn't in the game. She cut her finger dicing onions, forgot what the special was even though she'd been working on it for weeks, and then left tomatoes out of a batch of salsa.

Tomatoes. Out of a salsa!

"Trust" was a hard word to fall back on given the day's events, but Sara didn't have another choice. She clearly couldn't be trusted washing dishes, much less in her office confronting an employee. It would be better for everyone if she left.

So she handed the reins to Jose and called Joey to come pick her up.

A short while later, Joey pulled his truck behind the restaurant and hopped down, dark hair still wet and slightly curled from his shower. He'd been at the fire station the last two days, and Sara had hardly talked with him aside from a few quick texts.

"Are you bringing the whole restaurant?" he teased, eying the stacks of Tupperware around her feet.

Thank goodness Sara had prepped the food for the double Benson birthday party ahead of time. If she'd waited until this afternoon, they all would have ended up with food poisoning and a salty birthday cake.

"Feels like it," she said, pointing him to the heaviest boxes. "Those are all different cake layers and fondant decorations, though. So, it's not quite as bad as it looks."

"How big will this party be? Looks like a lot of cake."

"Just the family. I may have gone a little overboard," she admitted.

Joey laughed, his white teeth sparkling in the sun. "When don't you?"

He wasn't wrong. Sara took her role as the designated cake maker of the family very seriously. But she hadn't had a choice this time.

When Holly had suggested to Grady that maybe he'd like to do a separate party from Grandma this year—maybe one with his friends instead?—Grady had almost rioted.

"No way! Aunt Sara said last year that she'd make me a half-chocolate, half-red cake with green frosting and zombies eating the side of it."

Sara was impressed. The kid had a mind for details.

Holly had turned to her younger sister, eyes narrowed. "You said that?"

"I may recall saying something to that effect, yes," Sara admitted with a wince.

Grady had held a small finger under her chin. "You *promised*."

So Sara kept her promise.

The "red cake" he referred to was red velvet—her mom's favorite—and the perfect pairing for her cream cheese frosting recipe. Cream cheese frosting wasn't the easiest to decorate with by any means, but Sara was a chef, not a professional baker. No one could expect perfection. Plus, if zombies were going to be eating the cake, it was fine for it to be a little messy.

In the end, Sara had opted for four layers, alternating chocolate and red velvet. All covered in a green cream cheese frosting—and the requisite drooling zombies done in fondant, lest Grady have a fit if they were omitted.

Grady would love it and Sara would secure her title as the cool aunt. It should be a great party.

If she could get out of her funk long enough to enjoy it.

Joey helped Sara load the boxes in the back of the truck and then they traversed the cobblestone roads slowly, keeping the jostling to a minimum.

"How was your day?" he asked, his knee bouncing nervously.

He'd been around the Benson family plenty of times, so Sara didn't think he'd be nervous about the birthday party. It was more likely he'd had coffee while on shift again. The man could put out a forest fire without so much as blinking, but one cup of caffeine sent him jittering out of his skin.

Sara groaned. "Don't even remind me. It was miserable. I got into it with an employee because—"

"That sucks," Joey said, cutting her off. "I bet you showed them who was boss though, right?"

"Well. I mean, I kind of—"

"Good for you." Joey grinned and slapped the steering wheel. "Sometimes you have to drop the hammer."

It felt like the hammer had been dropped on Sara instead. Like one of those old cartoons where no matter how far the coyote threw the anvil, it always landed on his own head. Joey was usually a good listener, but he was distracted today. It was fine. Sara didn't want to talk much anyway.

"How was your day?" she asked instead.

Joey inhaled sharply and his eyebrows shot up like he'd been waiting for her to ask. Poised to answer.

He tipped his chin up at a sharp angle and batted his lashes. "What do you think about my profile? Handsome, no?"

Sara reached across the seat and pressed her hand to his forehead. "Are you feverish? You're being weird."

He rolled his eyes. "Just answer the question, Chef Sara."

She'd been joking, but his forehead did feel fine. "Of course you're handsome. Do you think I'd be dating you if you weren't handsome?"

"Good point. Plus, you literally swooned the first time we met."

Sara groaned, tired of reliving that particular memory. "My mom's inn was on fire. And I was exhausted. It had nothing to do with you. You just happened to catch me."

"Two sides to every story." He winked at her and waved one hand, redirecting her attention. "Anyway, I'm only asking because— drumroll please... I was discovered today!"

"*Discovered*?" Sara turned to him, paying full attention now. "What does that mean?"

"It means you are now dating a lifesaving firefighter *and* a movie star! I'm ready for my close-up, Mr. DeMille." Joey cocked his head at all kinds of strange angles, acting as though he was posing for the camera.

Sara just watched, confused. "You're going to be in a movie?"

He nodded eagerly, his teeth clicking together.

"Did you have an audition or something? You never mentioned anything."

"No, it was the funniest thing..."

He launched into the story, explaining that he'd been put in charge of the grocery run for the fire station. He was at the store, looking in the frozen food section for the hash browns everybody liked, when a woman had approached him.

"...Apparently, she is the casting director or something or other on the movie that's shooting at your mom's inn—the one based on Dominic's book."

"Yes, I'm familiar."

"Well, she liked the look of me and wants me to be in the movie!" Joey's mouth fell open, his eyebrows wagging playfully.

Sara couldn't find the right words. Mostly because the words that came to mind first were, *Are you serious?*

Yes, Joey was handsome. Borderline movie star handsome.

But he'd never acted a day in his life. And he'd just been standing in the grocery store.

In the freezer section.

Buying hash browns.

"What do you think?" he asked, nudging her with his elbow. "Are you starstruck?"

It was, of course, absolutely great news. Objectively so. No one could say this wasn't cool. So why did her stomach continue to twist into uncomfortable knots?

Why did her hands clench into fists and her toes press down into the thick foam of her shoe insoles?

Perhaps because it felt utterly, ridiculously, completely unfair.

Nothing in her life had ever landed in her lap like that. Sara busted her butt to earn her way into culinary school. She stayed late and showed up early to make sure she was top of her class. And even with all of that, it took her months to land a job in the city that didn't involve reheating frozen entrees and wearing a silly hat while she sang "Happy Birthday" to guests.

Then she'd worked her way up the ladder in Gavin's kitchen at Lonesome Dove, only to have him ruin everything by being a cheating, slimy, sexist pig.

No one had ever walked up to Sara while she was hash brown shopping, pointed at her, and said, "*I like the look of you. Care to own a restaurant?*"

That didn't happen to anyone!

So why Joey? Why should he get to be famous when Sara was the one who had worked her tail off?

When she was the one who had chosen the moral high road instead of selling her soul for a good review from a renowned food critic?

Why did he get to live his movie star dreams while Sara's dreams of being a big-time entrepreneur had practically crushed her earlier this afternoon just because a member of her waitstaff had gotten a little bit peeved?

"You okay, babe?" Joey asked with a cautious chuckle. "I was teasing about being starstruck, you know. Permission to speak and all that."

Sara knew her thoughts were unfairly bitter. Probably because she'd had such a rotten day.

She should be happy for Joey.

She would be.

In a sec.

"I'm fine. It's just the beginning of a bad headache, I think. It's been a day." She reached over and patted his knee. "But I'm happy for you."

"I still can't believe it," he sighed.

Sara swallowed the nausea that rose up in her. Casey had said very similar words only a few hours earlier, albeit for very different reasons.

"I can't wait to see you on the silver screen." Sara twisted her mouth into a smile.

Joey stared out the windshield, humming softly, clearly lost in star-studded fantasies.

Now, Sara really couldn't tell him how terrible her day had been. She didn't want to bring him down. No reason he needed to be crushed by her own personal anvil, too.

Like everything else, Sara would have to figure this out on her own.

7

ELIZA

THE NANTUCKET COTTAGE HOSPITAL

The surgery prep room was white and sterile and smelled like cleaning products.

This room had a window, at least. But the view was of the building next door. The gray stones were tinged green from moss and moisture and in desperate need of a power wash.

Eliza tried to open the window, but there was no latch. No way to let in a little fresh air.

She felt like she was suffocating.

The ambulance ride from the doctor's office to the hospital had been a blur. Eliza barely had time to register what the doctor was saying before she was being whisked away for emergency surgery.

"The baby has to come out today?" she'd asked. "Like, right now? This very second?"

"Yes," Dr. Geiger confirmed. "As soon as possible."

That had been an hour ago. Or was it two? Eliza didn't know.

But Oliver still didn't know anything was happening.

If Eliza could get the dumb window open, she could try to send him a carrier pigeon. Without her phone, that was the next best option.

Eliza knew Oliver's phone number. Had it memorized, of course. Or at least, she usually did. But whatever compartment of her brain that information lived in was firmly out of reach.

Try as she might, the numbers turned to a jumble in her head.

The woman working the check-in desk had given her a sympathetic smile like she was a simpleton when she'd been unable to provide an emergency contact.

Poor dear, her smile had said.

In New York City, Eliza had practically been hard wired to her telephone. She had to be available any time of day for questions from interns or clients or her boss. At any moment, she needed to be ready to handle business. Send over documents. Pull up facts and figures.

Maybe Eliza had fallen into the slow Nantucket lifestyle even deeper than she'd thought.

Oliver was almost always available. Even at work, he checked his phone during intermissions. At the peak of his worry about Eliza and the baby, he'd checked in between songs.

But now, her mind—usually a steel trap for numbers and data—felt more like a sieve. Somehow, she'd lost track of seven little digits. Seven vital digits.

She pressed her forehead against the glass window pane for a second, letting it cool her feverish thoughts, and then pushed the IV pole back to her hospital bed.

Oliver needed to be here for this surgery. She couldn't deliver their baby without him.

What if something went wrong?

Technically, something was already going wrong. Eliza wasn't supposed to have a baby today. It was too soon. Too early. She wasn't ready.

Winter had been a big, bouncing bundle of full-term joy. As had all of Holly's children. Eliza didn't know what to expect with a premature baby.

The whole time she was pregnant, each doctor's visit had contained an update about the size of the baby.

Oh, we've got a little sweet pea in there!

A plum in your belly!

Our little cabbage, our coconut, our pumpkin.

What would this one be when she arrived?

Dr. Geiger had no doubt done his best to tell Eliza exactly what was going on, but she hadn't caught it all. It was like standing in a wind tunnel on one of those game shows, dollar bills whipping through the air around you. She'd flailed around, grabbing as much information as she could. But it hadn't been enough.

Was the baby even ready to come out?

According to Dr. Geiger, it was best for her to be born now. Eliza wanted whatever was best for her unborn daughter, of course. But she couldn't get rid of the instinct that what was best for the baby was to stay inside of her for another month.

She didn't have a month. She didn't know how much time she had, but she knew one thing for sure: she wouldn't have this baby until Oliver was standing next to her.

A nurse opened the door, a look of concern pinching her features together. "Are you okay, honey?"

The woman had a Southern accent and a tall mess of blonde hair on her head. She looked like her sister Holly a bit, if Holly had more pronounced curves and hoop earrings.

"Fine," Eliza said. Her voice trembled as the word slipped out.

The nurse glanced at the machines around Eliza's bed. They were beeping loudly and often.

Somehow, Eliza had tuned them out. The noise in her head was plenty loud enough.

"That's fast enough to be the baby's heartbeat, but it's yours," the nurse remarked, eyes going wide. "Do you need something to settle you down, darling?"

"I'm okay."

She did feel out of breath, though. Like her lungs were too big for her chest. Like someone was tightening a vise around her ribcage.

"Maybe we could open the window?" she suggested.

"They don't open, I'm afraid." The nurse watched the monitor again and then plucked up Eliza's wrist, pressing two fingers to her pulse. "Hon, your heart is about to jump out of your chest."

Is this what served for good bedside manner these days? Surely these were not medically accurate terms. *Settle down. Jump out of your chest.*

Maybe she should have gone to the mainland to have the baby. Found a reputable doctor from a bigger city. Maybe these island people didn't know what they were doing, after all.

"I need to call my husband," Eliza said. "I think I need to get out of here."

She started sitting up, but the nurse placed a hand on her shoulder. It was a gentle touch, her fingers pliant. But the woman's arm was stiff, elbow locked. The heel of her palm pinned Eliza to the bed.

"We are working on finding his number," she said. "If you remember his number, just press the call button. We'll take care of it."

"I know his number," Eliza bit out.

"Great. What is it?" The nurse reached to the bedside table for the pad of paper with the hospital letterhead up top.

Eliza did her best to focus. Tried to make sense of the sudoku puzzle in her mind. Numbers whirled around, eights and fives and sevens and threes, but none of them stayed in place long enough for her to be certain they belonged.

And then the fruits came flying in—pumpkins and sweet peas and plums—and it was all chaos in her head and she had to open her eyes right away or else she was afraid she might vomit right on this poor woman's shoes.

"Well, I do know it, but not right now," she corrected. "I just need some air. I can't breathe. This place smells like bleach, and I'm—"

"Panicking," the nurse interrupted. Her brows were pinched together as she reached to hit the call button. "Take a deep breath for me, honey."

Deep breaths were extremely out of the question. Not when there was so little air in the room. Not when her chest felt like it was caving in.

It was the IV, Eliza decided. The tape around her elbow was too tight. Probably cutting off circulation, if she had to guess.

"In and out," the nurse said. "Breathe in and out. Nice and slow."

The woman's voice seemed far away. Like she was yelling down a long tunnel, her words an echo of an echo of an echo.

Eliza ignored her and reached for the IV.

"Oh, no. Let's not." The nurse grabbed her hand and pinned it to the bed. "You need that, honey."

"Don't call me that." Oliver had more creative pet names. They at least made Eliza laugh a little. This one was annoying. And patronizing.

She wanted Oliver here instead.

"Don't cry, dear," the nurse said. "Someone is coming to help. Okay?"

Cry? Eliza wasn't crying.

Except that, when she licked her dry lips, she tasted salt.

She *was* crying. A lot.

But Eliza Benson Patterson didn't cry.

No outward displays of extreme emotion. No jumping and screaming for joy. Certainly no crying.

But this? Weeping in front of a stranger? This wasn't Eliza. She didn't even recognize herself.

"I'm sorry, I—"

The nurse squeezed her hand. "Don't apologize. I'll be right back."

She turned and left the room.

Eliza let her head loll back on the pillows. She didn't know how much time passed as she stared at the thin slit of sunlight shining between the buildings and through the window. It seemed like it was moving across the floor quickly. Like she was in a time lapse, the sun arcing in fast forward across the sky.

Then the door opened and the same nurse returned with more of her colleagues in tow.

Eliza should learn their names. It wasn't polite to think of them all as "Nurse." They had names.

She tried to ask them, but they eased her back in the bed and hung a new bag from her IV pole.

"This will help calm you down, honey," the nurse who looked like Holly said.

Another nurse with spiky black hair nodded. "It's not good for the baby for you to be so worked up. An operating room is freeing up for you, so we'll move you in just a few minutes."

"We'll take care of you," someone else added.

A hand—which of them was it attached to? It seemed important that she know that—smoothed down Eliza's arm with the IV in it. Eliza tried to turn her head, but her vision swirled.

It was hard to even tell who was speaking. The comforting words seemed to come from everywhere and nowhere at once.

"Breathe."

"It's okay."

"Try and relax, honey."

Eliza had had a panic attack once before. It brought her here, in a weird sort of way. From Manhattan to Nantucket. And it felt just like this. Like she'd been locked in a cage, her mind and body separated by metal bars she couldn't get through no matter how many times she rammed up against them.

She felt that same disconnect now.

"Wait?" she slurred. "A medication?"

"Anti-anxiety. It will help you relax," another voice or voices said.

Eliza tried to speak, but an indistinct sound came out instead of words.

What she wanted to tell them was that she'd always responded extremely strongly to downers. A simple Xanax could knock her out for hours.

Blackness seeped into the edges of her vision. Eliza couldn't help but give in to the sensation. She let her lids fall closed, even as her mind warred against her body.

Stay awake.

Call Oliver.

Get up!

Eliza mouthed Oliver's name, hoping somehow, he'd be able to sense her need for him and show up. She couldn't do this without him. She needed him with her.

Then everything went black.

Eliza got her wisdom teeth removed her junior year of high school.

Her dad had driven her to Dr. Jackson's office and waited in the waiting room during her surgery. Afterward, he'd helped her to the car, but Eliza didn't remember that part. She didn't remember much, really. Just snippets. The sound of her dad laughing, amused by her clumsiness. A Nirvana song on the radio.

Her dad had buckled her into the passenger seat. But whenever he hit the brakes, Eliza started slumping forward.

Seatbelts were designed to stop a human body moving at a fast rate of speed. But, Eliza, still groggy and out of it from the anesthesia, had fallen forward gently, like a feather floating to the ground. So slowly that the seatbelt in her dad's pickup truck hadn't registered anything was wrong and just let her go, go, go.

Her dad laughed about it for years afterward, telling the story anytime anyone mentioned surgery or anesthesia. "The poor girl was helpless," he'd cackle. "There's a first time for everything."

And a second time, apparently.

Eliza felt helpless now. Like she was swimming in wet cement and moving an inch felt like moving a mile.

Then, suddenly, there was a hand on her arm.

A warm hand. Calloused. Roughened at the fingertips from years of plucking strings and tapping away at keys. Eliza knew that touch, even in her foggy state.

Oliver.

She strained against the heavy pull of her lids, trying to see him.

"Eliza?"

His voice was warm and smooth, but there was a tinge of worry there, too. Something Oliver's voice was usually free from.

That's one of the reasons their relationship worked so well. Eliza worried; Oliver eased. They struck a delicate balance that allowed each of them to be better.

Now that Eliza was unconscious, however, Oliver had to strike that balance on his own. He had to worry for her. Eliza didn't like being the cause of that.

Besides, she was fine. Whatever the nurses had pumped into her IV had knocked her out, but Eliza did feel more calm now. More in control. In control of her mind, at least.

Even if her body still hadn't roused, Eliza's mind felt sharp. She could even remember Oliver's phone number now. Though that hardly seemed necessary since he was sitting by her bedside. Someone must have called him.

"Liza?" Oliver asked, voice more urgent now. "Hi, babe. Can you hear me?"

She blinked. This time, light came through.

A blurry world came into more and more focus with each flutter of her eyelids. Eliza could tell she was regaining the use of her body.

She tried to lift herself onto her elbows to show Oliver she was okay. That she was in control of herself. He didn't need to worry.

His hand moved from her hand to her shoulder, pushing her down. "Whoa, cowgirl," he said, easing her back down to the mattress. Eliza could tell it didn't take much of his strength. Even though sitting up had taken all of hers. "Too early for that."

Too early? To sit up?

She didn't understand what he could mean. Why couldn't she sit up?

"You might rip stitches," Oliver explained, as though reading her mind.

Stitches?

Eliza wracked her brain for several second. His words made no sense in her hazy state. Then, suddenly, she realized.

The baby.

Oliver's hand rubbed from her shoulder down to her elbow. "Everything is okay. Relax."

The baby. Where is the baby?

"Breathe, Eliza. I've called a nurse."

Eliza realized she was talking out loud. She could feel her mouth moving, but only distantly. And her voice sounded like it was traveling through water to get to her.

She took a deep breath like Oliver said.

Finally, when she tried again, she found she could open her eyes.

Oliver stood over her, hair curled and long over his ears. His stubble was thick. He had on a t-shirt with a rip around the collar—the one he usually only wore when he was working on a house project like fixing a leaky pipe or cleaning the gutters. He must have dressed in a hurry.

His skin was even paler than usual, even after he'd caught some sun the week before at the beach. His green eyes shined with unshed tears.

The machine over her shoulder beeped along to the quick rhythm Eliza was setting. She took another deep breath, but the beeping picked up pace.

She licked her dry lips. "Where's the baby?" she croaked.

Oliver shushed her, smoothing a hand through her hair. "Everything is okay." He glanced at the machines behind her head, worry creasing his face.

Eliza wanted him to look at her, not the monitors. "Oliver."

"The doctor is on his way," he said. "I called the babysitter and Winter is fine, too."

Of course Winter was fine. Why wouldn't she be? Why was Oliver telling her things she didn't care about?

Eliza didn't want to know where Dr. Geiger was. She didn't want him to call a nurse. She didn't want to hear about the babysitter.

There was only one thing she wanted to know, and Oliver needed to tell her. *Now.*

She squeezed his hand as hard as she could—which, under the circumstances, wasn't very hard.

And then, with as much strength as she could dredge up, she rasped four words.

"Where is my baby?"

8

BRENT
114 HOWARD STREET

Brent shoved the mobile with the unfamiliar name back into the bag and did his best to forget about it.

Clearly, no one had intended for him to see it.

Besides, he needed to pick Susanna up from daycare. This would have to wait until later.

He brushed the dust and cobwebs from his shirt, closed and locked the workshop doors tightly, and drove across town to get in the pick-up line.

"We ate hotdogs in the shape of an octopus and played hair salon and Maggie didn't know the colors of the rainbow, but I knew purple because purple is my favorite color," Susanna said, speaking so fast in the backseat she had to stop and catch her breath. Her shoulders rose and fell with the effort. "Rory said it was violet, but Miss Katherine said we both were right, and I didn't even stick my tongue out at him."

Asking Susanna about her day at daycare opened the floodgates. She remembered everything and she spared no details.

"You did or didn't stick your tongue out at him?" Brent asked.

Susanna's eyes widened and she hesitated before shaking her head. "Didn't."

Brent raised a skeptical brow. "I'm thinking maybe you did stick your tongue out at him."

The girl's cheeks went pink, and she stammered through a few partial explanations before she heaved a huge sigh. "Only a *little* bit of my tongue."

She couldn't keep a secret. Like Brent's mom, Susanna wore the whole truth on her face.

When his parents threw him a surprise birthday party the year he turned sixteen, Brent had known about it for weeks. His mom's ears turned pink every time the topic of his birthday came up in conversation.

Mae Benson being an open book had always been a given. A surety.

But suddenly, Brent wasn't so sure.

As it turned out, she was capable of keeping some things very secret indeed.

"...See? Just a little bit. Like this." Susanna pinched the tip of her tongue between her front teeth.

Brent blinked, coming out of autopilot mode, remembering all at once he was driving. He looked at her in the rearview mirror and grinned.

"Well, that's better than your whole tongue, but worse than no tongue sticking out at all. Mixed progress."

The summer sun beamed down from straight overhead now, the shadows on the cobblestone streets almost non-existent. The breeze that rolled through the open window was refreshing and salty.

He wished he'd spent the day at work. It was a great day to be on the water. Being out on a boat always helped him clear his head.

Suddenly, Susanna gasped. Brent jerked the wheel slightly in surprise. "What is it?"

"I'm supposed to go to Jemima's house today!"

"Is that so?"

Susanna leaned out of her booster seat towards the window. "Mom told me she'd pick me up there. Oh no, we forgot!"

Brent laughed and shifted the car into park. "No, *you* forgot. I remembered." He tipped his head towards Jemima's two-story brick house in front of them. "We have arrived at your destination, young princess."

She sagged in relief and was unbuckled, bouncing in the backseat by the time Brent pulled the car door open. The moment he did, she lunged out, arms spread wide, certain he'd catch her.

And he did. Of course he did.

Brent swirled her through the air for a second before plopping her sparkly sneakers in the grass. Then she ran for the front door, knocking before Brent could even mount the steps in her wake.

Susanna's friend Jemima and her mom answered the door. Rose had told Brent the woman's name half a dozen times, but he couldn't remember. He was terrible with names. And Rose was usually responsible for scheduling the playdates, so he was out of practice.

Susanna and Jemima squealed like they hadn't seen each other in months, even though they'd just been at daycare together. They ran into the house, disappearing at the end of a long hallway.

"Sorry I couldn't bring Susanna home with us," Jemima's mom said. "My car is overflowing with cinnamon rolls that need to be delivered. This is the last time I sign up to be the delivery driver for a fundraiser."

"For the cheerleading team, right?" Brent vaguely remembered filling out an order form for a tray of cream cheese cinnamon rolls.

She groaned. "Yes. I keep telling people to find me in the daycare pick-up line, but no one does. I'm one day away from dumping them in front of the doors and putting a 'FREE' sign on them."

"Our order isn't one of those, right?" Brent asked, wincing slightly. "I forgot we got some."

"No, no, nothing to worry about. Rose took care of it two days ago." She pressed her hands together in gratitude. "Bless her."

"Great. There's a reason I let her handle those kinds of things."

"But feel free to take another! I'm positive half of these will never be claimed." She hitched a thumb over her shoulder. Brent could see a stack of disposable aluminum pans sitting on the counter.

"Tempting, but I'm actually headed into work."

Brent had made that decision all at once. He couldn't imagine going back to his house right now. Spending the rest of the afternoon alone with his thoughts.

He needed to *do* something.

"Perfect. Then you're definitely taking one." She jogged into the house and returned with a tray, practically shoving it into his hands. "These were for Isabel Morris, but I tried to wave her down yesterday, and she practically sprinted away from my car. I think she just started a new diet."

"If you're sure..."

"I'm positive," she said. She backed quickly into the house, as if Brent might change his mind and chuck the cinnamon rolls through the door like a grenade at the last minute. "Take care!"

As he walked back towards his car idling on the curb, Brent couldn't believe his life.

Dropping a kid off for playdates, buying fundraiser cinnamon rolls, and going into work on his day off.

If Brent could tell Past Him that this was how his days would look, he would have spewed his beer in the bartender's face.

Past Brent also would've done a spit-take at the news that he was the co-owner of his own business. One he shared with his best friend.

Yet sure enough, less than ten minutes later, Brent was walking through the front doors of a business that bore his name, his best friend and partner in crime lounging behind a real-life desk.

Talk about surreal.

"Triple B! What drags you in? I thought you took the day off."

Marshall Cook had a nickname for everyone he met. Even though Brent's middle name did not begin with a "B," Triple B had stuck.

"Had to make sure you weren't running the place into the ground and scaring away our newest hire."

"Too late. The new guy never showed. I had to call in Mary-Ann last minute to cover for him."

"Aw, drat. You could've called me." Brent peeled the top off of the cinnamon roll tray and dropped them on the desk.

Marshall's eyes lit up and he dug in immediately. His next words were muffled by the bite. "You were busy. Getting ready for your mom and Dominic to come stay, right?"

Brent nodded, feeling suddenly nervous about the visit.

His mom had seen him through some of his darkest times. She'd been there for him no matter how many times he ended up passed out on the floor or thrown in a jail cell for the night. She'd been a pillar for him. A lighthouse leading him through the dark, trustworthy and sure.

Now, that light flickered.

"And need I remind you," Marshall continued, wiping the back of his hand across his sleeve, flakes of cream choose frosting scattering across his desk, "I built this business from the ground up. You came in after all the hard work had been done. You're just riding on my coattails."

"Tell that to the sign out front. Whose name comes first?"

Marshall flipped his wrist dismissively. "We went in alphabetical order, not order of importance."

"Whatever you say, pal."

The truth was, Benson & Cook Enterprises was a real team effort.

Marshall had started the chartered fishing company on his own. Nothing but his boat, *Tripidation II*, and a desire to never work a boring nine to five if he could help it. But together, he and Brent had turned it from a successful side hustle into a full-blown enterprise.

It started out with a few minimum wage part-timers and some rented boats, but now they had full-time employees who ran tours on their own, giving Marshall and Brent a much-needed break.

They could actually take time off. And still make money! Wonders never ceased.

They had a storefront near the marina with a fresh coat of paint and their names vinyl-stamped across the front window. And desks. With honest-to-goodness *nametags*.

Marshall leaned back at his desk and kicked his feet up, a stack of papers crunching under his heel. "Did you lay out a red carpet for your A-list guests?"

"What?"

"Dominic and your mom," Marshall explained like Brent was slow in the head. "This movie is all I've heard about all day. Half our bookings right now are cast and crew. It's a big deal."

"Oh. No, not really. I took down the old swimsuit posters in my room for them. Does that count?"

Marshall snorted. "They're staying in your old room?"

"Yeah. Where else would they stay?"

"Fair enough," Marshall said with a shrug. "It's just weird, isn't it?"

"Maybe a little."

Brent knew when he bought his childhood home that they might run into some potential downsides, but until today, he'd steered clear of that.

He loved the familiarity of 114 Howard Street. For years after moving out on his own, Brent had felt lost. Unmoored. It felt good to settle down someplace he knew inside and out.

Or rather, nearly inside and out. Apparently, one little corner had remained a dust-covered mystery.

Marshall looked up at the ceiling and chuckled. "I remember sneaking your drunk behind down that hallway outside their bedroom door more than once during senior year. And now that room is yours. The whole house is yours."

"Almost."

He hadn't mean to say it out loud. But it seemed there was a limit to how much even Brent Benson could repress.

"The sale is final, right?"

"Yeah, yeah, done and dusted. It's nothing," Brent said, pasting on a smile.

Marshall didn't buy it. He dropped his feet and leaned forward, brows pulled together. "What's up, Triple B? Talk to me."

"It's nothing," Brent said again. But once again, the harder he shoved everything down, the more it seemed to want to bubble to the surface. "I was cleaning out my dad's old workshop, and I found something."

"Like...?"

Marshall wasn't prying. After a lifetime of friendship, there were very few secrets between the two of them.

Still, this felt like something that wasn't Brent's to share.

"Something my parents lied about."

The words seemed harsh, but Brent didn't know how else to describe it.

It sure felt like his parents had lied to him. How many times had he asked them for a brother when he was younger? He hated being the youngest. Hated being the only boy in a family of girls.

At Christmas when he was five, he asked Santa for a baby brother. And they never told him he already had one. Not once. His mom had bought him a G.I. Joe instead.

Marshall's eyes went wide. "Are you adopted?"

"No," Brent snorted. "Well, not that I know of."

"But it's a big family secret?" Marshall asked.

"Pretty big."

"And it's the reason your forehead is all creased up like that?"

Brent ran a self-conscious hand over his face, feeling all of the ridges. He made a concerted effort to relax. "Yeah."

"Then you should talk to your mom about it. Clear the air."

Marshall was saying exactly what Brent knew he needed to do. But that didn't change how little he wanted to do it.

Hadn't his family been through enough in the last few years without dredging up old drama?

Marshall leaned forward even further and dropped his voice low. "Is Sara adopted?"

"No one is adopted!" Brent laughed and shook his head.

"I had to ask. She's always been an odd one."

"Why? Because she wouldn't date you when you were a pimply freshman?" Brent asked, one eyebrow raised. "That doesn't make her weird. It makes her like every other girl on the island."

Marshall gasped, a hand pressed to his chest in mock offense. "I had a crush on her for one second. And I never asked her out, so my one-hundred-percent dating acceptance rate remains intact, thank you very much."

"You're good at convincing girls to go out on one date, but how many have taken you up on two?" Brent teased, grateful for the change in conversation.

"Those stats aren't interesting to me," Marshall said, balling up a piece of paper and throwing it at Brent's chest. "The only thing that matters to me is that Lean Machine and I have been on too many dates to count."

"Lean Machine? That's the nickname you're going with?" Brent sighed. "I can't believe Lena lets you call her that."

"She loves it," Marshall argues. "Almost as much as she loves me."

"Things are going well, then?"

"Great." Marshall grinned like the lovesick puppy dog he was. "She's great. We are doing great. Everything is—"

"Great?" Brent finished.

"Exactly. I mean, I'm dating a doctor. Can you believe that? Never saw that coming."

"A veterinarian."

Marshall raised a brow in warning. "Are you saying there's a difference?"

"No, just specifying," Brent said, holding up his hands in surrender. "It explains a lot. Vets usually have an affinity for stray animals."

Marshall laughed. "You got me there, amigo. But speaking of stray animals, Roger came in earlier. He wanted to talk with you."

"You better not let Roger hear you talk about him that way. He may be older than both of us by a few decades, but he could fight you."

Roger was the tattoo-covered Navy vet who owned the marina. Despite the fights Brent had been in over the years, he was fairly sure Roger could take him, too.

Marshall stood up and swatted Brent's ear on his way to the door. "I wasn't talking about Roger. Let's go, Mutt."

Brent groaned and followed Marshall outside. He sensed his friend was testing out a new nickname for him.

God forbid this one stick.

Benson & Cook headquarters was only a block away from the marina, but Marshall insisted they needed a golf cart to zip back and forth.

Brent felt a little ridiculous, but he had to admit it made it easier to find parking.

The day was clear, high sun reflecting off the gentle Atlantic waters. Bouncing down the cobblestone street towards the marina, the water sparkled like a pile of sapphires as far as the horizon.

Then a speedboat roared across the scene, slicing the smooth water in two with a foamy white gash.

Summer was the busy season. Tourists visited Nantucket all year round, of course, but in the summer, they invaded.

Marauded, really. Locals trying to get out on the water for sport or work had to navigate around out-of-towners who drove their barely-used boats way too fast through the harbor and sent waves crashing against the docks.

Still, Brent liked the hustle and bustle. Especially since tourists made up almost one-hundred percent of Benson & Cook's clientele. Locals had no need for anyone to hold their hands on a chartered fishing trip. But tourists could always use the help. Brent and Marshall took them to the best fishing spots, provided all of the equipment, and made sure they had a good time. If not, there was a money-back guarantee (though to date, it remained mercifully unused).

Just as they passed the marina, Marshall pointed out one of their boats pulling into the harbor. The company boats were all painted the same turquoise blue with their company name imprinted on the back and side in navy script.

Today's vessel was driven by Mary-Ann. She was a local, a born and raised fisherwoman, and she absolutely did not appreciate the constant *Gilligan's Island* jokes lobbed her way by clients.

Still, she did her best to humor them. They tipped better when she laughed and played along.

The clients with her today were an older couple. The woman was stretched out on a chair with large sunglasses on her face and a book in her hands. The man, clothed in a vest, cargo shorts, and a matching fishing hat, stood at the helm of the boat, chest puffed out.

From Brent's vantage point, he could see a price tag still dangling from the hem of the vest, flapping in the wind.

Brent and Marshall were waiting for the boat when it docked.

"How did Mary-Ann treat you?" Brent asked the guy.

"The ride went a little over three hours, but she didn't get us stranded on a deserted island," he chortled. "So we give her five stars."

Mary-Ann grimaced in his direction. Brent winked at her in solidarity. "She's one of our best."

Brent and Marshall were both long past cleaning duties, but they hopped on board to assist the guests disembarking with their fishy prizes and help Mary-Ann scrub up.

The cooler of customary beer and soda remained untouched, but the bottle of white wine was empty next to the deck chair. That explained the wife's wobbly steps down the dock. Her nails had bit into Brent's arm as he led her down the stairs.

"You two don't have to do this," Mary-Ann protested. "I can handle clean-up on my own."

"I called you at five-thirty AM this morning, and you were here in twenty minutes. It's the least I can do," Marshall said, pressing an earnest hand to his chest. "Forever grateful."

"Forever grateful you didn't have to haul your tired butt out here that early," Brent snorted.

Marshall grinned and nodded. "Isn't that what I said?"

Coming down to the water had been the right idea.

Even when he was mopping dirty water off the deck and throwing away used plastic cups, being this close to the water and feeling the sway of the boat beneath him made Brent feel grounded. Better than he had all day.

It was only when he stepped back on dry land that his pesky thoughts came rushing back.

Marshall noticed right away. "You came into work on your day off, which means you're even more messed up than you're letting on."

"I'm fine," Brent said.

Marshall rolled his eyes. "How many times have I heard that before? I'm not buying it."

There were pros and cons to having a lifelong friend. Marshall knew Brent too well.

"I'm just saying," Marshall said, swinging into the golf cart and slamming his foot down on the brake pedal to release it, "talk to your mom. The sooner you get this cleared up, the sooner I can be sure you're fine."

Brent had always thought of Marshall as his brother. Or rather, the closest thing he had.

Marshall had two older brothers of his own, though. Brent had always been jealous of that.

"You only care because I run half this business. You don't want me being a liability."

"Hey, I never said my intentions were pure." He laughed and nudged Brent in the arm.

They were just starting to pull away when the weather-warped marina door banged open and Roger came hustling out, waving his arms. "Leaving without saying goodbye?"

Sheriff Mike followed him out, a mug of coffee in his hand. No doubt sourced from the ancient pot in Roger's office that never seemed to empty. "Or are you running off because you saw the law around?"

Brent laughed. "Honest men don't need to run from you, Sheriff."

"Then why aren't you sprinting, son?"

All the men chuckled together. Brent's past featured a few run-ins with the local law, but Sheriff Mike had been a good friend of his dad's and treated Brent more as a wayward son than a ward of the state.

Now that Brent was sober and thriving, however, there was no need for any tough love. His activities remained well above-board.

Roger tipped his head to Brent. "I came by to see you, but you weren't in the office."

"Well, you got me now. What's up?"

"Sometime in the next few days, send me the dates you have open for a tour. Not with one of your young employees. With you."

"You want us to take you out on a boat?" Brent shot a disbelieving look at Marshall, who looked just as bewildered as he felt.

Roger had been in the Navy for years and running the marina for even longer. If there was anyone in Nantucket more experienced on the water, Brent didn't know them. Why he'd want a chartered fishing tour was beyond him.

Roger snorted. "Of course not. It's for my lady's father."

Brent had no idea Roger had a lady. He couldn't quite picture what that lady would look like, either. Something like a manatee, if he had to guess.

But good for Roger nonetheless.

"He's an old coot," Roger said, rolling his eyes. "I'd take him out myself, but I'm worried I'd chuck him off the boat a half hour in."

"You aren't making this sound appealing," Brent laughed.

Roger shrugged. "That's because I'm being honest. I figure I'll just get suddenly busy the day they come into town and have no other choice but to send him out with you lot instead. I suppose you two could assign him to an employee if you want. But they're liable to quit. So make sure it's someone you can stand to lose."

"What about me?" Marshall asked. "I was in the office this morning when you came in. Why does it need to be Brent? You don't trust me?"

"With your sense of humor, the old man would throw *you* overboard," Roger said flatly. "Brent's the only one I figure is up for the job. He can be serious. And he can handle him."

"I'll send over dates as soon as I get back to the office. Pick one and I'll get it on the schedule," Brent intervened.

"Much obliged."

Marshall threw up an invisible cowboy hat as he hit the gas and squealed away from the marina going a full twelve miles per hour.

Brent was honored Roger trusted him, but he wasn't so sure Roger was right. How much could Brent really handle if he was afraid to talk to his own mom?

He would see his mom at her party tonight. And Brent figured it was as good a time as any to find out what he was really made of.

9

MAE
THE SWEET ISLAND INN

Try as she might, Mae couldn't sit still.

She spent the rest of her birthday afternoon securing butcher paper to easels and scrubbing dried paint off of her supply of brushes so the kiddos could fingerpaint. She re-stocked marshmallow shooters and positioned them covertly around the party area along with a healthy pile of marshmallow ammunition.

Never one to slack, she also created a scavenger hunt that would take the kids all through the Inn, eventually leading them to the tree line just behind the garden where a treasure trove of candy and soda lay in wait.

Despite Dominic's many objections that the party was ready, Mae knew there was more to a party than tablecloths and balloons. The grandkids would need entertainment. And she was not the type of grandma to leave them disappointed.

After placing the last bowl of marshmallows on the snack table, Mae turned to Dominic. He'd flopped down into a folding chair ten minutes earlier, tongue lolling out the side of his mouth.

"We're done," she said excitedly.

Dominic didn't move.

She patted his shoulder. "Are you going to have enough energy to enjoy the party?"

"Barely," he groaned, letting his head flop to the side dramatically. "I'm not sure how you're still standing."

"Practice."

Usually, when it came to hosting wedding receptions and rehearsals, birthday parties, and luncheons at the inn, Mae brought in outside staff to help. But still, she'd more than prepared herself for the task of throwing a family birthday party.

Dominic, unfortunately, hadn't had her same level of training.

"Mom?" a familiar voice called out from inside the house.

Mae gave Dominic a quick kiss on the cheek and hurried for the back door. "Not a moment too soon. Our first guests have arrived," she cooed. "In the backyard, Brent!"

Her son appeared a moment later in the back doorway, Rose at his side. He threw his arms wide and grinned. "Happy birthday, Mom!"

"Thank you." Mae moved in for a hug, but before she could, a small figure broke from between Brent and Rose and sprinted for Mae, a blur of long hair and freckles.

"Happy birthday, Gramma!" Susanna wrapped her arms around Mae's legs. Mae bent down and pressed a kiss to the girl's head, pulling her close.

"Thank you, sweet girl. How can it not be happy now that you're here?"

"Looks like we're the first ones, too," Brent said with a glance around the backyard, eyebrows raised. "Eliza will hate that I beat her here."

Mae had been so busy all afternoon she'd forgotten she was expecting a call from Eliza earlier in the day.

"To wish you a happy birthday and tell you how my appointment went," Eliza had said the night before.

"You can wish me happy birthday at my party," Mae had insisted. She didn't want to be a burden to her kids.

Eliza had tsked. "A birthday morning phone call is tradition."

"From when you lived further away."

"Still," she'd said, "I'll call you in the morning."

The fact it was now late afternoon pushing into evening—with nary a peep from her eldest—planted a seed of worry deep in her gut.

"Well, Eliza can blame me for us being here on time," Rose said, stepping forward to pull Mae into a quick hug. "I almost had to drag Brent out the front door."

Mae laughed. "That sounds more like it. Brent has always moved at his own pace. Learned that from his father, despite my best efforts."

"And we're the first ones here, so clearly, I had plenty of time to spare," Brent said with a smug smile tossed in Rose's direction.

Rose spun around. "Would you rather be sitting in front of the ball game at home or standing here to lord this victory over your sister's head?"

Brent wrapped a casual arm around Rose's shoulders and grinned. "You know me so well. I do love to lord."

Mae smiled and shook her head.

As the baby of the family, the older girls complained that Brent got special treatment, but it wasn't true. Goodness know he spent a fair chunk of his childhood in timeout or grounded.

It was just that he'd always been able to make Mae laugh—even when she was steaming mad. It never lessened his punishment, but it made it awfully hard to stay stern.

Brent was still just as charming and funny as he'd always been. That little rascal never faded. But he was different, too. More mature.

Rose had something to do with that. A willowy, soft-spoken woman, Brent loved her with his heart and soul. Mae desperately hoped she felt the same way about him.

"Where should I put these?" Rose dangled the gift bags from her finger. One was pink, trimmed in silver. The other was blue, covered in dinosaurs wearing party hats. Mae didn't have to wonder which gift belonged to her and which belonged to Grady.

She pointed. "The table to the left will be perfect, love."

Brent plucked the bags from his girlfriend's hand, pressed a kiss to her temple, and sauntered off towards the table in question. His route took him past the army of chairs arranged around the main table.

"Looks like we're expecting half the island over, Mom."

Dominic chuckled from where he sat and nodded. "I've been helping her all day, and it sure feels as if that's the case."

"She put you to work, Dom?" Brent asked, grabbing a handful of Chex Mix from the snack table as he passed.

"I didn't ask him to do anything I wasn't willing to do myself," Mae cut in, narrowing her eyes playfully at Dominic.

"Gotta go easy on your fella. Not everyone can run around in high gear like you do, Ma."

Rose snorted. "Who are you to talk? You went into work on your day off."

"You did?" Mae asked in surprise.

"After he cleaned out the guest room upstairs and the workshop to make room for the things you need to store," Rose continued. "He should be exhausted, but he's as wound-up as ever."

Mae turned to Brent. "You used your one day off to clean for us? You know you didn't have to do that."

He ran a hand through his blond hair, sending the right side of it sticking up at odd angles. "It needed to be done, anyway. I got rid of some junk furniture. And the workshop was full of scrap wood."

Brent took a deep breath, casting his eyes quickly to Mae and then away again before adding under his breath, "...and old memories."

Her heart tugged.

She'd cleaned out what she wanted from the rest of the house after Henry died, but she hadn't been able to go into the workshop. The entire time she and Henry had lived on Howard Street together, the workshop was his space to do with what he would. Mae couldn't stand the idea of going in there once he was gone and deciding which pieces of him to get rid of.

Though she shouldn't have saved the task for her son, either.

She frowned. "You could have called me," she said softly. "I would have come to help."

Brent studied her for a second, his usually light expression weighed with something Mae couldn't place.

But in an instant, it was gone, replaced by an easy smile, and she wondered if it had ever been there at all.

"And leave Dominic here to set up the party by himself?" he balked. "I wouldn't dream of it."

"Thank you," Dominic called over. "There's a reason you're my favorite, Brent."

Susanna, having found one of the marshmallow shooters, streaked by and fired off a marshmallow at Dominic. "I thought I was your favorite!" she screeched.

"You are!" Dominic laughed, shielding himself. "Especially when you have a weapon in your hands."

Rose went chasing after Susanna, laughing while also dispensing some motherly advice about never aiming marshmallow guns in anyone's face.

Meanwhile, Dominic was scanning around, looking for his own weapon to retaliate with.

It was good to have company. The place felt alive when there was a bustle of activity and lots of happy chatter. Even though her children had been grown and gone for years now, Mae had never grown used to the quiet.

Brent sidled up next to Mae, hands in his pockets. "Anything left you need me to help with? It seems everyone else is busy waging marshmallow warfare."

"You know me. There's always something left to do." She directed Brent inside and loaded his arms down with more food to carry outside.

Sara had volunteered to take care of the main courses—since, according to her, "No one should have to cook their own birthday dinner." But Mae couldn't keep herself from making a large serving bowl of her famous potato salad, a dish of Boston Baked Beans, and some coleslaw.

When she saw Brent helping, Susanna dropped her marshmallow shooter and wanted to help, too.

"I can carry lots of things," the little girl boasted. "I'm very strong."

"I know you are," Mae said as she handed her plates, cups, napkins, and forks. She did her best to direct Susanna on how to set the table, but most of the settings ended up scattered haphazardly around the table.

Mae didn't mind, though. This was a family affair, after all. It was only right all the family got to pitch in.

By the time she made it back to the party area, Dominic was no longer sitting at his spot at the table.

"Where'd Dom go?" she asked, spinning in a circle, more surprised that he'd stood up on his tired legs than anything else.

"Grandpa went inside." Susanna pointed up at the second story window, and Mae could see Dominic standing in front of the open window fussing with something.

Dominic wasn't Susanna's grandpa in any technical sense of the word, but he had earned the title in every way that counted. Mae thought it was sweet that Susanna had taken to the two of them so readily. She was more than happy to add Susanna into the Benson clan mix.

She only hoped Brent would make it official by asking Rose to marry him sooner rather than later. Another grandchild or two would draw no complaints from her, either.

"What are you doing up there?" Mae called up, cupping a hand around her mouth.

Just as she asked, the question was drowned out by the first strains of an Elvis song filling the warm afternoon air.

Brent clapped his hands. "Now it's a party. Music!" He grabbed Rose's hand and twirled her once before pulling her against his chest.

Dominic padded out onto the grass a moment later and winked at her.

"Wanted a little ambience?" she asked.

Instead of answering, Dominic bowed low and held out his hand. "May I have this dance?"

"The party hasn't even started yet."

Dominic leaned in close and smiled. "With you, life is always a party."

She rolled her eyes as he took her hand and pulled her close. As Elvis crooned about falling in love, Dominic hummed along with the words in Mae's ear.

Even with Brent taking turns twirling his two laughing girls across the lawn, it felt as though Mae and Dominic were the only two people in the world.

When she'd first met Dominic, Mae had expected him to be shy and introspective, with all the grace of most writerly types—that is to say, dexterous of fingers, not of foot. That was mostly true enough.

But my, the man could dance!

One morning, soon after they'd made their feelings for one another clear, Dominic had put on this same Elvis record in the front window of the Inn. A moment later, he'd appeared on the porch to ask Mae to dance.

"I love Elvis," she'd said, resting her head on his shoulder. The King's voice had purred over Mae's skin like warm velvet.

"Of course you do. Everyone with taste does."

The memory made her laugh, even now all these many months later.

When the song ended and Dominic still held her close, not yet ready to let her go, Brent whooped and cackled at the two of them. "Get a load of the lovebirds!"

Over Dominic's shoulder, Mae saw Rose nudge her son. "Don't embarrass your mom."

But Mae didn't mind in the slightest.

"I didn't know you could dance, Mom!"

Mae turned and saw Sara in the doorway, her arms weighed down with bags and to-go containers. Her boyfriend, Joey, was carrying a stack of warming trays just behind her.

Brent gasped. "*Sara* is here before Eliza, too?" He made a big show of scanning the sky as he muttered under his breath, "There's gonna be a pig flying past any second now."

"Eliza isn't here yet?" Sara asked, looking shocked and then pleased in quick succession. "Good for me."

"If Holly and Pete make it here with the kids soon, then this could be a day for the record books," Brent chimed in. "It's never been done."

The kids were just teasing, but it brought Eliza to the forefront of Mae's mind.

Where *was* she?

It was funny—after so many years of Eliza living in New York City and only being able to reach her in pre-scheduled five minute increments—how quickly Mae had grown used to seeing and talking to Eliza every day at leisure.

"Have either of you heard from your sister?" Mae inquired.

Brent pursed his lips. "Not since last night. Well, I talked to Oliver. He texted me a video of a dad using a vacuum cleaner nozzle to put a ponytail in his daughter's hair."

Susanna's eyes widened and she clutched at her hair in horror. "No way!"

"Not since Wednesday when I dropped off a lasagna," Sara offered.

Brent stopped chasing Susanna and turned on his heel with a gasp. "Where's *my* lasagna?"

"When you learn to play the piano and can fill in last minute if my Live Music Sunday slot falls through, you'll get a lasagna," Sara retorted.

"Or when you date her," Joey said, wrapping his arm around Sara's shoulders.

Brent wrinkled his nose. "I won't be doing either of those things."

Mae waved her hand, drawing attention back to the topic at hand. "Should we call Eliza?"

"Definitely not!" Brent practically shouted. "Not until Holly and Pete get here. Once everyone is here before her, *then* we call and remind her about the party."

"You think she forgot?" Sara asked, extricating herself from Joey's grip and moving to the food table. "That's not like her."

"Pregnancy brain," Rose interjected. "I had it so bad with Susanna. I ruined two gallons of milk because I put them in the cabinet instead of the refrigerator. I also got to know the locksmith very well. I locked myself out of the house constantly."

"You should've gotten one of those little turtles with the spare key," Brent said.

"I did. But then I forgot where I hid it."

Sara groaned. "I'm already a mess. I don't want to imagined what I'd be like pregnant."

Joey was next to Sara, spacing out the chafing dishes while Sara lit small flames beneath them, but he froze at her comment. "No plans for that, right?"

"Definitely not." Sara shook her head and shivered dramatically.

"Good. Good deal. Because I just got my big break. I'm not sure I have time to pursue acting and raise a baby."

Sara turned her head away, rolling her eyes so Joey couldn't see.

Mae didn't miss it, though.

"You're an actor?" Dominic asked politely.

Joey puffed out his chest. "As of earlier this afternoon. The casting director for your movie was hiring locals."

"Well, it's not *my* movie," Dominic corrected with a shudder. "But I did hear they were hiring locals as extras. Well done, Joey."

Joey walked around the table to talk with Dominic about the movie, leaving Sara to set up the rest of the serving dishes by herself. Brent and Rose got pulled into a game of tag with Susanna that also included dodging flying marshmallows.

And Mae was distracted enough by all of it that her worry for Eliza slipped away.

Everyone would arrive soon enough.

10

ELIZA
THE HOSPITAL

"Where is my baby?" Eliza asked again, her voice wavering. "Where is she?"

She tried to look at Oliver, but her eyes danced past him to the nautical wallpaper bordering the ceiling. Little sailboats breezed past red-and-white striped lighthouses and fish jumped between the waves.

She decided she didn't like it at all. As if the wallpaper itself was telling her to calm down, to breathe, not to worry so much.

She'd had quite enough of the world telling her not to worry.

Oliver squeezed Eliza's hand, smoothing his calloused thumb over her knuckles. "She's okay, Eliza. The baby is fine."

Wrong. She'd had a baby before and she knew what "fine" looked like.

This was not fine.

"Where is she?"

"She's—"

"Oliver!"

He sighed. "She's in the NICU."

Not fine.

Not fine.

Eliza inhaled sharply and forced the air out slowly between her lips.

It didn't make her feel any better.

The events of the day were still a jumble in her head. Eliza was usually good in a crisis, but it was difficult to handle a crisis when you were unconscious. When you didn't understand the basic facts of what was happening.

Eliza needed to understand. She needed to fix this. She needed to make it fine.

"I had a C-section." She said it as a point of fact, not a question.

Oliver answered anyway. "You did. Thankfully, one of your nurses, Ginny, knew you. She was able to track me down."

Eliza faintly remembered Ginny from high school. A shy brunette who played the cello and sat behind Eliza in Senior English.

On the day of a book report, Travis Martin had knocked over Eliza's water bottle with his football bag and drenched the front of Eliza's pants and her notes. Ginny had volunteered to go in Eliza's place when no one else would to save her the soggy embarrassment.

She hadn't spoken to Ginny in years.

"I made it to the hospital just as they were wheeling you into the OR," Oliver continued. "I barely had time to get the scrubs on."

"You were in the room."

Oliver nodded. "Holding your hand."

"They gave me something to calm me down, but—"

"You can't handle anesthesia," Oliver finished. "Yeah, they picked up on that when you went unconscious. I confirmed it when I got here. Apparently, you were panicking in pre-op."

Eliza couldn't admit she didn't remember his number. Even though the nurses had no doubt relayed the entire embarrassing ordeal to him when he'd arrived.

Maybe Ginny had told him.

Eliza pushed her embarrassment down. It wasn't useful now.

"She is in the NICU," Eliza repeated, finding a small scrap of comfort in stating the facts as she knew them. "Not in here with us."

"She's okay, though," Oliver said.

Eliza was glad he hadn't said 'fine' again. It felt like a lie.

He swallowed and continued, "I asked the doctor and he said she's healthy. She, uh—shoot, what else did he say? You've always been better at remembering the details than me. I tried, but all of the technical stuff went right over my head. You were still unconscious, and..." His voice broke.

For the first time, Eliza realized how hard all of this must be for Oliver, too. The realization made her feel less alone, but not altogether better. She felt selfish.

"I'm sorry," she said.

"For what?" he asked. "For being unconscious?"

Eliza shrugged.

"How dare you!" Oliver said, wagging a finger at her before dragging a weary hand down his face. "*I'm* sorry. I should have come to the appointment with you."

"You couldn't have known."

"Neither could you," he said quickly. "This wasn't exactly the birth plan we discussed."

"Well, I'm sorry I forgot my phone."

Oliver laughed. Eliza relished his smile. It gave her a sense of normalcy in the midst of the abnormal.

"Remember when we first started dating and I had to convince you two phones were unnecessary? Now, you leave without even one."

Getting rid of all of her workaholic tendencies had been difficult. Eliza had always had two phones—one for work, one for personal use—but that became overkill when she moved back to the island.

Work and personal became far too intertwined working with her mom at the inn. Not in a bad way. It was just that when your mother was your boss, it felt silly to have her call one number to discuss business and another to tell you she made lobster ravioli for dinner.

Suddenly, realization dawned on Eliza all at once. "Where's my mom?"

"At home, I'd guess." Oliver blinked.

"We have to call her," Eliza balked, reaching down to her hip as though her phone might be in the nonexistent pocket of her gown. "She was supposed to be in the room with me."

"Only one guest allowed in the OR for a C-section."

"And Holly," Eliza carried on, ignoring him. "Holly was going to keep Winter at her house while we were in the hospital. She had activities planned for the girls. Coloring pages she was going to print out."

Oliver smoothed a hand over Eliza's shoulder. "I called the babysitter. Julie's watching Winter."

"Holly was going to bring Winter to the hospital to meet the baby. And I asked Sara to make freezer meals for us. Nothing is ready."

"What about Brent?" Oliver teased. "What was his role in the big day? He'd be annoyed to be left out."

"I'm serious."

"I know you are, babe. Which is why I'm not," Oliver said gently. "Like I said, this was hardly our birth plan. Everyone will understand that things didn't go the way we expected. You just need to focus on what is most important right now."

Eliza took a deep breath. "You're right. Can I see the baby?"

Oliver knelt down and brought Eliza's knuckles to his lips, kissing them. "You, too, Eliza. You're important, too."

In her husband's words, Eliza heard her father's voice: *While you're taking care of everything else, don't forget to take care of yourself.*

Henry Benson said those words too many times for Eliza to count.

Mom would run around the house like a madwoman some days, checking and double-checking that everyone in the house had what they needed—sunscreen for the kids, fresh coffee for Dad, a pie for a charity pot luck, a million and one things for a million and one people.

But she wouldn't take care of herself until Dad grabbed her by the shoulders and forced her up the stairs to shower and dress and let him handle things.

That's what Oliver was doing: forcing Eliza up the stairs.

Or, y'know, forcing her to lay in bed, given she'd just had a major surgery. But the sentiment was there.

Tears welled in Eliza's eyes, but she fought them back, damming her eyes to keep the pesky emotions from spilling over. Now was not the time for that.

Moments later, a knock at the door sounded. Dr. Geiger poked his graying head through the crack.

"Awake, I see." He smiled at her, one of the few times his face wasn't buried in a chart. His dark leather boat shoes squeaked on the linoleum as he stepped into the room. "How are we doing?"

"Good."

Her doctor had no doubt heard about her panic attack. And given he'd been the one to perform emergency surgery on her, surely he knew Eliza was lying.

But she couldn't help herself. She had to maintain the façade.

For herself more than anyone.

"Baby is healthy, and after a quick check up, I'm sure I'll be saying the same about you, yes?" He winked at her and ran through a series of questions so rapid-fire she couldn't remember them a second after they'd been asked.

Either way, by the end of it, Dr. Geiger gave her the thumbs-up of approval.

"By the way, I'm adding to your chart that you have a strong response to benzodiazepine," he added before leaving the room.

It felt like an understatement.

A minute later, Ginny filled the space Dr. Geiger had vacated, pushing a wheelchair.

She had the same shoulder-length brown hair she'd always had, but she'd filled out in the cheeks and around the middle. Her bright pink scrubs shone in contrast with the quiet girl Eliza had known in school.

Back then, she'd seemed intent on blending in. Now, she stood out vibrantly in the pale blue and white room.

"Glad to see you," Ginny said warmly, "and to see you're awake. There's someone who wants to meet you."

"There she is," Oliver whispered, his words tinged with reverence.

"She's so small."

White medical tape covered their baby's little cheeks to hold the oxygen tube in place. It made it hard to see her.

What little of her there was to see.

Could this really be the same baby who beat on her ribs at all hours of the night? It didn't look like she'd have the strength for something like that.

When Winter was born, Eliza could remember a nurse toweling her off and laying her, slimy and purple, on her chest. Still, she'd been the most beautiful thing Eliza had ever seen.

And huge.

Later, she learned Winter was average-sized at just over seven pounds, but Eliza still couldn't believe something—someone—that large had come out of her.

Now, her instincts had her wanting to put the baby back inside of her to let the child cook a little more. She didn't seem done yet.

"The doctor said she was healthy. Doing better than expected, given, you know... everything."

Oliver's voice was bright as he tried to force Eliza to see the positives. But how could she see the positives when her "healthy" baby was connected to tubes and wires and sitting inside of a clear box like a science experiment?

Eliza had failed.

The thought rang in her head like a gong, deafening her to anything else.

She was supposed to be the one to keep the baby safe and protect her until it was time, but she'd failed. Her body had failed, and now their daughter was roasting in a petri dish on the other side of glass and Eliza could not reach her no matter how much she begged.

Suddenly, the wheelchair turned and Oliver was kneeling in front of Eliza, eyebrows drawn, expression stern.

"Eliza Patterson, you did not fail."

Had she said that out loud?

"You carried this beautiful baby for thirty-six weeks, and she is going to be fine. So are you."

"You don't know that," she whispered fiercely through tears.

Oliver pulled the wheelchair closer, the brakes squealing slightly against the force. "I do know it. We are all going to be fine because we have you."

Eliza couldn't help it; she wrinkled her nose.

She only liked promises people could actually keep. Vague statements that things would work out weren't actionable. Weren't reliable.

No matter what she or Oliver did, they had zero control over this situation.

Yet despite all that—despite a lifetime of trusting the numbers and nothing else—Eliza felt better somehow. She believed Oliver.

"What are we going to name this one?" Oliver tapped a finger on the glass. She wished he wouldn't. It made her feel like they were middle schoolers on a field trip at the aquarium, trying to make the otters do something funny.

She took another deep breath. *We're all going to be fine,* he'd said. She wanted so badly to believe him.

"My mom suggested Mildred."

"Pass."

"It was my grandma's name."

"God bless her heart and may she rest in peace," Oliver said, voice full of mock sympathy.

Eliza playfully slapped his leg. "It's better than Brent's suggestion. Regardless of gender, he offered up 'Brent.' Said it was gender neutral."

Oliver laughed and then tapped his chin with his finger. "We really should have given this more thought. How do people usually name babies?"

"Months in advance," Eliza joked.

In truth, she and Oliver had tried to pick a name, but they just couldn't agree. As the clock on the pregnancy was winding down and they only had one month to go, Eliza was prepared to go nuclear. She had baby name websites bookmarked on her computer, and she'd planned to cuff Oliver onto the couch and not let him up until they'd come to an agreement.

The baby, however, had other ideas. Luckily for Oliver.

"The name should be something we like, obviously, but it should also capture this moment in time."

Eliza looked around the room, dubious.

The NICU was empty aside from them. Their daughter's incubator was the only one occupied. Eliza couldn't decide if that was a good thing or not. Hopefully, it spoke to the number of healthy babies being born on Nantucket.

"Not this exact moment, though," he clarified, waving his hands in the air as though washing away the image of the hospital room around them. "The bigger moment. Beyond."

She closed her eyes and let herself see beyond the room. Beyond the hospital.

The last time Eliza had been outside—on the hectic venture from the doctor's office to the awaiting ambulance—she'd felt the salty, damp air against her skin.

With so many moving parts and people circling around her, Eliza had focused on the air. On the way the sun cradled her in a blanket of warmth.

Nothing could beat summertime in Nantucket. The mornings started out with a slight bite in the air, the wind off the water enough to make you reach for a sweater. But by the afternoon, the weather would be picture perfect. Any trace of chill gone.

Down in this stuffy hospital room with its unnatural whirring and beeping, far from the sun beyond the limestone walls, Eliza looked down into the incubator and realized with a start that her baby was awake.

And looking up at her.

She blinked slowly, her pink lips moving and working around sounds she couldn't quite form yet. Her wrinkled fingers opened and closed.

Eliza reached her hand into the hole cut into the glass. When the tiny hand closed around her index finger, Eliza's throat closed, too.

The grip was firm. Strong.

Her little arms hardly looked capable of it, but she clung to Eliza, surprising her.

"Summer." She turned to Oliver, a smile flickering across her face for the first time in hours. "Her name should be Summer."

Oliver considered it for a moment, his forehead wrinkling.

Eliza worried he'd turn it down or that she'd have to fight for it. That she'd have to try to put words to something unspeakable, something that just felt right.

Then his face lit up.

Oliver beamed at her and nodded, his wavy hair bouncing around his ears. "It's perfect, Eliza."

"You think so?"

"It's a beautiful name for a beautiful girl."

A tear slipped over Eliza's cheek as she looked down at her daughter. She didn't bother wiping this one away.

"Hear that, Summer? Daddy said you're beautiful."

Summer just squeezed a little tighter.

11

SARA

THE SWEET ISLAND INN

Sara could hear Grady crunch through a fried tilapia fish stick from all the way across the lawn.

The sound may as well have been a hallelujah chorus. It meant her crust hadn't gone soggy during the reheat.

She probably didn't need to be overly concerned. Ten-year-olds were not the most discerning of eaters. Sara had seen Grady eat a handful of rocks once. He'd only been four, so she couldn't hold it against him.

Still, no one liked soggy breading. Especially after it had taken Sara a week of banging her head against the wall to come up with the kid's menu in the first place.

In an act of desperation, she'd finally gone to the frozen section of the grocery store and stared at boxes of pizza bagels and beef and bean burritos in search of inspiration. (During which time not a single casting director had come along and "discovered" her.)

Eventually, she'd spotted a box of fish sticks and today's menu had been born.

In all reality, the kids would have appreciated frozen fish sticks just as much as anything else. But as the resident foodie in the family, Sara had to train them up in the ways of good eating. She'd ended up making a parmesan-covered, peppery, slightly elevated version of fish sticks complete with a sweet chili, honey, and mayonnaise sauce for dipping.

Even though, after all that effort, Grady might've still preferred the rocks.

The adult menu suited Sara's skillset much better. Almost as soon as she'd volunteered to make the food, spicy grilled shrimp had cemented itself in her mind as the perfect entrée.

It allowed her to repurpose the leftover sweet chili and honey from the fish stick sauce. And with the addition of some lime juice, soy sauce, and a few herbs and spices, she had the marinade. After a twenty-four-hour bath in the fridge, Sara threw the shrimp onto the grill and watched them brown and caramelize to perfection.

It was a cookout, after all. The law of the universe required that *something* had to be grilled.

And it was the perfect day for exactly that. A slight breeze to carry away the smoke, but still enough that it wouldn't fan the flames.

The temperature was just right, too. Standing over a hot grill in dead heat could be killer. But as day gave way to evening, the sky was turning a velvety blue. A splash of yellow and orange lit up a thin stripe along the horizon.

In another hour, the temperature would be low enough that gathering around a fire would feel wonderful. Especially with the cool air coming in off the water.

Maybe they'd pull out the fire pit. Sara had brought supplies for s'mores just in case.

Nothing elevated about Hershey's milk chocolate, of course. But some classics ought not be messed with.

"Anyone want this last shrimp skewer?" Brent asked as he placed it on his plate.

"The last one?" Mom chewed on her lower lip, her eyes scanning the rest of the food table. "Eliza and Oliver aren't even here yet."

Sara could tell her mom was taking stock of the food on the table and how many people there were left to feed. She wouldn't say it out loud, but she was entering into problem-solving mode.

Even though Sara had told her repeatedly not to worry about a thing, Mom had made several side dishes.

Two servings of potato salad had made it discretely onto Sara's plate, but it shouldn't have been there in the first place. No one should cook their own birthday dinner. Including side dishes.

Sara held back an eyeroll and instead piped up cheerfully, "It's not the last one. I have two more trays inside."

Brent fist-pumped in celebration.

"I had a sneaking suspicion Brent might hog it all," she teased loudly in his direction.

He lowered his fist and said, the words garbled around a mouthful of shrimp, "I did ask if anyone wanted it first..."

Rose had the decency to give Sara an apologetic smile on Brent's behalf, but she could only laugh and shake her head when Brent shoved another shrimp in his mouth.

"I should have known you'd have it all under control." Mom winked at Sara.

Sara nudged Joey in the side. "Can you go grab the second tray of shrimp from inside?"

Joey threw his head back and laughed at something Dominic said, ignoring her entirely. "...I've got to read the book before the movie starts shooting."

"I doubt it's necessary," Dominic remarked. "They'll give you a script."

"I want to do my research. Sara has a copy, but I've been slacking on picking it up."

Dominic waved a hand. "You've been busy putting out fires and saving people. Believe me, I'm not offended. I'm a mere writer. You're a hero."

Oh, good, Sara thought. *More compliments.* That's exactly what Joey's ego needed right now.

Since arriving at the party, Joey had barely said two words to Sara.

He'd promised to help her bring in the food and set up the catering equipment, but once conversation switched to the movie, that all went out the window. He'd been too busy recounting his frozen section origin story.

Every time he told the story, it escalated. In the latest iteration, the casting director had apparently mentioned the way the lights from the freezer section caught him in profile.

It had been years since she said this out loud, but *Gag me with a spoon* felt like an incredibly appropriate sentiment.

With Joey otherwise occupied, Sara had been left to assemble the four-tier cake herself, standing on a chair to drop the top layer into place.

"No, you're *my* hero," Joey smarmed with so much sincerity Sara thought she might upchuck her dinner on the spot. "I've always wanted to try acting, and now I have a chance. Thanks to you."

It wasn't that Sara didn't like Dominic. Far from it!

But describing him as a hero made it seem as though Joey had been in desperate need of saving. As if his miserable life was so pitifully unfulfilled before this opportunity to be a non-speaking extra in a low-budget indie movie had come along.

It was ridiculous.

The men's conversation carried on nonetheless. Sara pushed her chair away from the table.

"Never mind," she snapped, "I'll do it."

She ran a kitchen all day for work, so why shouldn't she do it on her time off, too, right?

Besides—at the rate she was pissing off employees, it wouldn't be long before she was manning Little Bull all on her own as well.

Who needed dependable employees or supportive boyfriends? Not Sara. No siree.

Joey turned his head as she walked away, his eyes still focused on Dominic. "What'd you say, babe?"

She didn't answer. *See how he likes being ignored.*

The interior of the inn was cool and silent. The lights were all switched off inside, except for a single can light over the sink. Sara couldn't remember the last time she'd heard it so quiet.

She was happy for Dominic. Really. He'd worked hard on his book, and he deserved success. Plus, as the business manager and person in charge of all things marketing for the Inn, Eliza seemed to think the movie would be great for business. She'd been pushing the movie angle all over the Sweet Island Inn's social media pages.

But what had Joey done to deserve being swept up in the success?

Sara knew she was being petty, but that didn't stop the thought from blaring through her mind like a bullhorn and drowning out every other thought.

What did it say about her that she couldn't muster up a little enthusiasm for her boyfriend's exciting new opportunity?

And what did it say about their relationship that this opportunity had immediately made Joey too important to pay any attention to Sara and her problems?

Nothing pleasant. Nothing good.

She groaned and pressed her forehead against the cool front of the double-wide refrigerator.

"Tough day, sis?"

The sound of Brent's voice sent Sara jerking upright. She pulled open the fridge as though that had been her intention all along. "Just tired."

"Apparently. You left a smudge on the stainless steel. Better wipe that before Mom kills you."

She closed the door halfway and used the hem of her shirt to wipe the grease smear. "You're only here because you want first dibs on the new tray of shrimp. But I gotta tell you, they don't taste as good cold."

"That was part of it," Brent laughed. "But Rose also told me to come help."

"That was nice of her."

He hesitated. "She noticed your boyfriend was a bit... preoccupied."

"Perceptive, that one. Keep her close," Sara said, putting as much brevity into her voice as she could.

Sara hoped Rose was the only one who had noticed.

Brent's girlfriend was sweet and quiet—and the woman was observant. At times, she made Sara feel like a fish being filleted. She could see straight to her insides.

"He's pretty excited about his big break," Brent said.

Without meaning to, Sara snorted.

"Ouch." Brent winced. "I sense you aren't as excited?"

"That's why you and Rose go well together," Sara said, hefting the tray out of the fridge. "You're perceptive, too. Well, when you choose to be."

She kicked the refrigerator door closed with her foot and dropped the tray of shrimp on the counter.

Suddenly, the thought of grilling shrimp was wildly unpleasant.

She didn't want to be in any kitchen right now. She wanted to be at the beach. Somewhere quiet and warm and far away from the pounding headache taking up residence in her temples.

Maybe she'd ditch the party for a few minutes and take a walk along the private beach behind the inn. Joey certainly wouldn't notice her absence.

She always felt an odd simpatico with the ocean. She didn't make it out there often enough, though. Work kept her at the restaurant and tourists kept her away from the beach.

But when she did find the time, it was cocoa butter for the soul.

No one shamed the ocean for being tumultuous. For throwing a fit if it felt like it. They simply accepted it as it was.

Sara was a lot like that.

She wasn't cool under pressure like Eliza or steady like Holly. And she couldn't hide her feelings behind a smile like Brent.

Maybe the ocean was the only one who would understand her right now.

It knew what it was like to feel stormy.

Brent leaned his elbows on the countertop, his chin in his hand. "Well, if you don't want to date an actor, speak now or forever hold your peace. It sounds like your beau is seconds away from calling an agent."

"I think I'm done with confrontations for today, thank you," Sara said icily. "Besides, between you and me, I don't think exactly think the front cover of People magazine is Joey's next stop."

She peeled off the aluminum cover and gave the shrimp a good mix with the metal tongs. Brent made no effort to help.

"Something else going on, sis?"

Sara sighed. She didn't want to talk about the theft at the restaurant.

Number one, it made her look like an incompetent businesswoman who couldn't keep her own employees in line.

Number two, she might have been wrong to confront Casey in the first place.

The whole debacle was embarrassing. But Sara was ready to burst. She had to release a little pressure or she'd go insane.

"Something shady was going on with the books at work, and I had a… talk with the person I thought was responsible. It didn't go well," she said, stabbing a shrimp with the poky end of the tong. "To put it mildly."

"Did they quit?"

"No."

"Did you fire them?"

She shook her head.

Brent frowned. "So what happened then?"

"I think I messed up," she admitted, hating how bitter the words tasted on her tongue. "I'm not sure the person actually did it. And they were really angry I suspected them. Felt like I accused my own family member of stealing from me."

"Oof. That sucks."

"Yeah." Sara sagged forward. "It really does."

"But you were right to ask them, no? Family shouldn't keep secrets from each other."

Brent seemed more serious than usual, but Sara couldn't help but laugh. "Tell that to every family in the world."

"What does that mean?"

"It means families keep a ton of secrets!" she said. "Maybe that's my problem. Maybe I treat my staff too much like family. Now, they're comfortable enough that they're stealing money from the register the way I used to filch twenties from Mom's purse."

Brent's eyebrows shot upwards. "You stole from Mom?"

Oops. Sara hadn't meant to say that.

"Didn't you?" she asked like it was nothing.

"Absolutely not."

Sara blanched. "It was only a few times," she muttered. "Dad caught me once and I stopped after that."

"He didn't tell her?"

"He said it could be our little secret."

Brent turned his blue eyes on Sara, brows pinched. "Did you and Dad have any other little secrets?"

"None that come to mind. Why?"

"No reason," Brent answered quickly. A bit too quickly.

On a normal day, Sara would have pressed him. But she was tired of talking, and she couldn't handle anyone else's drama right now. Especially if they weren't keen to share it.

She slid the aluminum tray across the counter to him. "Take this outside."

Brent grabbed it and rolled his eyes. "Sir, yes, sir."

"Please!" she shouted after him as he marched through the kitchen like a soldier on patrol.

When she was alone again, she pressed her forehead to the cool granite countertop and closed her eyes.

It'll be okay, Sara girl, she urged herself. *It'll all be okay.*

Joey was still gabbing on about the movie when she returned outside. Dominic had escaped across the party to sit with Mom. Pete, however, had wound up fully entrapped in Joey's orbit, the poor guy.

"...The casting director said I had the exact right look, so I'm supposed to show up in the same outfit I had on in the store and have it approved."

Pete hummed feigned interest and then turned to Sara, seeking a reprieve. "The food was a hit at the luncheon. Hopefully, you'll see some business out of it."

"Really? That's great."

"Oh yeah, it was delicious. And it was nice to eat your cooking again," he said. "Alice has been going through a picky eating phase, so we haven't been in for a while. The cod you delivered last week warmed up amazingly, though. I loved the salsa."

Joey groaned. "I've eaten so much cod and salsa, I'll probably bleed lime and tomato juice if you cut me. Being a tester for Sara's meals has its downsides."

"If you're sick of it, feel free to let me tap in," Pete offered.

"We may have to take you up on that. I'll want to get in better shape for the movie," Joey said, patting his perfectly flat stomach. "I may have to skip Sara's cooking for the next two weeks to keep my diet clean."

"Cod fish is really healthy," Sara grumbled, stabbing at a chunk of her mom's potato salad—her third helping.

"Not when it's slathered in butter, babe."

Even after the release in the kitchen, Sara's steam level was rising again. The events of the day were compounding on her temper and her patience. She opened her mouth to respond, a flurry of arguments and accusations ripe and ready on her tongue, when Holly whistled.

Sara looked up to see her older sister was waving her over to the cake table, eyes wide and panicked.

Swallowing her frustration, Sara excused herself from the table. She couldn't help but notice the way Pete's shoulders sank in disappointment as Joey picked up right where he left off. "So apparently there's free catering on set…"

She felt bad for him, but not bad enough to stick around and say something she'd almost certainly regret.

Holly was half-hiding behind the four-tiered cake when Sara made it over to her.

"What's up?"

Holly beckoned with a jerk of her head. "Come over here."

"I am over here," Sara said.

"Over. Here," Holly hissed, her eyes darting down to the cake.

The side of the cake facing the party was bland. Just four tiers of alternating red and green-iced layers. No decoration. No flourishes.

Sara had watched Grady notice the cake and then sag in disappointment.

What he didn't know, though, was that the back of the cake would blow his ten-year-old mind.

Sara had hidden blood-covered fondant zombies on the back of the cake to be revealed during the cake cutting. Just like she'd promised him.

Well, technically, Little Bull's talented pastry chef had made the zombies, but what Grady didn't know wouldn't hurt him. And after the day she'd had, Sara needed this win.

Except, when she walked around the back of the cake, one of the zombies in question was more mutilated than he'd been an hour earlier.

Holly had the upper half of his body cradled gingerly in her palm. "I came back here to get a picture and a bug landed on the cake. I tried to swat it away, but I misjudged the distance and took out the zombie. He landed on the table and split in half."

"That explains the dent in his skull," Sara said, bending down to study the zombie's corpse.

Holly sighed. "I'm so sorry, Sara."

Sara plucked the zombie out of Holly's hand and tried balancing it on top of his legs, but the whole thing began to deteriorate at the slightest touch.

"I tried that," Holly admitted. "I was about to use the toothpicks from the bacon-wrapped dates to hold him together, but I thought I might just make a bigger mess of things. Can you fix it?"

Sara laid a hand on her sister's arm. "For the first time today, you've given me a problem I am more than equipped to fix. I should be thanking you."

Holly was too relieved to be concerned by Sara's statement. "Good. Grady would have been so disappointed."

"Actually, I think he'll like this better," Sara said. "So long as you don't mind your son's birthday cake being a little heavy on the gore?"

"Better the zombie be bloodied than me," Holly grimaced. "Grady has been talking about this cake for a month."

Sara hid the zombie in her palms and hustled across the lawn and back into the kitchen, the solution fully formed in her mind.

If every problem could be fixed in the kitchen and every person could be as easy to please as her nephew, Sara's life would be a dream.

12

MAE

String lights draped from the house to the branches of the black-and-white oaks, setting the backyard party aglow as the sun dipped behind the water. The orange sherbet sky turned to a rainbow of pastels.

Dominic's Elvis records still crooned from the record player in the open upstairs window, the gauzy white curtains blowing in the salty breeze. He'd gone up a few times to flip the record, but no one seemed to mind listening to the same songs. They set the right mood.

Mae couldn't have magicked more ideal weather. She'd run inside to grab a light cotton sweater after her first plate of food, but otherwise, it was the kind of Nantucket summer evening that made her grateful to live here.

Eliza ought to be here. She'd no doubt be running around with her camera, taking pictures for the Sweet Island Inn's website and social media pages.

But Mae's worry for Eliza had nothing to do with the business side of things.

It wasn't like Eliza to be late. Or to be out of reach.

Oliver could run late. He often did. Especially when he was coming to family dinner from a gig. The man was humble and kind, but he could never refuse an encore.

The other kids weren't worried about their sister. But only because they were all distracted.

Holly and Pete were busy trying to get Alice to eat something —*anything*. But the strong-willed girl refused.

"I could run inside and make her some cheesy noodles," Mae offered. "The elbows with shredded cheese. She loves that."

"She needs to learn a lesson, mom," Holly grumbled back, running her hands through her blonde hair to smooth it. The summer humidity always made waves in the underside of Holly's hair, giving it extra volume that Holly hated. "She hasn't eaten anything but cheese slices and applesauce for a week. It has to end."

"You went through the same phase. After a week of dry cereal, you got tired of it and ate dinner."

Pete smirked and wrapped an arm around his wife. "I knew this came from your side of the family. I never once turned down a hot meal."

Holly glared up at him and then set her jaw, nostrils flared. "I will not be using the appeasement strategy. This is a battle of wills. I intend to win."

When Mae walked around the side of the house a few minutes later to see if Eliza, Oliver, and Winter had arrived yet, she found Sara hunched behind the four-tiered cake.

"One of Grady's zombies fell apart," she said without prompting, squeezing a piping bag of red royal icing all over a prone zombie.

"Looks gruesome."

Sara grimaced. "I hope you don't mind."

Once upon a time, birthday cakes for her grandchildren meant barn animals or race cars. But a zombie-themed cake came with the territory of turning ten, Mae figured. He couldn't love cartoon bears and tractors forever.

That was the same thing Mae told herself when a teenage Brent hung the first swimsuit model poster on his bedroom wall. She'd wanted to fight it, but Henry had warned her it would only make things worse.

"The harder you push back, the more he'll want it. Believe me. I've been a fourteen-year-old boy," he'd said, patting her on the arm. "It's better if we say nothing at all."

So long as Mae never had to share a bikini model-themed cake with Grady, she could handle a little blood.

"I don't mind one bit. Grady will love it."

"I want you to love it, too, though," Sara said, frowning.

She'd been doing that a lot tonight: frowning. "Everything okay with you?" Mae asked.

Sara let out a long, frustrated breath. "Long day. To say the least."

She squeezed the piping bag harder than necessary, a stream of shiny red icing pooling on the edge of the cake layer and dripping down the side.

"We can talk about it if you'd—"

Before Mae could even finish the sentence, Sara shook her head. "No. It's your birthday. I'm not going to ruin it complaining."

Mae shrugged. "It wouldn't bother me. It's my birthday, and I say it's fine."

"No again. It's a day for being happy. And jolly. And bright."

"It's my birthday, dear, not Christmas."

But Sara set her shoulders and clenched her lips together tightly.

After years of butting heads with Sara, Mae knew better than to push her youngest daughter into talking when she wasn't ready. It was like icing a cake before it was completely cool. It would save you time in the short-term, but in the long-term, it turned into a melted, goopy mess.

Never worth it to rush the process.

Mae would know when Sara decided to tell her. Until then, nothing to do but wait.

She walked around the table and marveled at the cake. "I really do love it."

"Really?" Sara asked, sounding surprisingly uncertain. "I know it's a little plain on the front and a little, y'know... morbid on the back."

"It's perfectly on-theme," Mae insisted. "At sixty-four, the possibility of immortality is growing more and more tempting by the day."

Sara snorted. "That was not what I was going for, but I'm glad you like it."

"I love it, honey. Most of all because you made it for me."

Sara rolled her eyes, but she smiled, and Mae was happy to see it.

The best birthday present she could imagine was all of her children being happy. Though, when she told the kids that in the weeks before her birthday while they were trying to sleuth out what to buy her, they always groaned.

Sara dropped her piping bag on the table and wiped her red-stained hands on a paper towel. "Now, let's cut this cake before Mr. Zombie decides to decompose further. I'm not sure I'll be able to patch him together again."

"But Eliza isn't here yet." Mae turned in the direction of the front door, listening for any sign of knocking.

"We'll save them a slice. They'll understand. It's your birthday, after all."

Mae wasn't worried about Eliza being upset. She was worried about Eliza. "Has anyone heard from her?"

"Brent texted her after Holly and Pete got here. To gloat, I'm sure." She rolled her eyes, a tinge of fondness in her expression.

"What did she say?"

Sara shrugged. "Probably nothing. I'd ignore Brent, too."

Brent was across the lawn rolling on the grass with Susanna. Mae skirted around the edge of the tables, avoiding the squeals and flying marshmallows. Her son playing father was still new for Mae, but she couldn't be prouder of the job he was doing.

Right now, though, Mae had something else on her mind.

"Brent, dear," she said, "hate to intrude, but did you ever hear back from Eliza?"

"Watch out, Gramma!" Susanna cried.

Mae ducked as a marshmallow went streaking past her ear.

Her youngest son rolled onto his back, chest heaving from exertion. "I don't think so." He pulled his phone out of his back pocket to double-check and shook his head. "Nope. No word yet."

"Have you tried Oliver?"

Susanna, sensing that the time for marshmallow warfare was over, curled up against Brent's side with her head on his chest. They made a cute pair. Another photo-worthy moment for the Inn's social media pages.

Another moment Eliza was missing.

"Maybe I'll text Oliver," Mae mused.

Brent lifted his head for a moment. "I'll do it. You have fun. It's your party."

Everyone kept saying that. As though Mae's birthday precluded her from all of her usual activities. As though she was supposed to flip some party switch in her mind and turn off all of her busybody tendencies and her worrying.

Impossible, of course. In Mae's experience, a mother never took a break from worrying about her kids.

"I didn't ask how the kids were doing, Mae. I asked how *you* were doing," her friend, Lola, would always say on their weekend walks along the beach.

Truthfully, Mae didn't know how to separate herself from her children. How to focus on herself and her own happiness without it being intricately tangled up with the happiness of her little Benson brood.

But maybe the night of her sixty-fourth birthday was the evening to try. Even hummingbirds have to land sometimes, right?

"No, it's okay," Mae said, waving Brent away. "You've texted them once. That's enough."

"Twice," Brent corrected, swallowing Susanna's hands in his grip to keep her from poking him. "And a phone call."

Mae's stomach turned, but she ignored it. "Right. Of course. I'm sure they'll be here soon."

As soon as she walked back towards the tables, Dominic was waiting, his sights set on Mae.

"What's going on?" she asked.

"Sara is asking if we can cut the cake now."

Sara was waving nonchalantly from the cake table, but her smile looked more like a wince than anything else. Mr. Zombie must be in bad shape.

Before Mae could answer there was a shriek of excitement behind her. "Cake!"

Alice was still sitting at the table in front of her untouched plate of fried tilapia sticks and potato salad. Holly sat across from her, looking defeated.

"I think we have to wait on cake until everyone has eaten dinner, darling," Mae said.

Holly lifted an arm and waved it in the air like a white flag of surrender. "I concede. It's fine. Cake time!"

So much for the battle of wills, it seemed.

"And presents!" Grady added, jumping up and wagging his brows at the gift table.

"Cake first, then presents." Pete ruffled his son's hair.

The news of cake spread fast. Soon, everyone was gathered around the table. Sara stood behind it at the ready, large cutting knife in hand.

Mae couldn't ask them to wait on Eliza now. Not when Alice and Susanna were bouncing on their toes with excitement. Not when Grady's troublesome zombie was clinging to the precipice of the third cake layer by one crumbling fondant finger.

"Are we ready?" Sara asked, making special eyes at Grady.

Joey sauntered up to the back of the gathering next to Brent. "Is there a fruit tray around here?"

"At a birthday party?" Brent snorted.

"Just, like, with filming coming up," Joey mumbled, "I'm not sure about eating cake."

Sara glanced his way for a second, her smile faltering. Then she rebounded and bulldozed right over the fruit tray objection. "Here we go!"

Slowly, she removed the lock from the cake stand and began spinning the cake around. As soon as the blood icing dripping down the frosting came into view, Grady roared with pure delight.

"A zombie cake!"

The little girls screamed in terror, but they still wore smiles as they scrambled away from the cake and to their parents.

"You didn't think I'd make you a boring old green cake for your birthday, did you?" Sara taunted.

"Maybe," Grady laughed. "But this is so much cooler!"

"And bloodier," Pete remarked under his breath.

Grady nodded enthusiastically. "You're the best, Aunt Sara!"

Seventy-four balloons had been festive party décor, but seventy-four candles seemed like a fire hazard. So they opted for two sets of candles.

After they sang, Grady went first, scrunching up his eyes like making a wish required maximum concentration before blowing out his ten candles.

Then it was Mae's turn.

She only got one candle, but it was rather special. As soon as Sara lit it, sparks began shooting out of the top, spraying into the air like a thousand tiny stars. The light danced across the smiling faces of her whole gathered family.

Well, *almost* whole.

"Make a wish, Mom!" Brent shouted.

"No wishing for more wishes," Sara warned seriously.

"And make it for yourself," Dominic added with a stern finger point.

Mae smiled. Silently, she wished Eliza and her family would arrive soon.

Then she blew out the candle.

13

BRENT

Sara cut the cake slices while Holly plated them. In stark defiance of birthday protocol, Susanna and Alice ran back to the tables with the first two slices of chocolate cake.

Brent would have said something to Susanna about waiting her turn, but he'd learned fast that it was best to choose his battles with the kiddo. And she had already taken two messy, frosting-filled bites.

Grady didn't mind, anyway. Sara gave him a slice topped with the zombie and puddles of red icing. Brent had never seen a kid's eyes go wider with pure glee.

"This is grotesque," Holly said, wrinkling her nose at some red icing on her fingers. "Impressively done, but grotesque."

"Come on, Holls, it's cool," Brent said. "You used to watch zombie movies back in the day."

"I was a teenager," she argued, voice a low whisper. "Not ten."

"Kids are maturing faster these days. You can thank the internet."

"Don't remind me," Holly groaned. Then she levelled a plastic fork at Sara and Brent like it was a knife. "And do not encourage this."

"Encourage what?" Sara asked innocently, swiping the bloody icing from her plate and smearing it on her tongue.

"I swear," Holly warned, "if either if you show Grady a zombie movie, I'll... I'll tell your children every bad thing either of you ever did."

"I don't have children," Sara reminded her. "And even if I did, I'm as pure as the driven snow. No secrets to be told."

"Bah! Future children, then. I'm fine playing the long game."

For his part, Brent just shrugged. "I'm pretty sure everyone in this town knows my secrets. All they had to do was read the crime blotter in the newspaper."

Sara dropped another slice of red velvet cake on the plate Holly was holding, but when Brent reached for it, Holly yanked it back. "Fine. Then I'll toilet paper your house in vengeance."

Brent barked out a laugh. "You wouldn't."

"Try me." Holly narrowed her eyes. "If he has nightmares, I'm the one he wakes up in the middle of the night. As soon as I get him back to bed, I'll be heading to your house with my toilet paper rolls and a thirst for justice."

Brent shuddered. "You've got a twisted mind for torture. Fine, fine. No zombie movies. Scout's honor."

Sara scoffed. "Since when were you a Boy Scout?"

"Close enough. I had Dad. He taught me all the same stuff, no uniform required."

That seemed to be good enough for Holly. She finally relinquished Brent's slice of cake.

Teasing aside, Brent liked being with his siblings. It was easy to talk about Dad with them. To bring him up casually without bringing down the mood of a conversation or getting pitying looks and sympathetic eyes thrown his way.

Sometimes, he just wanted to remember his father without it turning into A Big Thing. They understood that.

Though, today, being with his sisters—minus Eliza; wonder where she's at?—came with a sting in the tail.

What if there was one more Benson sibling at the party?

The name on the mobile appeared in Brent's mind as though he was holding it in his hands, staring down at the letters his dad had carved out by hand.

Christopher.

An older brother, based on the name and the date carved on the back. He'd be the oldest of all the Benson's.

Brent could've had an older brother to teach him how to skip rocks, how to arm wrestle, how to talk to girls—or, failing that, to laugh at him when he flubbed it up. He would have welcomed either. Anything would've been better than his mom pinching his cheeks and assuring him he was the "most handsome boy" after Maria Carver turned him down for eighth grade formal. A brotherly noogie would have been far more preferable.

But he didn't know what that was like. He couldn't know. He'd never know.

And the not knowing was driving Brent bonkers.

Maybe a few years earlier, he would have wrapped the thing back up in the trash bag and hid it away again, forgotten about it entirely.

But now, after everything he'd been through, he needed to know the truth.

He needed closure.

"The Scouts were not a waste of time," Pete said, joining in the conversation. "I was an Eagle Scout, and I learned some incredible life skills."

Holly smirked and nudged her husband with her hip. "Like how to slip the switch for the electric fireplace at home?"

"You make fun now, but wait until the apocalypse comes."

"The zombie apocalypse?" Sara fake-gasped.

Pete shook his head, only half as amused as everyone else. "Mock all you like. The grid will go down, and I'll show you all."

Brent was only halfway through his slice when Grady finished devouring his helping—zombie and all—and tossed his plate in the trash can by the table. "Can we do presents now?"

"Everyone else is still eating their cake, buddy," Holly soothed. "Why don't we wait a little longer?"

His shoulders slouched in disappointment as he walked off.

"The excitement over the zombie cake faded pretty quickly," Sara said, a hint of bitterness in her voice.

"That's the trouble with edible art. It doesn't last as long."

"Or at least, not as long as all the toys everyone bought him that'll be broken within the next week," Pete added.

They were all laughing when Mom's voice cut through the party noise. "Brent, have you heard from Eliza?"

At that moment, the bugs hiding in the trees roared to life, drowning out even the sounds of Elvis crooning from the upstairs window.

Instead of responding, Brent shook his head.

Mom frowned, and then Susanna tugged on her grandma's arm, pointing to the balloon that was coming untied from around her wrist.

The adults had spent the last ten minutes tying half a dozen party balloons to each of the little girls. Rather than finishing their cake, they'd been dancing around the tables, watching the balloons bounce and trail behind them with glee.

"Stop playing and eat faster!" Grady urged his sister, growing impatient. "So we can open presents."

"None of the presents are for me," Alice fired back, dropping down into her seat and taking the smallest possible bite of her cake in defiance. Her eyes were locked on her brother's the entire time. Grady glared daggers right back.

"Maybe we should call her one more time," Mom suggested. "I don't want to open gifts until all of my kids are here."

All of my kids...

Brent shuddered.

"Sure, Mom," he mumbled. "Can do."

For the third time, he called his sister. And for the third time, she didn't answer.

It wasn't like Eliza to go MIA, but Brent wasn't worried. He did want to talk to her, though. She was the oldest, wasn't she? Maybe she knew something. Maybe she'd heard something, seen something, cajoled the truth out of Mom or Dad at some point and then been sworn to secrecy.

He wished he could let it go. Just untie this particular thought balloon from his wrist and let it float up in the night sky.

But it bobbed and tugged at him. Refused to be set aside.

A familiar hand gripped his shoulder gently. "Did she answer?"

Brent shook his head and spun around to face Rose. "Not yet."

"Are you worried?" she asked.

"Not really."

Rose frowned.

"What?"

"Nothing." She dragged her hand down his arm. "You just seem... distracted. Like something is bothering you. I noticed it at home, too."

Sara wasn't wrong—Rose was perceptive. She paid closer attention to his moods than even he did.

"You don't miss a thing."

She smiled up at him and wrapped her arms around his waist. "I'm a mom. It's my job."

"Is that so?"

She hummed confidently. "Yep. For instance, I know Susanna is eating the extra frosting I scraped off my cake right now."

Sara just happened to be walking by and stopped cold, turning to Rose. "You scrape off the frosting?"

"Nothing personal," Rose assured her. "I'm not much of a dessert person."

Sara narrowed her eyes suspiciously. "Noted." Then she walked away with her double portion of red velvet cake.

Brent and Rose laughed quietly together at how strange his family could be. After a moment, though, the laughter faded. Her expression turned serious and she squeezed his waist. "But really, are you okay?"

"I am," he assured her. Because it was true. True enough, at least. "I just need to talk to my mom. Maybe my sisters first."

Rose poked a finger into his stomach, making him flinch, and then winked. "Okay. You'll tell me later?"

He bent down and kissed her nose, grateful to her for understanding what he didn't even have the words to say. "Later. I promise."

He told Rose everything, and he always would.

But this still felt like his mom's secret. Like something he didn't have the right to share.

As everyone finished eating their cake, Mom did her best to distract the grandkids with the scavenger hunt. Ten minutes later, they emerged from the trees with arms full of candy and soda, taking turns trading long, pirate-y "Arggghhs!"

Then, the sun finally dipped below the horizon and the sky entered the final slate blue phase before going black. The period when lightning bugs came out to play.

All of the kids, even Grady, ran around the lawn trying to catch them in their hands, breathless and giggling as they made dizzy circles in the grass and tried to catch a little bit of starlight.

Grady's attention wavered first. He staggered over groaning to his mom. "The moon is out. It's almost Alice's bed time. When are we going to open gifts?"

Pete knelt down next to his son. "Bud, I know it's your birthday, but the day is about more than gifts. It's about being together with your family."

"And I've been with my family forever. I want to open gifts now."

Brent couldn't help laughing. When Holly shot a warning look at him, he held up his hands in apology. What could he say? The kid had a point.

Eliza and Oliver were excessively late.

Alice had been yawning for the last thirty minutes and Susanna's frosting-induced sugar high wasn't going to keep her afloat much longer.

"Mom," Brent called, laying an arm over his mom's shoulders. "I think we've got to call it. Eliza isn't gonna make it. We should open gifts."

Mae chewed on her lip for a moment and then relented. "You're right. I'm sure she's fine, right?"

"Sure," Brent agreed. "Just busy. I'll tell her we waited as long as we could."

Mae nodded and clapped her hands, though she didn't look overly pleased about it. "Gift time!"

Grady sprinted away from his dad's sage advice and straight towards the gift table. The little girls trailed after him.

"Can I hand out gifts?" Susanna asked, raising her hand like she was in school.

Rose smiled and rushed to help her. "Sure. Here. This one is for—"

"Grady, duh," Susanna finished. Her eyebrows were raised as though it was more than obvious. "It has dinosaurs."

Everyone laughed, and within a few minutes, the gifts had been distributed.

"Well, Grady," Holly said, "you've waited long enough. Go for it!"

The kid had made one solitary rip in the wrapping of the first box when Brent's phone rang. He pulled it out, and Eliza's name flashed on the screen.

"Oh, hold on!" he called, holding up his phone. "Eliza has phoned in to explain herself."

Grady groaned, but everyone else was riveted. It wasn't every day Eliza screwed something up.

"Hey, sis. Long time, no hear. You're missing a great party," Brent said, conscious of everyone's eyes on him. There was a long pause, and he frowned. "Hello?"

"Hi," Eliza said, her voice soft. "Sorry, hi. Sorry I missed your calls. My phone was dead."

"No electricity where you're at?" he teased.

"I've been busy."

Brent noticed her voice was strange—soft and slow, almost like she'd just woken up.

"What is she saying?" Mom whispered.

Susanna turned to Rose. "Will we eat cake again when Aunt Eliza gets here?"

Trying to tune them out so he could hear Eliza, Brent half-turned away, pressing a finger to his other ear. "What's going on? Everything okay?"

"Yes," she said. "Well, no."

Brent listened as his sister relayed everything. In classic Eliza style, she recounted the day's events as though she were reading from a time log. Like she'd taken notes prior to calling him.

When Brent hung up, the reality still not quite having sunk in, the words didn't come out as cleanly.

"The baby is in the NICU."

Mae gasped, hands clapped over her mouth.

Holly and Sara looked at one another, communicating wordlessly over the heads of everyone else at the party.

Rose moved towards Brent, laying a hand on his elbow as he stared down at his phone like it had more answers left to give.

"She had to have an emergency c-section this afternoon," Brent mumbled.

Mae was standing up, her body tense like a too-tight bow string. "Is she okay?"

Yes. Well, no, Eliza had said.

Brent didn't think his mom would want to hear that.

"Eliza and the baby are okay, but they're at the hospital," he said. "She didn't call because her phone died."

Instantly, the mood of the party shifted. Everyone moved with an anxious excitement, gathering their things to go to the hospital. No one had suggested it out loud, but going to see Eliza seemed like the only reasonable thing to do.

"I was supposed to watch Winter," Holly whispered to Pete as they hurriedly dumped the trash from the tables into the dumpster. "I can't believe Oliver didn't call."

"I'm sure they were busy," Pete said.

"Yeah, but they island didn't lose cell coverage. He could have sent a text."

"I'm sure Winter is fine, Hol." Pete laid a hand on his wife's back, soothing the tension from her shoulders. "There's nothing you could have done, anyway."

A few feet away, Dominic was offering the same assurances to Mae. "...You couldn't have known."

"But I did know," Mae protested. She pressed a hand to her heart and smiled, though her eyes were filled with bitter tears. "I can't believe I was so worried about this party when Eliza was in surgery."

"I can't believe we have three birthdays on the same day," Sara said, staring at the remnants of the cake as she passed by with a bundle of half-deflated balloons. Brent could practically see her wheels turning as she imagined whether she could get away with making one cake for three conjoined birthday parties.

"A mother knows when her kids need her. I should have tried harder to find her." Mae sighed and straightened her spine.

As she passed Brent, she rubbed his shoulder. He wondered if she'd sensed anything from him today.

He wasn't selfish. He knew Eliza was and should be his mom's main concern.

But still, he wondered.

Everyone was heading towards the side gate, working their way to the cars in front of the Inn, when Grady called out from behind them. "Hey! What about the presents?"

In the commotion, they'd left Grady with a half-opened gift on his lap. The poor kid couldn't catch a break.

Pete sighed. "Bring them along. You can open them in the waiting room."

He jogged back and helped his son carry the boxes to the car, and then the entire crew loaded up and headed to the hospital to see what on earth had happened.

14

ELIZA

The NICU felt like a world unto itself. Like the teddy bear-covered linens and pastels could swallow reality. Only the coming and going of the nurses showed the passage of time.

Someone in scrubs with a yellow Pediatrics badge came into the room every fifteen minutes to check on Summer. After eight nurses had come and gone, Eliza finally remembered her phone.

Oliver retrieved it from the charger in the post-op recovery room and handed it over to her. As soon as Eliza powered it on, the phone began to vibrate nonstop.

Brent called four times, Holly called once, and her mom had texted her three times.

Eliza went to call Brent back, but her thumb hesitated over the button.

"I should have called sooner," she mumbled aloud.

Oliver squeezed her shoulder. "Don't feel bad about anything. It's been a long day."

"Yeah, but still—"

"No. If anything, I should have made the calls. Out of the three of us," he said, pointing to himself, Eliza, and Summer, "I'm the only one who didn't give birth or get born today. What's my excuse?"

She knew she should call her mom first—Mae deserved to hear the news before anyone else—but Eliza took the coward's path and called Brent back instead.

She wanted to talk to someone who wouldn't freak out and throw her off kilter again. Someone she didn't feel like she'd let down.

Brent picked up after the first ring. "Hey, sis. Long time, no hear. You're missing a great party."

There were muffled voices in the background and a rustle against the mouthpiece that sounded like wind.

Brent was outside with other people. A party, apparently.

It took Eliza a few seconds to register what her brother meant. When she did, her stomach turned with guilt.

The birthdays.

Eliza had forgotten about her mom's birthday party. And Grady's.

"Hello?" Brent asked.

"Hi. Sorry, hi," she said, shaking her head to clear it. She'd apologize to her mom later. If nothing else, Mae Benson was forgiving. Right now, Eliza needed to focus and relay the facts. "Sorry I missed your calls. My phone was dead."

"No electricity where you're at?"

She glanced at Summer. At the beeping machines and flashing lights. Her daughter was surrounded by more electricity than Eliza had ever seen before.

"I've been busy."

The voices in the background of the call faded. Eliza could picture her brother pacing away from the party to better hear her.

"What's going on? Everything okay?"

"Yes. Well, no." She sighed and launched into it. "I had a doctor's appointment this morning and they did a scan to check on the baby. Something had gone wrong. I'm okay, and Summer is... she's here. I had an emergency C-section a few hours ago. Now, we're in the NICU. The doctor is worried about her lungs right now, so they are monitoring her. Oliver and I are both here, which is why we aren't at the party. Sorry again for not letting you know sooner."

Eliza didn't know what she expected Brent to say, but he responded with a measured, "Okay. See you soon."

Then, without waiting for her to say anything, the line went dead.

"How did it go?" Oliver asked nervously.

"It's my mom's birthday," she said. "And Grady's."

"Oh, right. The party. I knew I was forgetting something."

She rubbed her daughter's hand between her fingers. "And now Summer's, too."

"Guess this is the last year we'll be able to claim we forgot," Oliver chuckled. "Did your brother say anything else?"

"'See you soon,'" Eliza repeated with a shrug. "Then he hung up."

"Okay..." Oliver frowned. "I expected more, to be honest."

So had Eliza.

But then again, she'd dropped an information bomb on Brent, and he'd never been the fastest processer.

And secretly, perhaps, that was why Eliza had called him. She knew he wouldn't freak out because he'd be too stunned to formulate a response right away.

Her mom would have cried. Or asked too many questions.

Holly would have jumped into action, trying to help.

Sara would have gotten nervous and passed the phone to someone else.

And Eliza didn't feel capable of handling anyone else's emotions. She had enough trouble figuring out where to stash her own.

"Three birthdays on the same day," Eliza muttered, mostly to herself.

"That's got to be a record."

"I just hope Grady won't be bothered by it."

Oliver looked down at Summer and smiled softly. "How could anyone be bothered by anything to do with this little one?"

"He already has to share his big day."

Oliver waved away her concern. "Grady will love her. And so will everyone else."

Eliza had her doubts. She'd nearly come to blows with two other girls in Mrs. Johnson's third-grade class over whose name should come first when the class sang "Happy Birthday" to the three of them. It came down to a fiercely contested rock-paper-scissors tournament. Had Jessica Ratley won, or was it Mariah Munes? Eliza couldn't remember.

She glanced at their daughter again.

Over the last few hours, the shock of seeing Summer connected to tubes and wires had worn off. Even the squeaky gurney wheels, distant mechanical beeps, and whispering nurses had become a comforting ambient noise.

But Summer's size still shocked her every time. *My sweet pea. My plum. My pumpkin.*

Not so big as a pumpkin, though. Not by a long shot.

Wanting to let her know someone was there with her, Eliza and Oliver never let a second pass without one of them stroking her arm or holding her hand. She felt impossibly fragile beneath their touch.

"Her fingers are so small. Like Tic-Tacs," Eliza said, counting them off one by one.

"They aren't going to fall off," Oliver teased. "She had ten when she was born, and she'll go home with ten."

Home.

It should be an anchor Eliza clung to. A promise of good things to come, of the normalcy she'd been craving all day.

But really, Eliza was riddled with guilt because she didn't know if she even wanted to take Summer home. Not when she was still so small.

The glass encasement Eliza had at first hated now seemed like the only place her delicate little girl would be safe. She wasn't ready for whatever came next.

At that, another memory bubbled up from nowhere at all.

The day Eliza had moved into her room at UPenn, her mom had cried and cried. Mom clung to Eliza on the wide lawn in front of the Rodin College House. Eliza's room was on the first floor, blinds open. She knew her roommate, Alisa, could probably see their spectacle. Eliza tried hard not to be embarrassed.

"I'm planning to bus and ferry back in just a couple months for Thanksgiving," Eliza had muttered, patting her mom's back. "Plus, Dad bought me a plane ticket for Christmas."

"Thanksgiving!" Mom's eyes had gone wide. As if it was a prison sentence, not a holiday.

Alisa's parents had barely stayed ten minutes after helping her move into the eighteen-by-eighteen-foot room. Almost like they'd been glad to see their daughter be independent.

It had been hours since Eliza's parents had helped her unpack, and there they were still—lingering.

"If we're going to catch our flight, we should go," Eliza's dad said, trying to gently peel Mom away.

Mom stroked Eliza's golden hair in a way she hadn't since she was a little girl. "If you want us to stay another day, we can. We can get a hotel room. Take you out for dinner. Walk around campus with you. Do you know where all of your classes are?"

"My sister can only watch the kids for today. And I'm not sure she could handle Brent much longer than that, anyway," Dad had said. "Nor would she ever forgive us if we made her."

"Yes, go be with the little kids." Eliza was no longer a child. She didn't need her parents the same way Brent and Sara did. "Besides, classes don't start for another week and the R.A. said there would be a pizza social in the lobby."

"That's great," he'd said with a clap. "You'll get free food and make new friends. Every college kid's dream."

Mom had hiccupped and shaken her head. "My baby is in college. I can't believe it."

"Believe it." It came out more like a demand than a joke. She papered it over with a pat on her mother's back.

"The thought of you alone in the world is the scariest thought I've ever had," Mom had admitted—more to herself than to Eliza. "But I know you'll be fine."

Back then, Eliza had rolled her eyes at the hysterics.

Now, she understood. Looking down at her daughter laying inside the incubator, Eliza understood completely.

She knew Summer would be fine. But that didn't ease the ache beneath her ribs. It didn't settle the yawning pit of worries that opened up in her stomach when she thought about strapping her tiny daughter into the pink car seat they'd bought.

"We should get one of those 'Baby on Board' signs for the car," Eliza blurted suddenly.

"We never had one with Winter."

Oliver was leaning back in his chair, his head resting against the low headrest in a way that set his neck at a strange angle. He'd have a kink in it in the morning.

"Winter was different. Bigger."

"Summer will get bigger, too."

"But until then."

"Can we talk about this later?" Eliza could hear the exhaustion in his voice. "This seems like a later discussion. We have enough to worry about."

Eliza knew he was right, but she couldn't turn her brain off. "And baby gates. We need baby gates."

"We have baby gates." Oliver sounded exasperated now. "The cabinets are baby-proofed, and we have those locks on every doorknob. I feel like I'm robbing a vault every time I try to open the closet."

"I still think we should get the sign for the car."

Oliver leaned forward, elbows on his knees. "Are you okay, Liz?"

"Fine. I', fine," she said again because the first one hadn't sounded as convincing as she'd wanted. "Just trying to plan for the future."

"Well, stop."

Eliza turned on Oliver. "We need to make sure everything is ready."

"I can tell you right now it's not," he said with a weary chuckle. "Nothing is ready because we thought we had four more weeks."

"I know! That's why I'm trying to get ready now."

Oliver sighed and reached out for Eliza's hand. She pulled away at first, but he insisted, chasing her down and sandwiching her fingers between his. "Right now, your only job is to relax and recover. And stare at our daughter."

"But—"

"No," he said firmly. "No buts. Relax. Recover. Stare. I'll do everything else."

Eliza couldn't just sit here and do nothing. All of Winter's old baby clothes were still in boxes in the attic, and Eliza hadn't had time to wash them yet. The nursery was in disarray, one side of the crib laying in the middle of the floor where Oliver had abandoned it after Winter had run off with one of the screws in her fist.

They didn't even have diapers yet.

But before Eliza could say anything, there was a knock at the door.

Ginny smiled in at them, her brunette ponytail bouncing around the side of the door frame. "How are you feeling?" she asked, pressing her stethoscope to Eliza's inner arm and glancing up at the goofy giraffe clock hanging above.

Eliza had grown to hate the *tick-tock* of that clock. She wanted to rip it off the wall.

"Fine."

"What's your pain level?" Ginny gestured to the chart on the wall, where a line of ten faces ran the gamut from smiling to tears.

Eliza felt just south of neutral. The corners of her mouth were turned ever so slightly downward. Not a frown, not a straight line. "A six, probably."

"That sounds about right. We're fifteen minutes past time for more pain meds." Ginny grabbed a cup of pills from the tray she'd rolled in and handed it to Eliza.

Eliza had heard Ginny got married not long after graduation—to a boy two years older who played trombone in the marching band—but Eliza didn't see a wedding ring. Not even a tan line to show where it might sit on her finger when she wasn't at work.

"I'm about to leave for the night," Ginny said, glancing at the clock again. It was getting late. Winter would already be asleep by now. "My replacement will be here in fifteen minutes, but until then, I wanted to make sure you were up for visitors."

Not a second later, Eliza's mom appeared in the doorway.

She looked older than Eliza remembered. Her eyes were bloodshot like maybe she'd been crying. And did her hair have more gray in it? That seemed impossible. But who knew anymore?

Regardless, Eliza's mom was here. Familiar and comforting and *here*. Finally.

It felt like a weighted vest had been lifted off her shoulders. Like her lungs could expand for the first time all day.

"Mom."

Her mother rushed into the room and towards Eliza, stooping awkwardly to hug her where she sat in her wheelchair. She buried her face in Eliza's neck and squeezed tight.

"Honey. I'm so sorry I wasn't here. How are you feeling?"

"Fine."

Ginny gave Eliza a small wave and slipped out the door quietly.

"You had emergency surgery," Mom chastised.

"To save the baby, not me."

She smoothed her hand over Eliza's forehead and assessed her from head to toe, taking in the wheelchair with a scrutinizing eye. "Do they have you on pain medication?"

"I just took some." Much like that day at UPenn, Eliza suddenly wanted to push her mom's hand away, but she was trying to be generous. She just needed a second to absorb the sudden intrusion. "I should have called, but my phone died."

"You were busy, honey."

"Yeah, but you were supposed to be in the room, and—"

"No apologies," Mom interrupted. "So long as you and the baby are okay, I'm okay. Everything is okay."

Holly came in quietly, hands folded behind her back. "Did I hear everyone is okay in here?"

"Fine," Eliza said again. Hoping if she said it often enough it would feel true.

Holly nodded in understanding. "I'm sure. We won't stay long. You all need your rest."

"*Isn't she lovely, isn't she wonderful?*" Sara came into the room crooning the Stevie Wonder song, sashaying back and forth. Then, she pushed their mother aside and hugged Eliza. "I'm talking about you *and* the baby. How are you feeling?"

"I'm fine," Eliza said. She feel neither lovely nor wonderful, but she kept saying fine and maybe part of her was starting to believe it. "I'm not the one in the incubator."

"It's probably just precaution, right?" Mom asked, running her hand over the glass that separated her from her newest granddaughter. "She looks healthy."

"She looked perfect," Holly whispered, almost reverently.

"The doctors are optimistic her lungs will catch up quickly," Oliver said. "She'll be fine."

How many times could the same word be used before it lost all meaning?

Fine. Fine. Fine. Fine. Fine. Until it was melted butter in everyone's mouths.

"And what have they said about you?" Mae asked, turning to Eliza.

"Ginny was just in here, and she didn't have anything to say. So I must be fine."

Holly's eyebrows lifted. "Ginny Abernathy? Or, I guess, she's back to her maiden name now. Morris, I think?"

Sara nodded. "Ginny Morris."

"You all know her?"

"She was my counselor at Camp Eldritch in sixth grade." Sara sneered. "Such a goody-two-shoes. I tried to leave a frog in Meghan's bunk bed, and she assigned me to kitchen duty for the rest of the week."

Holly laughed. "Good for her."

Another knock at the door. "How is my oldest sister doing?" Brent asked, entering the family reunion.

"I'm fine," Eliza said, hopefully for the last time. She was happy her family was there, but going from a nearly empty room to a packed one in the span of only a few minutes was jarring.

"If you need anything, I'm your guy." Brent pointed both thumbs at himself. "Hospital food is terrible and the cafeteria is closed, but I saw some of the kitchen staff cleaning up. I bet I could talk them into making you a mostly edible sandwich. Charm is my superpower."

Oliver backed away from the incubator and glanced at the door. "I think we're only allowed two visitors at a time. I'll give you all some space."

Brent waved a dismissive hand. "I took care of it. One of the nurses and I have a bit of history."

Holly gasped and playfully slapped their brother's arm. "Did you date one of your niece's nurses?"

"No," he laughed, rubbing at his arm where she'd slapped him. "I gave her—and her *husband*—a fishing tour when they moved here six months ago."

"If he'd dated her, she never would have helped us," Sara drawled. Ignoring Brent's protests, Sara knelt down next to the incubator. "Look at how perfect she is, Eliza. You made her. Can you believe it?"

"Absolutely perfect," Holly echoed, pressing her hands to her heart. "She looks like Winter, doesn't she?"

"But with Oliver's coloring," Mom added. "Look at her dark hair."

Eliza leaned forward and looked in on Summer. She did have dark hair. She'd been so distracted by—well, by everything—she'd hardly noticed.

Summer had dark hair like her daddy. Why did that make her want to sob?

"She's small," Eliza murmured.

"Totally normal," Holly said right back. "She's four weeks early."

Mom agreed. "Winter wasn't a big baby, either. Even full-term, she was just over seven pounds."

"Exactly. Nothing to worry about."

"I guess so. It's just hard to see anything beyond the wires and the incubator."

"It's an illusion. The tubes make her look smaller," Holly theorized. "Once her lungs are good to go and they take those off, she'll look much better. Look at the rolls above her elbows. Little biscuit dough rolls."

"She'll be as chunky as Grady was in no time," Sara laughed.

Eliza hadn't noticed the rolls, but sure enough, there they were. Pinchable little bundles of baby chub just like Winter had when she was born.

Dark hair like her daddy.

Rolls like biscuit dough.

My sweet pea, my plum, my pumpkin.

She was so close to crying, but she wouldn't. Not with everyone around. That would have to wait until later.

"Oh, yeah, Grady was a beast. My little Michelin Man," Brent said with a smile. "Now he's ten! Time sure flies."

"Believe me, I know." Mom looked at all of her children and shook her head. "I remember being in the hospital with each of you. Like it was yesterday. Now, you're having babies of your own. It's unbelievable, really, it's just—" Her voice broke in a choked half-sob.

Brent wrapped their mom in a side hug and rested his cheek on the top of her head. "You can't cry on your birthday, Mom."

"Leave her alone," Sara jabbed.

Mom wiped at her misty eyes. "I'm just so proud of all of you. For sticking together and growing into good people. It's the best birthday present I could have ever asked for."

Holly joined the hug with Brent and Mae first. Then they shuffled closer to Eliza's wheelchair, and Eliza threw her arm around her family, too.

Worry for Summer still gnawed at her, but she suspected that would be there for a long time. Maybe the rest of her life.

But all the obstacles she'd been struggling with before seemed more manageable now.

Her family had been through worse. They'd get through this, too.

15

MAE

FRIDAY MORNING—ONE WEEK LATER

The Sweet Island Inn would only be closed for a couple weeks, but the overflow of boxes littering the entryway suggested Mae was closing up shop.

The set designer had kindly but firmly requested all personal effects be out of sight.

If only she'd known how hard that would be.

Guests of the inn often smiled at the entryway picture of Grady and Alice running through a sprinkler wearing goggles too large for their face. They'd gesture to the wall and ask, "These all belong to you?" Mae would proudly respond that they did.

The movie, however, didn't care about sentimentality unless it was fictional.

So into the box went the pictures. Into the box went books and ornaments and Mae's best cooking spoon.

The boxes were also loaded down with the sun-bleached Sweet Island Inn sign from the front porch and each of the three back-to-back-to-back Best of Nantucket Hospitality Awards Mae had won.

Stripping any trace of herself from the business that had become her home over the last three years made Mae more uncomfortable than she'd expected. How quickly evidence of a life could be erased.

"How much room is left in the storage closet?" Mae called across the spotless kitchen.

"None. Why?" Dominic's voice wavered, nervous to even ask.

"I have another box of pictures that need to be put away."

He groaned, the sound echoing off the unusually bare walls. "Shove them under a bed. Or in the oven. No one's going to be using the oven, anyway."

"I don't need another kitchen fire, thank you very much." Mae shivered at the thought.

The previous fire had been small. An annoyance more than a disaster. But the thought of spending another two weeks washing and scrubbing away the smoke smell had turned her into a real-life Smokey the Mama Bear. *Only you can prevent Inn fires.*

"Let's just take it with us to—"

"No!" Dominic cut her off sharply, a raised finger all Mae could see sticking out from the storage room door. "I'll find room. We can't possibly take anything more with us to Brent's house."

"He won't mind. Brent cleared out space in Henry's old workshop for us. It's really fine."

Suddenly, Dominic burst out of the room and into the kitchen, arms raised in triumph. "Not necessary. I've made space."

"Let's hope I don't find anything else to pack up."

"God forbid."

Dominic was fanning himself like he was about to slump over from heat exhaustion. Slightly warm for June, the temperature still hadn't crested seventy-five degrees. And with the damp breeze off the water and the cottony white clouds offering some protection from the sun, it was a gorgeous day.

But Mae allowed for Dominic's dramatics. He'd been hard at work all morning.

"I know we're packing a lot. I'm sorry. This could be a great opportunity for the inn, so I want to make sure I do it right. Everything has to be spotless."

"Everything was already spotless," he said over his shoulder. "That's why the film crew chose this as a filming location. You keep an immaculately clean house."

"I know, I know. You sound like Lola and Debra." Mae's friends had come over for an evening of wine on the porch the night before, and they'd teased Mae for wiping up the water rings on the table between every sip.

Mae had heard it all. From Dominic. The kids. Henry. Mostly when they were complaining about having to pick up their rooms or help clean the bathrooms again.

Everything is fine the way it is, Mom! The never-ending chorus of the last thirty years.

"Tease me all you want," she said. "But it's what earned me all those awards we had to pack away."

She stopped and surveyed the living room once more. Every corner empty and scrubbed to within an inch of its life.

Immaculately clean, yes. But wrong. So wrong! This place was meant to be filled to bursting. Without all the things in their proper places, Mae felt like a string without a kite.

Dominic stopped and stood next to her, hands on his hips as Mae turned to gaze out the front window. A line of tulip trees acted as a privacy screen and sound break from the road, making it difficult to see or hear anyone approaching until their tires crunched over the white gravel drive that horseshoed in front of the inn.

"Brent texted. He'll be here in ten minutes," Mae said, the thought twisting her stomach nervously.

The film crew asked about using Sweet Island Inn as a location months earlier, but it was only now hitting Mae that strangers would be in her home without her.

What if they needed help setting the tricky thermostat upstairs?

Or what if they missed the note she'd hung inside the fridge that said to not turn on the ice machine? There was a leak in the line and it spilled water all over the floor. A replacement part wouldn't be in for another couple weeks.

"We can always come back if something goes wrong or gets left behind. I'm sure it wouldn't bother anyone on set," Dominic said, as though reading her mind.

"That's right! You were invited to set."

Mae could picture it now—professional cameras and folding chairs with names stitched into the back. The director would wear a baseball cap and people would hustle around, touching up makeup and handing out lunch deliveries. Clipboards as far as the eye could see.

Maybe they'd even ask Mae to help with something around the set. She could be their Inn Expert on hand, ready to answer all questions hospitality. *"Oh, yes, I'd be delighted to show you how I manage a new booking..."*

Dominic wavered back and forth uncertainly. "I was invited, but I'm not sure I want to go."

The image in Mae's head flickered to black, disappointment wrinkling her brow. "Don't you want to see your vision come to life?"

"I want to see the movie," he clarified, shoving his hands in his jean pockets. "I'm just not sure I want to be involved in the process."

"What do you mean?"

"I'm a writer, not a movie-maker." He shrugged. "I'd hate to make anyone uncomfortable."

"They're professionals. I'm sure they'd be fine."

"A lot of people from Nantucket will be part of it, too. Joey couldn't stop talking about his 'big break.' I don't want to make him nervous."

Mae smirked. "I'm not sure that's possible. Sara has herself one confident beau."

Finally, Dominic sighed. "It's more than that. I don't know if I want to see my house turn into a movie set."

"But you'll see it when the movie comes out, no?"

"Yeah, but that will be different. I'm excited to see it as a fictional place on screen. But seeing it as a working movie set would be like seeing the puppeteer's hands during a puppet show. It would ruin the magic."

Mae loved seeing the strings. The more she could know about how something worked and how it was made, the better. She wanted to know all of the behind-the-scenes secrets.

No matter what she wanted, though, she wouldn't go to the movie set without Dominic. Her Inn would be featured in the movie, but it was his book being brought to life. She would only go if he was comfortable with it.

"You don't have to decide right now," Mae said. "After a few days sitting around the house, you may become so bored you change your mind."

Dominic chuckled. "I think you may be projecting. You are the one who will get bored. I will happily sit and read the entire time."

At home, Mae wouldn't mind Dominic spending the day with his nose in a book. Running the Inn kept her plenty busy, what with cleaning and cooking, readying rooms for check-in and seeing guests off at checkout.

In Brent and Rose's place, though, Mae would be transported from her life and plopped down in a museum of old memories. A living monument of the years she'd spend raising her children. Of something she used to take care of and tend to everyday, but that was no longer hers. Not anymore.

An idle mind could be a dangerous thing, and Mae suspected she'd be in need of a diversion or two.

A familiar horn honked three times. Dominic angled himself so he could see out the window. "On that note, I think our moving truck has arrived."

Mae had been so lost in thought that she hadn't noticed Brent turn down the driveway in "the moving truck," which was actually Brent's old beater.

Dominic and Mae stepped out into the balmy day to meet Brent on the porch. The wooden steps, worn smooth from years of guests and ocean spray, squeaked beneath their feet.

"Your chariot has arrived," Brent said, waving his arms with a flourish and a bow. The exhaust blew dark smoke and the whole truck seemed to hiccup and shake as it idled.

"Are you sure the chariot can handle the trip?" Dominic asked, voice raised to be heard over the rumbling engine.

Brent patted the side of the truck. Two loud bangs shook loose a small puff of rust. "I've been driving her without a bit of trouble for the last six years. Old girl will be glad for the chance to strut her stuff again. She's gotten shelved lately in favor of the hatchback. Turns out little kids are fragile and safety ratings are important. Who knew?"

That reminded her: Susanna! Mae would be playing live-in grandma for the next two weeks. She'd nearly forgotten. Hours of entertainment she could count on, for sure. Craft projects and no-bake cookie recipes flicked through her mind, dusting away the anxiety that had clung to her like a cobweb.

Dominic looked dubious. "We do have a lot of luggage."

"That's definitely not a problem," Brent said. "I cart tools and lumber all over the island when I'm on a construction job."

"If you're sure..."

Brent patted the truck again. "Positive. Maybe a more sensible person would have scrapped her by now, but she's the first car I bought with my own money."

"A first car is a special thing," Dominic said warmly. "We'll be sure to treat her with respect."

Mae chuckled. "I'm not sure Brent was treating her with respect when he took her out on all those late-night beach races?"

"You know about that?" Brent's eyes went wide.

"A little bird told me you and your truck nearly ended up in the ocean once."

Brent ran a nervous hand through his dirty blonde hair. "Haven't the faintest idea what you're talking about. Anyway, where are the boxes?"

"Nice transition," Dominic laughed. "She'll never suspect."

The two men walked into the house together ahead of her, laughing and whispering, and it gave Mae hope for the days to come.

Maybe her worries were unfounded. Maybe it would be nice to have a two-week break from normal life.

Mae followed them in and grabbed her suitcase just inside the door, but Brent plucked it right from her hands. "I'm here to do the heavy lifting, Ma. Go grab a mimosa or something."

"It's one suitcase!"

"Nuh-uh." He wagged his finger. "Think of my house as the Howard Street Inn, and me as your concierge. Your stay with us begins now."

Then, without waiting for her retort, he trundled away, banging her suitcase down the stairs and tossing it into the back of his truck.

She could do this.

It was as simple as letting go.

~

Turned out, Mae's idleness would begin even earlier than she thought.

While the boys loaded up the vehicle, Mae busied herself double-checking all the lights in the inn were off and turning the thermostat up so she wouldn't waste money cooling an empty house.

Padding through the inn doing last checks, Mae couldn't get past how bizarre it felt to see the place empty. Without muffled voices slipping out from under doors and water surging through the pipes, the house felt lonely.

Mae moved down the hallway, running her hand over the gold number plates next to the guest rooms and swiping a stray bit of dust from the antique writing table next to the banister.

The next two weeks yawned opened in front of her, unusually and disturbingly sparse. With a mental "X," Mae checked off Day One of her two-week exile.

"What are you going to do while the Inn is closed?" Brent asked the moment Mae scooted into the bench seat of the truck. The interior smelled like wood shavings and saltwater.

"No idea," Mae laughed, trying to hide the depth of her concern. "Eliza thinks it will be amazing free advertising. If I'm lucky, talk of the movie will send guests rushing to make reservations."

"Before you start thinking about work again, I'd suggest you enjoy your break," Brent said.

"Hear hear!" Dominic cheered.

Brent nodded, even more certain his advice was solid. "The inn will still be here when you get back, Mama. Might as well try to enjoy yourself."

Of course the Sweet Island Inn would go on existing without Mae. Mae's concern was whether she could exist without it.

The first thing she saw was the wall.

As soon as she walked through the door of the Howard Street residence she'd once called home, Mae noticed the wallpaper had been replaced with a dark moody floral print.

Gone was the gold- and navy-striped wallpaper she and Henry had picked out less than ten years earlier. In its place loomed large flowers nearly the size of Ma's head. They were drawn in rich jewel tones with thick vines draping from bud to bud.

The wallpaper was beautiful and no doubt very modern—though a little menacing, in Mae's opinion.

Before she could notice anything else, Rose appeared, buzzing with energy.

"Welcome, you two! Leave your bags here and Brent will carry them up to your room. I left towels in the guest room and bought shampoo and conditioner for the shower."

"Oh, we brought our own, darling," Mae said. "You're nice enough to give us a bed. We don't want to bother you beyond that."

"Of course, of course—but just in case. I don't want you two to worry about anything while you're here."

Mae smiled and patted Rose's elbow. "And I don't want you to worry. Just pretend we aren't here."

"See, hon?" Brent said, adjusting a box under his arm to let it rest on his hip. "I didn't need to spit-shine the floors and clean all of the ceiling fans."

Dominic laughed. "Especially since your mom would have loved that chore. With the inn closed, her hostess energy is all dressed up with nowhere to go."

"For the record, he used a wet mop pad, not actual spit," Rose said, rolling her eyes even as her cheeks flushed. "And the fans needed to be cleaned regardless. There was decades' worth of dust up there." Suddenly, Rose's eyes widened in alarm. "Not to say you didn't clean them, of course! I'm sure you did. I just—"

"I actually didn't," Mae said, hoping to put Rose at ease. "Henry never let me do anything involving a ladder. My balance is terrible. But getting him on the ladder to clean the fans was like herding a cat through a sprinkler."

Rose let out a relieved sigh. A moment of awkward silence followed.

"Onto the unpacking, I suppose," Dominic said. "Ready, Brent?"

"Aye-aye."

The two men left to unload the truck. Mae could hear their voices growing softer through the thin walls. She always thought this old house needed more insulation. She could hear the two of them laughing, at ease with one another.

Which was more than she could say for herself and Rose.

Rose hovered in the threshold of the living room, hands clasped behind her back. It was unclear if she wanted Mae to follow her into the living room to sit or whether she expected her to go on up to the guest room.

"Well, maybe I'll head on up—" Mae started to say just as Rose said, "Would you like some tea?"

Mae nodded. "Sure, that would be—"

"Oh, of course. Get settled," Rose said, waving Mae towards the stairs.

The women stared at one another for a second, neither wanting to speak in case they spoke over the other again.

Finally, Mae smiled. "I have all day to get settled. I'd love some tea."

Rose nodded and led Mae back to the kitchen.

Let it go, dear, she told herself as they walked down the narrow hallway single-file. *Take your hands off the steering wheel.*

But it was proving awfully hard to shake the feeling of being in a place she'd once known so well—especially when the map in her head no longer quite matched reality.

The kitchen at Howard Street seemed smaller now than ever before. Especially with new barstools taking up space, wide-set with tall backs and white, tufted upholstery.

"We have a few different teas. Anything specific you like?"

"Anything decaffeinated," Mae said. "I can't handle caffeine this late in the day. Maybe a fruit tea?"

Rose opened what used to be Mae's junk drawer to reveal a neat rack of tea bags. She looked back over her shoulder, lower lip pinched between her teeth. "I have chamomile?"

"That sounds perfect, dear."

"Sorry. I should have asked what kind of tea you liked. I can run to the store—"

"No, no, nonsense," Mae said. "Chamomile is fine. I'll get the mugs."

Mae turned to the cabinet just to the right of the sink. But when she pulled it open, instead of mugs, she was met with a fully-stocked spice rack and a pasta roller.

"Sorry!" Rose cringed from the other side of the kitchen, pointing a hesitant finger at the cabinet closest to the back door. "I did some rearranging when we moved in. That cabinet was the only one with a shelf tall enough for my spice rack."

Mae smiled. "No need to apologize. I didn't assume everything would be the same as I'd had it."

Except, hadn't she? Perhaps a little. Not consciously, of course, but somewhere in her gut. In her bones.

Rose's face was still creased with worry, but before she could say anything else, the back door opened and Dominic came in, cheeks red.

He saw the mug in Rose's hand and raised his brows. "If you're taking orders, I could go for some ice water. I'm parched."

"Coming right up." Rose set to work boiling water, dropping a tea bag into a mug, and cracking ice from the tray into a tall glass for Dominic.

Dominic thanked her and drank his water in one long gulp. Rose refilled it instantly, folding her hands behind her back when she was finished like a waiter anticipating another request.

When none came, she sighed.

"Brent got his room ready for you. It's a guest room now, I suppose," she said. "But we can accommodate if you would be more comfortable in the master. It was your room first."

"But it's your room now," Mae prodded as gently as she could. "The guest room is fine with us."

"A guest room is the perfect place for guests," Dominic teased.

"Important guests," Rose qualified. "I want you to be comfortable here."

Mae chuckled. "I was comfortable enough here for thirty years, so I'm sure the next two weeks will be fine."

The quip was meant to be a joke, but Rose's face reddened again. "Of course. It's more your house than mine."

"No, not at all," Mae said quickly. "This is your house. We're just happy to be your guests. Speaking of, we should head on up and unpack, Dom."

Rose jumped and spun towards the stove. "Wait. Your tea!"

She filled Mae's cup to the top with steaming water, and Mae took it, careful to not let her fingers brush the hot ceramic sides. "Thank you very much."

When they made it up to their temporary living quarters and the door was shut firmly behind them, Mae let loose the sigh that had been building in her chest.

Dominic understood it implicitly. "She'll relax after we've been here for a while. Brent told me in the workshop how nervous Rose has been. She just wants us to be at ease."

Rose was always quick to help out and pitch in when she, Brent, and Susanna came by the inn. But there, she was friendly, relaxed.

Now, she was a rumbling volcano of tension. Mae worried she'd explode under the pressure.

"She only wants to be a good hostess," Mae said, rubbing at her temple. "I know that. And I know things will work out. It just feels strange being treated like a guest in my own house."

"I thought it was their house now," Dominic said, his mouth pulled back in a gentle, knowing smile.

Mae covered her mouth with her hand, surprised by the slip. "It is their house! Of course it is. I didn't mean—"

He laid a hand on her shoulder. "I know you didn't. This is a large adjustment. For everyone."

"Not for you," Mae said, a tinge of bitterness in her tone.

"For me, too. I mean, we're temporarily homeless and our house is being used as a movie set. It's only fair we all have a little anxiety about it."

"You have anxiety about it?" Mae asked, turning to him.

Dominic ran a hand along the back of his neck. "My fair share, I suppose. I sympathize with Rose, actually. This is the most time I will have spent with Brent. I want him to like me."

"He does like you!"

"I know he does, but what I know and how I feel aren't always working in tandem," he said. "Just like you know this house isn't yours, but it doesn't make it any less strange that there is now a contour line drawing of a naked human body hanging in the front hallway."

Mae smiled slyly. "How do you know that wasn't mine and I just left it behind?"

Dominic raised a brow and snorted softly. "That would be off-brand for you, dear."

"Okay, you got me. It's not mine. But there's something Rose and I can bond over. I like art."

"You do not."

"Well, I could learn to like it." Mae patted Dominic's knee and stood up. "You're right that this is a large adjustment, but I can be flexible and try to make Rose more comfortable. Everything will be fine."

"Everything will be fine," Dominic echoed.

"First step, no hiding out in this room," Mae said. "I'm going to ask for a little tour of the house. Let Rose show me all the changes they've made."

When she walked back downstairs, Mae smelled citrus and mint—an unfamiliar smell in a familiar space. Rose was sitting at the kitchen island, chin in her hands, scrolling through her phone.

As soon as she noticed Mae, Rose jolted to standing, nearly knocking the hefty barstool over.

"Sorry, dear," Mae said. "I didn't mean to startle you."

Rose righted the barstool and smoothed her hands down her loose white t-shirt. "Did you need something?"

"I just decided to unpack later. I'd rather spend a little time seeing what you've done with the place."

"Oh, there's not much to see. Brent and I don't have the design sense you had. Everything looked so cohesive before. Now, it's a bit of a mess."

"It looks great," Mae assured her. "But I left so much of my old junk behind that I'm not surprised you feel that way."

"No, that isn't what I—"

Mae interrupted. "Don't keep any of it on my account, okay? I didn't take it with me for a reason. Sell it. Trash it. It's up to you."

"This house just has a lot of history. For all of you," Rose stammered. "And I want to, you know... respect that."

Mae stepped forward and laid a hand over Rose's, patting her knuckles. "This house does have a history, but it also has a future. *Your* future. And nothing would make me happier than to see you and Brent make this place a home of your own."

Rose blinked several times, nodding slowly. "Okay."

"I'm a guest here," Mae continued. "I may come into your kitchen and think I know where things are, but that's because I'm an old woman now."

"You are not old!"

"Sixty-four, if my birthday party last week is to be believed," she said. "It's hard to teach us old dogs new tricks. But don't let me make you uncomfortable in your own home."

Finally, the tension in Rose eased, and she sagged forward with a smile. "Is it that obvious I'm nervous?"

Mae held her finger and thumb up, a small sliver of space between them. "Only a little."

"I tried so hard to hide it."

"You're hosting your boyfriend's mother and her boyfriend for two weeks. A few nerves are expected. But I think we'll have a wonderful time together."

"I think so, too," Rose agreed. "We're so happy to have you."

The women smiled at one another warmly, and then Rose leaned forward. "Can I hug you? I'm a hugger."

Mae laughed and pulled the woman into her arms, squeezing her like she was one of her own children.

"Now, where's that rapscallion son of mine?" Mae asked. "Because if he thinks he's getting away with leaving my baggage at the foot of the stairs, he's got another thing coming."

Rose pointed to the workshop. "Still organizing. I told him to clear out more space in there before you arrived, but he didn't listen. He's trying to make room for all of the boxes now."

"Stubborn man, just like his father."

Rose rolled her eyes. "Don't even get me started."

With a laugh, Mae relinquished her hold on the woman and went to find her son.

Sometime in the last year, Brent had greased the squeaky hinge on the workshop door, so it didn't make a peep when Mae pushed it open.

The shop still smelled the same as it always had—a familiar blend of wood shavings and dust. The high windows along the top of the space let in light and created a damp heat that used to drive Henry crazy.

Every time he was in the shop, whether summer or winter, he'd throw open both garage doors for a breeze.

Seeing Brent in the corner of the shop, his back to the door, Mae could almost imagine for a moment it was Henry. Her son and late husband had the same build—tall and lean with wide shoulders and trim hips. The same dirty blonde hair, too.

Mae was about to tell Brent as much when she noticed him looking down at something, studying it as he turned it in his hands.

It was a mobile. One of four Henry had made for their children. A personalized mobile for Eliza, for Holly, for Sara, for Brent.

Except that this mobile wasn't one of those four.

Mae saw a small lighthouse Henry had carved dangling between Brent's fingers.

Henry could always carve anything, but his painting skills left much to be desired. He'd recruited Mae to paint the white and red stripes around the body of the lighthouse.

Mae remembered dragging the small brush around the figurine. Imagining her first child staring up at it as he fell asleep.

It was a vision that never came to pass.

And after everything had happened, Henry never brought the mobile in from the workshop. Mae always assumed he got rid of it, too heartbroken to look at it anymore.

But here it was, in her youngest son's hands.

The idea of turning back into the house and pretending she'd never come into the workshop crossed Mae's mind. She ought to put this moment away for a while. Find a way to approach it when the time was right.

But before she could follow through with her cowardly plan, Brent turned and met her gaze.

"What's this, Mom?" he croaked.

There would be no running from this now.

Just as Rose had said, this house did have a history. One she couldn't hide in the workshop any longer.

16

HOLLY

Predictably, ex-convict Rob was not the ideal houseguest.

It would be one thing if the kids were in school and Rob had any desire to ever leave the house. He'd told Pete he wanted to spend time with the ocean, after all.

But so far, most of his time had been spent with Holly's couch and the television. Holly worried he'd fuse to the leather.

The moment Rob had appeared on their porch with his overgrown hair and suspicious suitcase, she knew he would be trouble. Every day he'd been in the house since then had proven Holly's first impression correct.

On his first Saturday with them, Rob took one bite of his banana pancake—which Holly warmed up for him once he finally rolled out of bed after eleven in the morning—and muttered something remarkably colorful loud enough for everyone to hear.

Grady's eyes had bugged out like it was the greatest thing he'd ever heard. That night, when he learned they were having pizza for dinner, he'd repeated it at maximum volume.

Holly cringed at the memory.

On Monday, Rob poured the grungy clothes in his suitcase into the washer with a load of Holly's delicates. Once he'd dried and shrunk every single camisole, slip, and expensive pair of underwear Holly had ever owned, she caught him dropping them, unfolded, into her intimates drawer.

"You've got to talk to him about boundaries," she'd whispered to Pete that night in bed. "There have to be limits."

"He was trying to be helpful," Pete argued.

"We barely know this man! Even if we did, my underwear drawer would still be off limits."

"Rob has always been a—you know, like a loose cannon. He isn't the best with rules."

Holly snorted. "I'm sure you're right. I don't think rule followers typically end up in prison."

Pete had patted her arm and immediately rolled over to go to sleep, exhausted after an early morning and late evening at the office. "He'll settle in and things will work out. Don't worry."

That was less than reassuring. Rob "settling in" was exactly what Holly worried about.

On Tuesday, Holly had walked into the living room to find Rob giving Grady and Alice a crash course on the most popular street drugs and their colloquial names.

"There's a girl in my class named Molly," Alice had said, eyes wide. "Is she using drugs?"

As soon as Holly got home from dropping the kids off at the Nantucket Nature and Wildlife Kids Camp, she'd tried to talk directly to Rob.

"Grady and Alice are taking to you so well, and I just want to make sure your conversations with them are age-appropriate. You have real influence over them."

"That's great," Rob had said, grinning. "I want them to learn from my mistakes."

"That's sweet, but they might not be ready for conversations about drugs."

"I don't think we should shelter children from the harsh truths." Rob spoke with all the confidence of someone who had never raised children of their own. "The more they know now, the less chance there is it'll get 'em into trouble down the road."

Pete, home for lunch, had the nerve to agree with his cousin.

"Kids fall into that stuff when they don't know the consequences," Pete had said from the table, his work laptop open in front of him. "It's never too early to start having these conversations."

"The kids don't even ride the school bus yet. I don't think hard drugs are on their radar," Holly had mumbled.

Nothing much improved over the days that followed. She worked hard to keep the kids busy, but Grady was full of questions.

And dear cousin Rob seemed to have all the answers.

"Is Uncle Rob going to live with us forever?" Grady asked on Thursday night as Holly pulled his dinosaur comforter up under his chin.

"No, no, no. He's only here for a little while. And he isn't your uncle; he's your cousin." Holly frowned, trying to remember where Rob's apple fell on the family tree. "Maybe even your second cousin. Or once removed."

Preferably further removed than that, she thought.

"Can I stay home tomorrow? Uncle Rob said he'd teach me how to play poker."

"No way, kiddo. You'll have all weekend to hang out with Rob," Holly had said, knowing full well she was going to foist the kids on her mom and Dominic all day Saturday. Cousin Rob was not invited.

But all that was in the past. Now, it was a Friday afternoon, approaching the second weekend Rob had spent in Holly's living room.

Under normal circumstances, it would be Holly's favorite kind of day. The sun was high in the sky, yellow light filtered through fleecy white clouds. A soft northern wind was keeping things cool and bringing the smell of the ocean through the open windows.

That was all well and good. Saltwater was preferable to the odor steaming off the pile of Rob's dirty laundry in the corner.

But despite the day's cheery weather, Alice was sitting on the floor at Rob's socked feet. She'd woken up with a slight fever, so Holly kept her home from camp. Grady had been beyond jealous.

"Did you have to share a bathroom?" Alice was asking.

Rob scrolled mindlessly on one of Pete's old computers. Holly didn't even want to think about what he could be doing on there. "Only with my cellmate. There was a toilet in our cell."

"A toilet? In your room?"

"And a sink," Rob said.

Alice looked horrified. "Could you close the door?"

"No. The guards wouldn't have liked that." Rob kicked a foot up onto the coffee table and scratched at his chin. "They had to keep an eye on us to make sure we weren't getting into trouble."

"What kind of trouble?"

Holly jogged into the living room. "Do you want to go read some books, Alice?"

"I'm coloring." Alice held up a perfectly-sharpened colored pencil and a blank coloring sheet of a butterfly landing on a unicorn's horn as proof. She'd been "coloring" for twenty minutes.

"It's a beautiful day outside. Why don't you go find some caterpillars to put in the terrarium Uncle Brent bought you?"

Usually, Holly needed only press a mason jar into Alice's hand and her daughter would dart for the peony bushes that lined the fence. She'd hunt for bugs and critters until dinnertime.

Before Alice could respond, Pete tromped into the kitchen through the garage door, phone pressed to his ear and his work laptop tucked under his arm.

He'd promised the night before he'd be home early on Friday. Apparently, his work was coming home early, too.

"...Of course, Mr. Thomas," he was saying into the phone. "Like I said, I'll have to look over the details again, but I think you have a solid case. Goodwin & Payne would love to take you on as a client. I'll have my assistant call you on Monday to set up an in-person meeting."

Pete dropped his laptop on the gingham placemat on the table and pulled Holly in for a quick kiss on the cheek. She could hear Mr. Thomas's muffled voice on the other end of the phone.

"How's it going?" Pete mouthed to her before he pressed the phone back to his ear. "Well, uh, sure, Mr. Thomas. I mean, you already have my email address, but I can send the fax number, too, if that's easier for you."

Holly frowned and pointed to Alice and Rob in the living room. She wagged her brows, bobbed her head, jumped up and down—everything short of waving light-up traffic controller sticks—to help Pete understand how bad things were going.

It had only been a week, but Holly felt like she was losing control of her house. The delicate system of rules and expectations she'd established since school had let out in May was under attack. She needed Pete's help to rein the children back in.

Pete followed her jabbing finger and pulled the phone away from his mouth, covering the speaker with his palm.

Holly sagged with relief. It was nice to have someone else come home to do the laying down of the law. Pete would simply instruct Alice that she needed to go play outside, and then—

Instead, he broke into a warm smile. "I love to see my family bonding. You two having fun in there?" he called over to Alice and Rob.

Alice opened her mouth to respond, but when Rob gave a wordless thumbs up, Alice clammed up and followed his lead.

Holly wanted to scream.

Oblivious, Pete gave her an encouraging wink and sat down at the table to talk Mr. Thomas through the ins and outs of how to attach a photo to an email.

Holly grimaced as she tossed the dish rag into the kitchen. The rag landed in the sink and sunk beneath the soapy surface of the water. She wished she could dive in after it.

"Come on, Alice," she said instead, biting the words out between her smiling lips. "We're going outside."

Alice groaned. "But I'm coloring."

"Let's color outside." Holly snatched the plastic box of colored pencils off the floor and walked to the back door. When Alice didn't follow after ten seconds, she snapped her fingers. "Let's go."

Pete pressed a finger into his other ear melodramatically, brow furrowed as he tried to hear Mr. Thomas over Holly's voice. As if she was talking *that loudly*.

Alice crossed her arms and pouted for a few minutes in the backyard, but eventually, the sunshine and the promise of restocking her terrarium pushed away thoughts of Rob. At least temporarily.

As they played, searching through the thick grass and foliage around the yard for the fuzziest caterpillars, Holly kept on eye on Pete through the dining room window.

She could see him working at the table, hunched over his laptop. His phone was clamped tight to his ear on and off as he took calls.

The moment she looked over and saw he'd walked away from his impromptu work station, Holly made her move.

"I'll be right back, sweetheart," she said, kissing the top of Alice's head. "If you search the milkweed by the spout, you may find some caterpillars that will turn into monarch butterflies."

Alice squealed and ran off towards the corner of the house, occupied for at least a few more minutes.

When she walked into the kitchen, Pete was telling Rob about poor, technologically-challenged Mr. Thomas.

"Can I talk to you?" Holly interrupted quietly, pointing to the laundry room off the kitchen.

Pete took a long drink of his ice water and wiped his mouth with the back of his arm. "About what?"

Holly's jaw clenched tight. She shook her head and jerked her head toward the laundry room again.

Puzzled, Pete followed her into the humid laundry room. As soon as they were inside, she slid the pocket door closed, trapping them in with the heat.

"Can't we leave the door open?" Pete panted, pulling at his shirt collar.

"No, we can't. Because in case you forgot, you let your cousin couch-surf with us, and I don't want him to overhear."

In truth, Holly didn't want to blame Pete for how badly things were going with Rob, but it was getting hard not to.

Who else was there to blame?

Sure, she could blame Rob. But blaming Rob felt like being mad at a puppy for chewing up an expensive leather shoe. Puppies will be puppies, after all. The true blame lies with whoever left their shoes within reach.

In this case, the blame rested firmly on Pete's shoulders. For throwing open their front door and letting a stranger into their house.

"Things are getting out of hand, Pete," Holly said, fighting to keep her voice level. She'd been pushing down so much frustration over the last seven days she was at risk of it all bubbling out at once. "Rob is a slob, for starters."

Pete rolled his eyes. Holly barely resisted the urge to grab him by the collar. "He's a bachelor. Always has been, as far as I know. He doesn't know how to clean to your standards."

"Okay, fine, whatever! I shouldn't have led with that. His cleaning habits are the least of my worries," Holly said. "He's crass, too. He is teaching our children about drugs and prison tattoos."

"I thought we agreed it could be good for them to hear about some of this stuff."

"No, you and Rob agreed," Holly said. "I think it's ridiculous."

"Why didn't you say something?"

"I did! And I'm saying it again now." Holly sighed. "Rob doesn't have any sense of personal boundaries. I caught him in our medicine cabinet. Do we even know what he was in prison for?"

"I don't think expired antibiotics and children's fever pills are the stuff that fuels addictions," Pete scoffed.

He was treating this like a joke. Why couldn't he see it how she did?

he wasn't crazy. She wasn't a nag. This was a *problem.*

So she threw out the nuclear option.

"You don't know what it's been like because you're never here."

Hurt flashed across Pete's face. He recoiled back into the washing machine, and when he did speak, his voice was low and wounded. "I told you weeks ago that things would be crazy while Billy was gone on his cruise. You know this is temporary."

Pete had worked hard to balance work and life better and become more of a partner at home. Since starting the law firm with Billy, Pete spent more time with the kids, he cooked dinner at least one night per week, and he and Holly had even started making their way through the endless seasons of Grey's Anatomy together.

After all of that, talking about the time he spent at work could be a touchy subject.

Holly gripped Pete's elbow, wishing she could transfer her viewpoint into his brain. "Pete, honey, I'm not blaming you. And I understand. I just want *you* to understand that you haven't seen what I've seen this last week."

Surely he'd seen enough to generate the appropriate reaction, though?

Pete had been there for the street drug conversation. He'd even joked about the sudden locker room smell that had invaded their living room.

But maybe it wasn't enough.

Pete hadn't been home to see the way Grady threw his dirty socks on the living room floor next to Rob's clothes instead of putting them in the hamper.

Pete hadn't been the one to fight with Alice about eating her cereal at the table because she wanted to eat breakfast in bed like "Uncle Rob."

All that was moot, though.

Holly didn't need Pete to be a witness to everything. She just needed him to listen to her. To care about it.

"I'm not trying to kick Rob out, but I think you should talk to him."

"About what?" Pete asked, as though Holly hadn't just laid it all out for him.

"Tell him he needs to clean up his act a bit around the kids. And literally clean up his act in the living room. I don't want to sit at my dining room table and see his dirty underwear sticking out of his suitcase."

"He doesn't have much space in the guest room. The drawers are full of the kids' old clothes. What do you expect him to do, Holly?"

"Not throw his dirty clothes around my house!" Holly shouted, her frustration spilling over. She glanced at the door and took a deep breath, trying to remain calm. "Just talk to him. Please."

"I think you should do it."

She snapped her head up, unsure she'd heard correctly. "You want *me* to talk to *your* cousin?"

Pete shrugged. "Yeah. You are both adults. I think you can handle it between the two of you."

Holly gaped. "You're joking."

Pete shook his head. "Like you said, I haven't seen everything you've seen. You'll be able to argue your point better than I will."

"It's not a debate. I don't want to 'argue my point' with Rob. I want to tell him how life is done in our house."

"And I'm sure Rob will hear you out."

Holly stared at her husband. "What if he doesn't? I'm the one home alone with him most days, Pete. What if the conversation makes him angry?"

That might've been unfair. So far, Rob hadn't done anything to make Holly believe he was violent.

But that didn't mean he wasn't.

When Holly went to visit Eliza and Summer in the hospital, she'd taken the kids with her even though they'd had to sit in the waiting room while she went into the NICU. Not out of any hard evidence of danger. Just a gut feeling. A bone-deep fear.

No matter how many times Rob offered to watch Grady and Alice, she couldn't fathom leaving them alone with him.

Pete frowned and raised his dark brows. "Are you seriously suggesting Rob might hurt you? Come on, Holly. Now, you're going too far."

"Is it such an absurd idea? He was in prison. We don't know what happened in there. You're the one who said he isn't the best with rules. Enforcing some could make him angry."

Pete scoffed, pressing his hands to his hips. "I've known Rob my whole life. He's had a hard go of it, but he's a good guy."

"He *was* a good guy," Holly said, her voice low and harsh. "You haven't seen him in over a decade. You don't even know if he was married. We have no way of knowing if he's dangerous or—"

"Stop." Pete held up a hand and shook his head. "I wouldn't let Rob stay here if I thought he was dangerous. Whatever you may think, I wouldn't put you and the kids at risk. I can't believe you'd even accuse me of that."

Holly opened her mouth. And closed it.

Trying to find the right words, but they kept slipping through her fingers like minnows.

Pete could be too optimistic for his own good. He saw the best in people, which up until this very moment was something Holly had always appreciated about him.

But it could also lead him to trust the wrong people.

This was the perfect example of that. This was a *problem.* He needed to see that. He had to see that.

"If you could just—"

However, before she could finish her thought, Rob's voice boomed through the house, slipping under the laundry room door.

"Whoa, slugger. Who clocked you?"

Holly and Pete looked at each other, brows furrowed in twin expressions of confusion.

Then Pete slid the door open and stepped into the kitchen.

Holly had to press a hand into Pete's back to keep herself from running face-first into him when he stopped suddenly outside the door.

"What the..." Pete's voice trailed off.

Holly grabbed her husband's shoulders and moved him aside when she realized he wasn't going to move on his own.

As soon as she did, she saw Grady. Since Alice was home sick, she'd called Robin Schmidt to see if she could bring Grady home. Her son Tim was in Grady's class and at the same day camp.

Grady stood between the kitchen sink and the island, his hands held loosely at his sides.

There was a smear of dirt across his belly, like he'd been sliding on the ground, and a stain near his collar from the fruit juice she'd packed in his lunch.

Another dark stain dotted the middle of his chest.

Holly didn't know what it was until she looked up and saw the waterfall of dried red blood dripping from her son's nose down to his lip. It looked so red against his pale skin.

Grady tried to talk, but his lip was split. He winced instead. His eyes went glassy, a sure sign he was about to cry.

Then at last, he managed to mumble something. Holly had to strain to hear it. But the words were clear enough to make her heart drop.

"I got into a fight."

17

ELIZA

THE NANTUCKET COTTAGE HOSPITAL

Two days after Summer was born, Dr. Geiger recommended removing the oxygen.

Eliza watched it happen from behind the pane of glass. The tubes being carefully removed, the tape delicately peeled away. The first cry as her daughter's lungs filled with sweet, sweet air.

She felt like her own lungs were expanding. For the first time since her daughter was born, Eliza could breathe again.

Two days after that, Summer was moved out of the NICU and into a standard recovery room.

Eliza watched that happen, too. She tottered alongside Ginny as the team of nurses wheeled the sleeping infant down the hall. She kept a careful watch on her daughter's face, ready to swoop in if Summer showed so much as an inkling of discomfort—C-section stitches be damned.

She kept a brave face the whole time. But the truth was that Eliza was hurting, too. Heartache had a physical cost, and she was paying it in spades.

So, as much as she tried to keep track of time passing, the exhaustion softened the edges of her reality. Days began to bleed and blend together.

Feeding and changing diapers and tiny bursts of sleep caught wherever she could snag them.

Doctor's consults and lukewarm meals scarfed down off metal trays and long medicinal terms with menacing auras—surfactant and sepsis, bilirubin and bradycardia, gut priming and gavage feedings and gentamicin.

And the testing. Lots and lots of testing.

Hordes of nurses measured Summer's mobility, her sleeping, her breathing, her eating. If she cried, they tested it. If she twitched, they tested it.

Eliza felt her heart in her throat every time. *Was it bad? Is everything okay?*

They always said yes. *Of course she's fine. Of course she's okay.*

She hadn't yet decided if she believed their answers.

She supposed this was all part and parcel of parenting a newborn. Or rather, of parenting a *premature* newborn.

The first was familiar to her.

The second was something else entirely.

After Winter was born, Eliza's entire life shifted. The things she'd counted as important before—work and success and such—now felt insubstantial.

Because, after all—what could matter more than the big eyes that looked up at her? The eyes that trusted her, that depended on her?

What could matter more than giving Winter every opportunity to *succeed*?

At the time, that felt like a seismic change.

Now, Eliza's worldview had shifted even more. A new question took to the forefront: what could matter more than giving both her children every opportunity to *live*?

It wasn't exactly her first spin on this carousel, though.

Sometime in the last year, Eliza and Oliver had begun to note that Winter's speaking seemed delayed. Her tongue struggled to move around certain letters. They could see the frustration purpling in her face when she tried to communicate with them and couldn't.

"Is she too young for speech therapy?" Eliza had asked one night, her eyes strained from the glow of her phone screen in their dark bedroom.

They'd been lying in bed for over an hour, both restless. Oliver was tossing and turning and muttering in half-sleep; Eliza was researching speech impediments.

"That usually starts once they are in school, I think. I'm sure she'll be tested for it," Oliver had mumbled. "I wouldn't worry just yet."

Eliza knew *he* wouldn't worry. Oliver rarely worried about anything. Especially not academics.

Being a musician had been Oliver's only goal. To the point that he skipped school to take the train into New York City and busk for pocket change on street corners.

His parents had hired tutors and enrolled him in the best private schools. Oliver repaid that investment by skipping college and joining a band.

It worked for him, in the end. It was an unthinkable life for Eliza.

Growing up, school had been everything to her. She'd been the shining star of her family. The model daughter with straight As and a

1590 on the SATs. Everyone was always sure to tell her how smart she was. How successful she'd no doubt become.

"One day, she'll give us smart little grandchildren, too," her mom had said once. Not to Eliza directly—Mae was bragging to her friend Lola over glasses of wine on the deck. Eliza just so happened to be walking past and overheard.

She wondered now if her mother had any idea how often that refrain would go on to repeat itself in Eliza's head for the rest of her life.

When Eliza took Winter to the pediatrician and had to check "no" next to the question, *Is your toddler speaking in two- to three-word sentences?*, there it was.

Smart little grandchildren should be speaking sentences, she'd think. *Smart little grandchildren would get all "yeses."*

Maybe she should have read to Winter more. Maybe they didn't talk to her enough. Maybe she watched too much television.

Those things had consumed Eliza, day and night.

But now, sitting next to Summer in the hospital, praying she'd keep breathing on her own, Eliza could think of nothing more trivial. Winter could run and play. She could *breathe*.

She was a loud giggler, screeching whenever Oliver rubbed his beard on her belly or when Eliza dabbed a dot of brownie batter on her nose. And she mostly slept through the night. Eliza didn't have to peek in her room in the wee hours, anxiously checking to make sure her chest rose and fell as it should.

Winter was healthy. All else paled in comparison.

"Your baby girl is ready to go home," Ginny said, dropping her stethoscope against her fuchsia scrubs. "She passed the car seat test."

Eliza blinked and looked up at Ginny's friendly face. She'd been lost in thought all morning as Ginny bustled about the room. More testing was on the docket, of course.

But today's test was the last hurdle, or so Dr. Geiger had said. It only required Summer to sit in a car seat for an hour while her vitals were monitored.

"To make sure she can sit in a semi-reclined position for a long period of time," Ginny had explained. "It's a standard test for premature babies."

Eliza looked down at her baby where she sat, car seat propped up on a chair.

After all the poking and prodding the infant had endured, Eliza assumed this would be a cinch. What Eliza hadn't anticipated was feeling so helpless.

Something about seeing her tiny daughter sitting alone and untouchable, swallowed up by the straps and cushions of the car seat, nearly undid her.

Summer would have to go into a *car*. Out on the *road*. Where other drivers and cars could see them, scare them, strike them.

Summer would leave the hospital and be surrounded by strangers who had no idea she was a delicate piece of china. They wouldn't know how fragile she was. How careful they must be around her.

The reality of the dangers lurking just beyond the hospital doors hit Eliza all at once.

"She passed," Ginny said again gently. As if Eliza hadn't heard the first time.

She had heard, of course. But she'd only just begun to process what it meant.

Summer had cleared.

They were going home.

Only a matter of minutes later, it seemed, Eliza and Summer were discharged and being wheeled through the hospital.

Ginny told every nurse they passed the good news, beaming as though talking about her own baby rather than an old high school classmate's.

"Baby Summer is going home!"

And each one of them cheered, cooed, blew kisses, waved goodbye.

Eliza waved back at all of the nurses, thanking them for their care. Secretly wishing she could take them home with her.

The smiling cartoon teddy bears lining the fluorescent-lit hallways of the children's wing of Nantucket Cottage Hospital had taken on a sinister edge the longer Eliza had stayed in the hospital. They watched Eliza and Summer leave now, wide eyes hypnotic and unsettling.

If she never saw their fuzzy, grinning faces again, it would still be too soon.

Ginny pushed Eliza through the sliding double doors into a beautiful day.

The golden mid-afternoon light glinted off the asphalt and the cars in the parking lot. Fluffy white clouds floated through the blue sky, promising continued sunshine that wrapped her in a blanket of warmth. It felt like nature's way of telling her everything would be fine.

Eliza only wished she could take the message to heart.

I'm fine, she said to herself. *I'm fine, I'm fine, I'm fine-fine-fine.*

Ginny pushed Eliza to the edge of the curb. Oliver was waiting in the yellow-painted loading zone, engine idling. He hurried over to help her transition from her wheelchair to the passenger seat.

"I'm okay, honey," Eliza murmured. As expected, Oliver promptly ignored her and helped anyway.

Eliza glanced into the rear of the vehicle as she shuffled down the ledge of the curb. Winter was in her car seat, straining against the fuzzy pink straps to see out the window.

When she saw her mother, she reached out with chubby dimpled fingers. Bright and smiling. Her precious little girl.

But when the door opened and Winter saw Oliver click Summer's car seat into place, her little hand whipped back like she'd been stung.

"Is someone not too excited about little sister?" Ginny whispered, a hint of amusement in her voice.

"She didn't want to come pick her up," Oliver sighed, running a hand through his dark hair.

His waves were normally tousled, but today, they looked unkempt. Rumpled. Exhaustion had pressed dark circles under his eyes.

"I think she blames Summer for keeping Mommy and Daddy away. I'm afraid she may cry at any sighting of her babysitter now, too," he added. "Julie is an angel, but nothing beats your own mom and dad."

Eliza had wanted Winter in the hospital with them as much as possible, but a toddler could only be expected to sit by a newborn's bassinet for so long. She needed to move and play—two things Eliza couldn't offer from her recovery bed.

So Oliver had been splitting his time between the hospital and home as well as he could, but he'd been stretched thin. Their babysitter, Julie, had been a lifesaver.

Ginny pressed a hand to her heart, lower lip pouted out in sympathy. "Poor girl. Don't worry; she'll come around. They always do."

"You see this a lot?" Oliver asked.

"All the time," Ginny laughed. "Little kids don't understand why their mommies are hurting and why everything is different. But a few days at home with a routine will fix everything. Trust me."

It sounded nice and simple. But Eliza couldn't decide if she believed that, either.

When her sister Holly was born, Eliza was Winter's age. Only two years old. She'd no doubt had strong feelings about her sister's arrival, but she couldn't recall them now.

She could, however, remember Sara's entrance to the world.

Eliza was four by then, and she could grasp what it meant to share her parents.

Holly was pigeon-toed, an ailment that was later fixed with braces and insoles. But in the meantime, she tripped over her own feet often. Her lip was split open near-weekly on the edges of tables and chairs. On the cracked concrete sidewalk outside their house. She was carried inside, bleeding and screaming, too many times to count.

Consequently, Mom and Dad hovered over Holly, protecting her from herself. Warning her to slow down. Catching her before she could do any more damage.

Eliza didn't need the same oversight. They mostly let her be.

So, when Sara arrived, Eliza worried her parent's time would be even more divided. That she would receive even less of their attention.

Mae still loved to tell the story of how Eliza suggested they give Sara away to a family in need. "She wanted to donate Sara like an old dress," Mae would chuckle, inevitably wiping away a tear of laughter. "She said, *'You already have two girls. Some people don't have any!'*"

By now, it was a cute, charming story. *Precocious little girl with a precocious little suggestion.*

But at the time, Eliza was sure she'd been onto something. And if Winter could express all of her feelings, Eliza suspected she'd be saying something similar.

You already have me, the little girl would protest. *What more could you want?*

But just as Sara won Eliza over with her belly laughs and sunny blonde ringlets, Eliza knew Summer would win Winter over, too. Perhaps not permanently. Having a sister was, in some respects, a battle that never ended. Goodness knows that Eliza reconsidered her original proposal once Sara learned to talk back and express her (very strong) opinions.

But for the most part, their relationship was good.

Eliza wished the same for her girls. And she trusted it would happen.

They just had to get home first.

As they pulled away from the curb, Eliza started to plan. To parcel up her world into neat, manageable chunks.

Unpack the car.

Set up a diaper changing station.

Sanitize the baby bottles.

Wash the baby linens.

With each box she prioritized and plotted and prepped, she felt better. And as they rounded the final curve to their home, she let out a sigh that had a week of hospitalized anxiety laced through it.

Then Oliver opened the front door and Eliza saw her house for the first time in seven days.

And she realized she wasn't getting started on her list anytime soon.

"Home sweet home," her husband murmured. Winter giggled and ran into the house, navigating the maze of clutter and mess and toys with glee.

She hopped from couch cushion to couch cushion, which was made possible by the fact that they were scattered around the living room floor like stepping stones.

Scattered between the cushions were choking hazards like Lego bricks and cat's eye marbles. The containers they belonged in were overturned and stacked next to the entertainment center—a stepping stool for Winter to reach the power button for the television.

Beyond the immediate chaos, Eliza could see a mess of dry cereal and toast crumbs under the dining room table. Dishes stacked high in the sink. And, visible through the crack in her bedroom door, an overflowing laundry basket.

"Wow." Eliza was only half-aware she'd spoken the thought out loud.

"The place is a bit of a mess," Oliver said, hurrying ahead of Eliza to clear a path for her. "I hoped to clean up before you came home, but it all happened so fast."

Winter cried out as Oliver disassembled the obstacle course she'd been enjoying, stranding her on a cushion without another one to jump to.

"Winter hasn't been napping very well," he continued, "which is usually when I clean. And Julie had a big test today, so she let Winter do a lot of independent play yesterday so she could study. Don't worry; I'll clean it up."

Winter grabbed the cushion Oliver had just placed on the couch and returned it to the floor so she could continue her game.

"No, sweetie," Oliver chided gently. "We need to clean things up for Mommy and baby sister. We don't want them to trip over the mess."

Winter responded with crossed arms and a sidelong glance at Eliza and Summer, far more menacing than any toddler had the right to be.

Eliza tiptoed through the room to the worn leather armchair in the corner. "It's fine. I understand."

She nestled Summer into the crook of her arm. Oliver said he would clean, and he would. Eliza just needed to focus on her girls.

"Do you want to go find a book to read?" she asked Winter. "Maybe the bear and duck book you like?"

"I don't like that one," she said, eyes narrowed.

Eliza winced. That book was Winter's favorite since the first time Eliza read it to her months ago. They had to carry it with them in the car everywhere they went in case she wanted to flip through the pictures.

Not anymore, it seemed.

"Another book, then?" Eliza sighed. "Any book you want. We can read it to Sissy together."

Instead of answering, Winter furrowed her brow and ran past Eliza into the dining room. She dropped cross-legged onto the floor next to an empty diaper box bearing a jumbled pyramid of markers. Winter chose a purple one and began scribbling furiously on the cardboard.

"That's the only thing she'll do by herself for more than ten minutes at a time," Oliver muttered. "I've learned to take advantage of the window."

"Speaking of time, it's almost Winter's naptime," Eliza said with a glance at the clock above the extra-wide kitchen door.

The clock had been with Eliza since her very first apartment in New York. One of the few pieces she cared enough to keep through all the moves. When the minute hand broke one day, her dad had whittled her a replacement from a scrap piece of wood. No one could tell a difference, but Eliza knew it was there.

She'd always liked that. A tiny little secret between her and her father.

Oliver sighed and wordlessly pushed himself off the sofa. It took him five minutes to get Winter into her bedroom, twenty minutes to red her two books, and another ten minutes to convince her not to immediately roll out of bed when he closed her bedroom door.

Eliza listened to the whole exchange from the living room. She wanted to help, but Winter clearly didn't want to be around her right now.

So instead, she tried to clean up a bit. Her stitches pulled when she bent at the waist and her whole body ached from lack of use, but Eliza wanted to help.

No, she *needed* to help. To do something.

She kicked Legos to the edges of the room, careful not to step on them, and toed the marbles into a pile in the middle of the floor.

Bending down to use a dustpan was out of the question. But she could sweep the crumbs into a pile, at least.

She was in the linen closet reaching for the broom when Oliver came out of Winter's room and let loose a long, weary sigh.

"I think she might stay in bed. I really don't know. She's been afraid to nap the last few days, worried I won't be here when she wakes up." Oliver padded across the floor and then stopped, spotting Eliza. "What are you doing? I said I'd clean."

"I know, but I want to help. The place is a disaster, and—"

"I've been a little busy." Oliver sounded more defensive than he ever had before, his tone sharp and clipped. "I told you, Winter hasn't been napping."

Eliza turned around and offered him a sympathetic smile. "I know. I understand."

"But you're still cleaning when you should be resting."

"I want to help. You have your hands full with Winter and—"

"And I can't handle a kid and keeping the house clean as well as you can?"

Eliza blinked at him. She didn't know whether it was a question or a statement, but either way, it seemed excessive.

Oliver was usually so easygoing. She had no clue how to handle this flare-up.

She opened her mouth to respond when Winter's bedroom door opened. Oliver's shoulders sagged with exhaustion, but before he could turn around, Eliza moved around him.

"I'll take care of her."

Eliza met Winter in the hallway. Her eyes were puffy from crying. Winter was as exhausted as anyone else from the events of the last week.

Usually, Eliza would kneel down to get on her eye level, but the most she could do was brush her hand over Winter's cheek and lift her little face up to meet her eyes. "You need to stay in bed, sweetheart. Why don't we go lay down and sing a song? Maybe 'The Goodbye Song'?"

"I want Daddy's song."

Eliza stared at her daughter blankly for a moment. "What?"

"Daddy's song!" Winter repeated with a huff of frustration.

Eliza shook her head. "I don't know that one, baby. Why don't we sing—?"

Winter darted past Eliza and wrapped her arms around Oliver's legs. "Sing me your song, Daddy."

"I made it up," Oliver explained. "I was so tired I honestly forgot other music existed."

He laughed humorlessly, then carried Winter back into her room. Eliza gingerly lowered herself into the chair. She could hear Oliver start singing through the door.

In the hospital, Eliza had been out of her depth. As much as she'd wanted to care for Summer and take care of all of her needs, her baby had needed oxygen and a team of nurses and special tests. Eliza couldn't provide for her entirely.

That was hard. But the knowledge that Winter was at home, perfectly healthy and whole and understandable to Eliza, had comforted her.

Now, she realized that wasn't entirely true. There were things in her daughter's eyes she didn't quite recognize anymore. There was no telling if she'd ever recognize them all again.

Maybe no child is ever fully understandable to their parent.

Oliver came out of Winter's room again a few minutes later and sat on the sofa. This time, he was perched on the edge, prepped to stand up at a moment's notice.

"She sleeping?"

"Yeah," he sighed.

"Daddy's song, huh? I'll have to learn that one from you." Eliza tried her best, but she couldn't keep a bitter edge out of her voice. "You're doing a better job than you think you're doing. I think Winter was happier when I wasn't here."

Even as she was still in the midst of saying it, Eliza was surprised by her own vulnerability. She was tired and in pain—she'd stopped taking the pain medication two days earlier—and her usually stiff upper lip had gone a little wobbly.

Oliver laughed, to her surprise.

Eliza snapped her attention up to him with an arched brow.

He gestured around the room. "Have you seen this place? We've been a mess without you, babe."

Summer began to stir on Eliza's shoulder, making little whimpers in her sleep. "But you've made do. Ginny said we should make a routine, but you two already have a routine. And I don't know the rules anymore."

"We had a routine," Oliver said, gesturing between himself and Winter's bedroom door. "The two of us cobbled together a system that worked—for a few days. But now we *all* need a routine. All four of us. And that's going to take some time."

As if on cue, Summer began to cry. Wailing in the way only newborns could, a shrill siren call.

"She's hungry," Eliza said. "I'll make her—"

"No, *I'll* make her a bottle," Oliver cut in with a wry smile, pushing himself to standing. "You just stay there and look pretty, okay?"

Before he could even take a step, there were clumsy footsteps from the back of the house and then Winter's door opened once more.

When she appeared in the living room, there were purple marker streaks across her face like war paint. She'd even colored in her lips.

Oliver's eyes widened. Eliza gasped. Even Summer stopped crying for a just a second, as though surprised by the sight of her older sister.

"Is it morning time?" Winter asked, seemingly oblivious to why everyone was staring at her.

Eliza and Oliver made eye contact. He raised his brows. "See what I mean? Chaos."

Nothing had gone the way Eliza imagined it. Not Summer's birth. Not their stay in the hospital. Not their first day home.

Oliver was right. They needed a new routine. A new system. And Eliza would make it.

She held Summer out to Oliver. "Make her a bottle. I'll deal with this one," she said, hitching a thumb over her shoulder at Winter.

He bit his lip, nodded, and took their daughter carefully between his hands.

She used a quarter of a pack of baby wipes to get the marker off of her daughter's chubby cheeks. *Thank the heavens for washable markers.*

By the time she finished, Oliver was sitting on the couch feeding a now-content Summer.

The floor was still a mess of crumbs and toys, and as soon as Winter was released, she tore a cushion down off of the couch and jumped on it.

But soft afternoon light was coming through the white curtains covering the windows, washing across the blue shag rug. Oliver had his bare feet on the coffee table. Summer was swaddled in a soft muslin blanket—the same blanket Eliza had first brought Winter home in, decorated with smiling hedgehogs. And Winter's giggles broke through the air like music.

They'd figure the rest out eventually.

18

MAE

THE WORKSHOP AT 114 HOWARD STREET

Brent held the mobile out to her. "What's this, Mom?" he said softly.

Mae bit her lip. "Oh, dear," she murmured in a voice she hadn't used since Henry died. "Oh, dear."

Thirty-Seven Years Ago

Mae dropped down into the kitchen chair. "I'm sorry, what?"

"You aren't sick. You're pregnant," the nurse said again through the phone. "Congratulations."

Mae had woken up that morning feeling nauseous, which wasn't anything new. She'd been feeling sick for days.

Her favorite breakfast—scrambled eggs with strawberries and a coffee—made her gag. She couldn't even keep water down. It tasted like old pennies in her mouth.

"Go to the doctor and get a few tests done," Henry had said before dashing out the door of their one-bedroom beach cottage for work.

Henry's parents had owned the property for over a decade, renting it out to vacationers on odd weekends. The wood-shingled house had seen better days. The red paint was all but chipped off the exterior after years of salty spray and more shutters than not hung drunkenly askew off their hinges.

Perennials popped up in the yard every spring, looking more and more wild with each passing year, and pink roses peeked through the gaps in the fence like nosy neighbors.

Now that Henry and his sister Toni were grown and gone, his parents didn't make it over to the cottage as often. Fewer guests came calling and Willa's hip made it hard for her to garden the way she used to, anyhow. So the cottage had become a chore to them.

But Mae had always loved the humble place.

When Henry approached his parents with the idea of buying the house for him and Mae to live in, they'd refused him at first.

"It's one bedroom, Henry. You can't raise children in a one-bedroom house!" his mother had balked.

But he'd done his Henry thing—wheedled and charmed and chuckled—and eventually, he'd talked Willa into it with a promise that it wouldn't delay the family planning.

Six years later, much to Willa's dismay, it was still just the two of them.

Henry had been telling the truth. The cottage hadn't delayed them having children. They simply didn't want children. Yet.

Mae was busy running Mae's Marvels, her catering company, out of their small kitchen, creating menus for garden luncheons, family birthday parties, and small corporate gatherings. And Henry had been working for Nantucket General Contracting, slowly but steadily working his way up the ladder.

They were a young couple finding their way in the world. They would have children when they were both ready. When they'd had time to plan out their future.

Or rather, that *was* the plan. It seemed now that things had changed.

Mae was pregnant.

"Thank you," Mae said, surprised her lips could form the words. The rest of her body was numb with shock.

She thanked the receptionist for her time, then dropped the phone on the table with a clatter.

When Henry came home thirty minutes later, Mae was still sitting at the table. Only now, the kitchen was cleaned and spotless, and Mae was drumming her fingers on the red- and white- checkered tablecloth.

She couldn't sit still. Almost like the life inside of her was creating an excess of energy, something Mae of all people certainly didn't need.

As he walked inside, Henry had to duck through the front door to avoid hitting his head on the rafter beam. Mae had never understood how he enjoyed living in the cottage, given how clearly undersized it was for someone of his height.

But that was Henry. He hunched his shoulders and ducked his head and did so with a smile. *How much trouble could it be to bend my knees,* he'd say.

"How did the doctor go?" he asked, hanging his denim jacket on the old doorknob they'd fashioned into a hook on the wall.

"I'm pregnant," she blurted.

So much for a gentle delivery of the news.

Mae's heart thundered in her chest, and she wondered if it was good for the baby. She'd also had a glass of wine last night when her nausea had subsided enough for her to enjoy the bluefish Henry brought home. One glass of wine wouldn't hurt the baby, right? Mae made a mental note to ask the doctor.

Henry stared at her, blinking for a second. Then his full lips split into a grin. His bright blue eyes glittered like the morning sun off the water.

"Mae, that's incredible."

His long arms wrapped Mae in a tight hug, and for the first time, Mae let herself be excited.

"You're going to be a mom," he said, whispering the words against her hair. "I'm going to be a dad."

"We're going to be parents," Mae said when Henry held her at arm's length, taking in the sight of her as if he'd never seen her before. As if everything that mattered had changed.

The smile couldn't be wiped from his face. He tipped his head back and stared up at the ceiling of their cottage. His shoulder-length blonde hair swayed as he shook his head. "We'll have to move."

"We can't raise a baby in a one-bedroom cottage," Mae laughed, repeating his mother's words.

Henry grinned down at her. "No, we certainly can't."

Four months later, he was grinning down at her again.

"Henry, it's beautiful," Mae told him.

Mae held the handcrafted mobile in her hands. Gently, as if worried she'd break it. She knew she wouldn't, but there was a way one had to hold precious things. A way to look at them, too—soft eyes, soft heart.

"You made this?" she asked, blinking at him in awe.

Henry puffed out his chest. "I told you I'd gotten good at whittling. See the old mill and the lighthouse?"

"And the island," she said, rubbing her thumb over the sanded-down finish of Henry's carving. "It's perfect. It's home."

The new house at 114 Howard Street felt like a mansion compared to the old cottage.

They'd been living there for two months, but the big house still didn't feel like it belonged to her yet. This was a new home, though. She'd have to make it hers.

She wanted the kind of home that you could close your eyes and see, smell, taste. This mobile in her hands was the first step of that. Whenever her firstborn son looked up from his crib and saw the striped lighthouse idling above his bed, he'd know he was home.

Mae stretched onto her toes and kissed Henry, the beginnings of her baby bump brushing against his flat stomach.

He chuckled. "I couldn't agree more."

Present Day—Friday Evening On The Beach

Mae clutched the coffee cup between her palms, letting the warmth sink into her. Hoping to gather strength from it.

She didn't normally drink caffeine after noon. It would keep her up all night. But she was going to be up all night anyway, given the turn her afternoon had taken.

"Did you just find the mobile today?" Mae asked, staring down at her toes buried in the white sand.

She couldn't bring herself to enjoy the sunset the way she usually would. It seemed too cheerful for the moment.

The afternoon had been beautiful. A day to paste on postcards and send off to lure people to Nantucket. Even now, the clear blue sky was marbled—rich amethyst and sapphire shades over her head giving way to a warm wash of glowing citrine behind the clouds.

The splash of ruby at the horizon line said a dark sky was only a few minutes away.

"I found it last Friday. Before your party," Brent said, resting his arms on his bent knees. He had a coffee cup in his hands, too, but Mae hadn't seen him take a drink of it yet. "I was cleaning out the workshop to make space for your things when I found it in the corner of the highest shelf. Wrapped in a trash bag."

Mae's heart squeezed. She could hear the implication in Brent's voice.

Like they'd been trying to hide the mobile away. Shoving it in a dark corner like they were ashamed of it. Ashamed of him. Ashamed of Christopher.

"I didn't know the mobile was still in there," Mae admitted. "I thought your father might have gotten rid of it. Thrown it away or something. He never told me where it went."

Brent looked over at his mother, his brows pulled together. "We aren't really talking about the mobile, Mom."

Mae lifted her eyes from the sand. Brent looked so young.

He *was* young. Younger than she was when she first got pregnant.

The instinct to protect him from pain, from bad news, overwhelmed her. She wanted to change the subject. *Look how smooth the water is* or *How's work going* or *Caught any big fish lately?*

But Brent wasn't a child anymore, much as she may always see him as such. He was a man, a man who'd floundered, who'd seen bad things and maybe done some of them, too, but who'd long since learned the difference between hopes and heartbreaks.

She owed him that much respect, at least.

"It was a surprise when I found out I was pregnant. I went to the doctor thinking I had the flu. But it wasn't the flu; it was a baby. We weren't ready for children yet—I know, I know; who ever is?—but your dad was excited. I was, too. We were happy."

"So..." Brent ran a hand through his blond hair. The strands looked golden in the fading light. "So, you didn't... get rid of him?"

"No!" Mae reached out and wrapped her hand around his elbow. He was muscular now. She could barely wrap her fingers halfway around his arm. "No, no. We wanted Christopher. Very much."

Brent nodded. "I figured. Dad made him a mobile. He wouldn't have done that if he didn't want him."

"The mobile was a surprise for me." Mae could close her eyes and see Henry's young, smiling face. The way he radiated with pride.

He had bought a whittling set at an estate sale in 'Sconset and never used it. Mae tried to get rid of it twice, but Henry assured her he was a great talent and she'd regret it.

Turns out he'd been right. He usually was, the stubborn old goat. Goodness, how she missed him.

"He gave it to me two days before it happened." Mae swallowed down the emotion rising in the back of her throat. She shook her head. "I'm sorry. I haven't talked about this in a long time."

"Why not?" Brent laid a hand on his mom's back. It was comforting, but stiff. Unpracticed. Confronting tough emotions had never been his strength. Brent was Mae's sunshine boy.

When Brent came along, Eliza was nearing her teenage years, and their peaceful house on Howard Street was more tumultuous than ever. "Too much estrogen," Henry would joke when the girls argued or when Eliza locked herself away in her room to be alone.

Then Brent arrived, his white-blonde hair matching his happy demeanor. He was cheerful, and he wanted everyone else to be cheerful, too.

"You could have told us about Christopher," Brent continued, smoothing his palm in a circle on Mae's back. "He was our brother, too."

Mae sniffled and batted her lashes, trying to keep control of herself. "I went into labor early. Spontaneously. The doctors tried to stop it, but there wasn't anything they could do. I was only twenty weeks along. Christopher was too small."

More circles on her back. Slow and steady.

Henry's eyes, crinkling with a laugh.

The white and red stripes of the lighthouse.

Memory after memory like seagulls cawing in her head, each one forcing her to hear it, see it, acknowledge it.

"For a long time, it simply hurt too much to talk about him," Mae admitted. "Or to think about him. Maybe that's why your father hid the mobile away. So I wouldn't see it. Then, maybe a year later, Eliza came along. She fixed things up. And I suppose, if I'm being honest, I let myself hide in that for a while. I didn't want to be sad, so I tried to forget."

Brent let out a humorless chuckle. "I know that feeling."

"After that... Well, you kids were so little, and I didn't know how to explain something like that to you. It felt so big that I just couldn't find the words. Then enough time passed that it seemed too late to bring it up."

Mae pressed her coffee cup into the sand and folded her fingers together tightly. The sun was almost gone now and the wind off the water felt colder, biting through the thin cotton sweater she had on.

And in her head—*red and white, white and red*. The strokes of a paintbrush over softly sanded wood. A tiny little lighthouse dangling from fishing string.

"I'd erased Christopher from our lives, and I felt guilty. I still feel guilty. It was easier to pretend he'd never been part of our family than to admit I was being selfish."

Suddenly, Brent threw a warm arm around Mae's shoulders and pulled her close. "Grief is selfish."

Mae turned to Brent, surprised. "Where did you learn that?"

"School of hard knocks." His mouth turned up in a sad smirk. "I wasn't exactly thinking about what was best for the family when I buried my grief in a bottle and ended up in jail after Dad died."

Mae shook her head. "What you went through was hard, honey. It's understandable."

"Just like your situation is understandable, too." He leaned back and looked in Mae's eyes, raising his brows as he spoke the next words. "I won't say I wasn't upset this last week. I won't say I'm glad you never told us about Christopher. But I can tell you, without a single doubt, that I get it. I understand."

Guilt had been Mae's companion for so long. Nearly thirty-seven years.

Her thoughts of Christopher—of that time in her life—had been tinted with guilt. With regrets. With the desire to talk about her first child, but the knowledge that she couldn't without admitting to her other children that she'd lied, concealed, repressed.

For years, she and Henry would sit together on Christopher's birthday and remember him.

But then Henry was gone, too.

Knowing Christopher's memory would die with Mae had been gnawing at the back of her mind. And the realization that someone knew—that Brent knew... It meant everything.

The emotions Mae had worked so hard to keep under control welled in her eyes and rolled down her cheeks. Brent pulled her close and patted her arm. "Don't cry, Mom. Everything is okay."

The sun was gone now. The sky was dark and velvety, stars beginning to dot the sky above the ocean.

Mae leaned into her son, her sunshine boy, and nodded. "Say it again," she requested.

He laughed. "Everything is okay."

19

BRENT
114 HOWARD STREET

The house on Howard Street was quiet when Brent walked back up the driveway.

The gauzy white curtains on the first floor were drawn, all the windows dark except for the picture window that looked out onto the porch. Rose kept one lamp on at the base of the stairs so she wouldn't break her neck in the night going to the kitchen for a drink.

If it were a weekday, Brent would go inside and grab her car keys from the ceramic bowl just inside the door. He'd spent a few minutes rearranging the vehicles to make sure Rose could get out in the morning for work.

But tomorrow was Saturday. Susanna would still wake them all at the dark side of dawn, but instead of dressing in day clothes and rushing out the door, they would lounge in pajamas and eat banana pancakes.

Since his mom was staying with them, they'd probably be treated to homemade browned butter syrup, too, if she was feeling up to it.

"Thanks for walking me home," Mae said, reaching out in the darkness to rub Brent's shoulder. She chuckled. "Or, to your home, I suppose. Either way, thank you."

"Of course. Thanks for going with me. For talking."

Silence had hung like a curtain between them on the way to and on the way from the beach. But for different reasons each time.

On the way there, it was the nerves that kept him quiet. As they returned home, he was struggling to sit with the discomfort of the truth. Like shedding a layer of clothing on a cold day, Brent's body just needed time to adjust.

When Brent was ten, Grandpa Benson died. It was expected. A natural death at the end of a long life. Still, his father had comforted him, hugging Brent to his side while he'd processed the first major loss he'd ever had.

It wasn't until later, when Brent was walking down the hallway to the bathroom and peeked his head through the crack in his parent's bedroom door, that he saw his dad sitting on the edge of his bed.

Stooped over, face in his hands, shoulders shaking.

It was like looking at that old optical illusion, only ever able to see the two faces eye to eye—and then suddenly, the lamp appears in the negative space between them.

The man crying on the foot of the bed didn't even *look* like his dad.

His dad was the man who scooped up snakes with the shovel and flung them into the drainage ditch behind the house. The man who would pull the collar of his shirt over his head and bump around the house, pretending to be headless until Brent and Sara laughed so hard they couldn't breathe.

But the man slouched over and sobbing on the edge of his bed was Brent's dad, too.

That was a lightbulb moment for Brent. The realization that his parents were human beings. Complex people with thoughts and feelings that ranged beyond making him dinner and driving him to school.

Now, at twenty-four, Brent was being reminded of that lesson. Maybe it was a lesson he'd never be done learning.

Maybe no parent was ever fully understandable to their child.

Mae slipped her shoes off just inside the door and lined them up on the floor, the toes pressed against the wide trim on wall. The same place she'd always left her shoes when he was growing up.

When she turned around, her head tilted to the side and her smile was distant. She reached out her hand and cupped his stubbly cheek. "You're a man now, but you're still my sunshine boy, you know?"

Brent was well past the age for embarrassing childhood nicknames. But he wasn't going to tell his mom that. Not tonight.

"Goodnight, Mom. Love you."

"I love you, too." She patted his cheek one more time and headed up the stairs, taking them a bit more slowly than she once did.

Brent waited until he heard the door to her room close. Then he walked through the house to the workshop.

Over the last week, he'd only pulled the mobile from the top shelf twice. Bringing it down just long enough to remind himself it was real. That it existed.

Now, the mobile was sitting out in the open on the work bench. Exactly where he'd placed it after his mother had walked in and caught him holding it.

Before she'd opened the door to the workshop, Brent was busy trying to gather the courage to bring the topic up on his own. He'd been debating whether he should pull his mom aside and discuss it seriously, privately. Or whether he should mention the mobile casually, tossing it out in normal conversation as if he didn't have a clue what it meant or where it had come from.

Then he'd turned around and seen her watching him. The moment her eyes dropped to the mobile, the color in her face had leeched away.

And Brent knew there would be no casual way to discuss this.

Better to get out of the house for a conversation like that, though. A walk on the beach. Everyone in Nantucket knew the ocean was good at keeping secrets.

So they'd slipped out together. Neither said a word.

Mae had picked her way through the sand, leather sandals dangling from her fingertips. Brent had trailed behind and wondered what ought to be the first thing he said.

In the end, it didn't take much to rip the bandage free.

I erased Christopher from our lives, and I felt guilty. I still feel guilty.

Brent's role in the Benson clan had always been clear. He was there to lighten the mood. To make his family laugh. To ease the tension.

So when relaying the story of Christopher's tragic birth brought his mom to tears, Brent did what he'd always done.

And now, he would keep her secret.

Brent gently picked up the mobile from where it sat on the work bench and slid it back into the dusty trash bag his father had wrapped it in almost four decades earlier.

Like Henry, Brent couldn't throw the piece out. Instead, he would set it aside in a quiet corner. Out of sight, but not forgotten.

Upstairs, Rose and Susanna were cuddled together in "the big bed," as Susanna called it.

Susanna wore her favorite pink nightgown with neon yellow hearts printed on it. She had her head tucked against her mom's chest, dark curls wild and hanging in her face.

Rose held a finger to her lips and pointed wordlessly at Susanna. "Asleep," she mouthed. Her eyes widened dramatically. "Finally."

Brent carefully slid his arms under Susanna, tucking her head in the crook of his elbow and letting her legs dangle as he scooped her up.

When he laid her in her own twin-sized bed down the hall, her eyes flicked open for a minute. "Is it night-night time?"

"Yes, it's night-night time," Brent whispered, pulling her purple quilt under her chin.

"I waited," she said. "I wanted a goodnight kiss."

"I always come kiss you goodnight when I get home late. Even when you're already asleep."

She frowned. "You do?"

"Of course."

She blinked up at him, a realization washing over her until she smiled sleepily and closed her eyes.

"Goodnight," Brent said softly.

Susanna didn't say anything back. She was already asleep.

Rose didn't ask any questions when Brent and Mae had left for their walk. She'd known something had been brewing the last week, but she never pressed Brent to share.

She still didn't press as he walked back into their bedroom and swapped his sandy jeans for a pair of cotton pajama pants and a gray tank top.

He loved that about her.

Rose knew when to push him. Occasionally, she pressed the "feelings stick" she used with her kindergarteners into his hands. Brent always acted offended, but she knew what she was doing in those moments.

"You doing okay?" she asked when he climbed into bed. She reached over and curled her long fingers against his palm.

"I'm okay." The words came out on default, ringing false even to his own ears. He sighed. "I have a lot on my mind, but I'm okay."

She laid her phone down on the bedside table face down. "Do you want to talk about it?"

Did he? Brent didn't know.

A week ago, he'd been itching to tell someone about the mobile. If Eliza hadn't called and dropped the bombshell that she'd had Summer early, Brent would have told his siblings at the party. He was grateful he didn't do that now.

Part of it had come from a desire to not be the only person carrying this secret. Now, though, he realized it had never been his secret to carry.

Christopher's life and death belonged to Mae. They had for decades. Brent was simply sharing some of the weight.

"I want to be honest with you, but I'm not sure I can talk about it," he explained. "It doesn't feel like my story to share, if that makes sense."

Rose considered it for a minute, her full lips pursing in thought. Finally, she nodded. "Being honest doesn't mean sharing everything."

Brent frowned, working through that one.

Rose continued. "Everyone has secrets. I can know you without knowing every single piece of the world in your head."

He leaned back against the tufted headboard, his hands folded in his lap as he thought about it.

He knew his mother in every way that counted. He knew the weight of her love. She was honest with that. What other honesty mattered?

Brent peeked over at Rose, his mouth tipped up in a smirk. "You're smart. Did you know that?"

She lifted her chin with pride. "Duh. 'Bout time you noticed."

Chuckling, he leaned across the bed and took up the spot where Susanna had been curled just a few minutes earlier to lay his head across Rose's chest.

She curled her fingers through his hair, scratching his scalp, and he closed his eyes, content.

He didn't know every thought in her head, just as she didn't know every thought in his. But he knew he loved her more than anything. He knew his love was honest.

No other honesty mattered.

20

HOLLY

THE GOODWIN RESIDENCE

Holly was dabbing a third damp paper towel under Grady's nose, trying to staunch the bleeding, when Alice clamored through the back door. It slammed closed behind her.

"Mom, you said you'd be right back!"

"I'm a little busy," Holly said, lacking the bandwidth to come up with a lie to get rid of Alice before she saw her brother all bloody.

"I found a caterpillar, but it's climbing up the tree. I can't reach." Alice jerked to a stop at the end of the countertop, eyes wide. "Did you hit him?"

"No, I didn't hit him!" Holly snorted. She had never hit her children. She'd been spanked growing up, but she and Pete had decided against it for their own kids. Why would Alice even think that?

"Who did?"

"Someone else," Holly answered. "Someone from camp."

Truthfully, Holly didn't know. Pete had been trying to get the whole story out of Grady for the last ten minutes, but it was coming out in bits and pieces. And half-truths, Holly suspected.

"We can't help until you tell us who did this," Pete sighed.

Rob had grown bored with the spectacle after a few minutes and retreated to the couch, but he chose that opportunity to speak up. "Snitches get stitches."

"Nature camp is not the same as a prison yard," Holly murmured, dabbing at Grady's nose a little too hard. He winced. "Sorry, baby. I think it's mostly done bleeding, but hold this in place for a few more minutes."

Holly stood back. The sight of her son sitting on the counter with his legs dangling over the edge was both familiar and strange. She'd whisked him to the counter next to the sink plenty of times to take care of scraped knees and elbows, back when he was small enough to be whisked.

Except back then, his feet barely cleared the edge of the counter. Now, they hung halfway down the cabinet fronts below.

Plus, his bloody nose and muddy shirt weren't from a clumsy fall. Her son had been in a fight. A real fight.

And based on the way he pressed his lips together and looked towards the wall, Holly didn't think he was keen on talking about it.

"Take off your shirt. I'll throw it in the wash." She snapped her fingers at Grady. "While I do that, you can tell your dad who hit you and why. And be honest. We can't send you to a camp where you aren't safe, and—"

Pete laid a hand on Holly's shoulder. "Hon, I'll take care of the shirt and the conversation and… everything. You can go."

"Go where?" Holly asked, gesturing around the house as if that was answer enough. "Look at what's happening around here. I can't leave."

"You have to help me catch the caterpillar," Alice whined, stamping her foot. "He's probably at the top of the tree by now. I'm going to miss him."

Suddenly, Rob slammed his computer shut and lurched off the couch. "I could use some fresh air. I'll catch the caterpillar."

Apparently, he wasn't as oblivious to everything around him as Holly had thought.

"There you go. Rob can catch the caterpillar," Pete said, raising his brows at Holly as though this solved all of their problems. "You can leave. Go get a coffee. Or," he furrowed his brow, "go shopping. I don't know."

Holly knew Pete didn't mean anything by the shopping comment. He just couldn't think of anything else Holly might leave the house to do.

And she couldn't blame him.

She couldn't remember the last time she'd done something for herself. And as much as she wanted to stay and fix all this madness going on at home, she could feel the walls closing in on her. She needed a change of scenery.

Which is how Holly found herself, fifteen minutes later, sitting on Shelly Frank's front porch swing with a glass of sun tea in her hand.

She hadn't been aiming to go there. She'd just wandered out of the house and Shelly happened to flag her down from across the street. Maybe she sensed Holly's desperation radiating off her like nuclear fallout, or maybe Holly just had a look in her face that said, *Please somebody save me.*

Thus, the tea and the swing and Shelly's warm hand on Holly's forearm.

"I'm so glad you stopped by," Shelly crooned for the second time. "It has been ages since I've sat down and enjoyed this front porch. After all the hours I spend out here gardening and decorating, I don't have time to enjoy it. Isn't that about how it goes?"

"That is absolutely how it goes," Holly agreed—even though her own lawn had been neglected for the better part of a year.

Shelly's front lawn was fit for a Home & Garden magazine cover. Rather than mulch, she used a ground cover that sprouted a spray of small violet flowers. Dotting the length of her white brick home were topiary bushes perfectly manicured into spheres. And behind those, leaning against the side of the house, were wrought-iron trellises dripping with ivy and lovely white dangling flowers Holly.

It was the kind of garden you could have when you didn't have children getting in fistfights and ex-convict uncles sleeping on your couch.

Cousin! Rob was Pete's cousin. Nobody's uncle. The kids were rubbing off on Holly.

Shelly leaned in, voice low and a wicked smile on her face. "Ronny keeps teasing that I should call Mike up for help on the lawn. He says it would save me time and Mike takes such good care of his."

"The weed whacker," Holly hissed, hiding her laughter in her tea. "He wields that thing like a sword."

"Yes, like it's a sword," Shelly agreed with a cackle, "and everything with leaves is a dragon."

"I've never seen someone get so much use out of one lawn tool in all my life."

"Don't judge me," Shelly said. "But I sit in my dining room window and watch him do his yardwork. It's fascinating."

"No judgement. It's very entertaining." Holly had spent more than a few Saturdays peeking through her bedroom blinds at their neighbor,

Mike, who had a bit of a reputation for getting a little cavalier with the weed whacker. "He has to duck and dodge all of those flying twigs and leaves."

Holly knew it wasn't nice to gossip about him. Especially since Mike smoked meat he got from his cousin's butcher shop in New Bedford once every few months and always made sure to bring Pete a large cut of it.

But it did feel good to laugh at someone else's problems rather than stew in her own. If only for a moment.

"Anyway, what have you been up to lately?" Shelly asked, stirring her tea with a stainless-steel straw. "I always see you and Pete coming and going with the kids, but there's never any chance to talk. Ronny gave Pete's name to a man from church who was looking for a lawyer. Mr. Thomas, I think his name was."

Ronny was a pastor at the First Baptist Church of Nantucket. Shelly was a stay-at-home mom, like Holly, but her kids were in high school and middle school. The oldest boy had his driver's license, so Holly saw him ferrying the younger two kids to school and to other activities while Shelly waved goodbye from the front stoop.

During the school year—whenever she found herself wrestling Grady into the car with his homework or pleading with Alice to unpack her doll from her bookbag—Holly couldn't help but imagine Shelly lounging inside the house each morning in a robe. Probably sipping on her still-hot coffee and enjoying the quiet, slow start to her day.

Such luxuries were nothing more than a dream in the Goodwin residence.

"Pete was just talking to Mr. Thomas on the phone this afternoon, so I'm sure he appreciated the word of mouth." *And I'm sure he had a grand old teaching the man how to use the internet*, she added silently. "We've been good. Busy. But nothing compared to the rest of my family. Eliza had her baby, if you didn't hear. Just last week. And my mom's inn is closed down while the movie crew films. So yeah, just busy. Busy but good."

Unless you counted criminals invading your sofa and your first baby getting in his first fight, that is.

"Everyone cannot *stop* talking about the movie!" Shelly exclaimed. "No offense to your mom or Dominic, of course. I'm happy for him. But I'd like to talk about anything else. Even my hairdresser got hired as an extra."

"None taken. Mum's the word." Holly sipped her tea and tried not to wince. There was an awful lot of lemon squeezed into it. Enough that it made her jaw twinge with each drink. "Though I don't have much to talk about otherwise. I just needed to get out of my house for a little bit."

Shelly tipped her head forward and lowered her voice. "Trying to get away from a certain houseguest?"

"You know about him?"

Shelly nodded. "I thought I saw Pete walk outside in his boxers and a white tank top to get the newspaper the other morning. Took me a minute to realize it wasn't Pete at all. I saw him again yesterday doing push-ups on his knuckles in the driveway."

Shelly tried to deliver the information as though it was just a factual, non-judgmental relaying of events, but her nose wrinkled slightly at the memory.

"I'm sorry," Holly groaned, dragging a hand down her face and flopping back on the porch swing. "That was Pete's cousin, Rob."

In an uncontainable rush of information, more like an exorcism than anything else, Holly explained the last week of her life in minute detail.

She told Shelly about Rob's past and Pete's total trust and acceptance of his cousin, despite not having seen him in over a decade. About the dirty clothes in the living room, Rob opening her underwear drawer, the kids practically worshipping "Uncle Rob," and a thousand other miniscule, frustrating details she'd been saving up to use as funny anecdotes in the memoir she'd surely never write.

"Wow," Shelly said, eyes wide.

Holly nodded and then remembered the latest bit. "Oh, and Grady just came home with a bloody nose. He got in a fight."

With that final burden off her chest, she let out a heavy sigh and sunk back into the porch swing. "I'm exhausted."

"I can't imagine." Shelly's lower lip pouted out in sympathy. "I hate having anyone stay at my house for more than a weekend. Let alone a man who wanders around in hole-y boxers. When missionaries come to the island for church visits, Ronny always offers them our guest room. They are the nicest people, but that does not mean I want to wake up to find them sitting at my kitchen table in the morning."

Holly's mind clung to one detail in particular. "The boxers had a hole in them? You didn't mention that before."

"I was trying to be kind," Shelly admitted. "I didn't know if you liked him or not. Now that I know you don't, I can give you all my sympathy. Tell Pete to kick him out!"

"I tried, but Rob is his family. He wants to help him."

Holly understood Pete's instinct. She even respected it to a certain extent. But she certainly didn't agree with it.

Clearly, Rob was having a bad influence on the kids. On Grady, at least, though God only knows what Alice would cook up next.

It just couldn't be a coincidence that Grady had his first-ever fight the same week Rob was staying with them. There had to be a connection.

Holly was about to change the subject, not wanting to bad mouth her husband to anyone. But then she looked up and saw Shelly frowning at her.

No, not *at* her. *Over* her.

"Speak of the devil, isn't that him right now? With Grady?"

Holly spun around so fast her tea sloshed over the rim of her goblet and down her hand. The chain of the porch swing squealed, and Shelly yelped, reaching out to steady the swing from swaying side-to-side rather than front-to-back.

The houses between Shelly's and Holly's had landscaping of their own, so Holly had to squint to see beyond the white picket fence next door and the hedge bush Mark had weed-whacked half to death.

Setting aside the racket he made every Saturday morning, Holly was grateful for Mark and his chaotic lawn care methods now. Last week, he'd made a particularly nasty gouge in the upper lip of the hedge. And it was over that dip in the foliage that Holly could see Rob and Grady sitting on her front porch.

Their heads were bowed together. Rob was illustrating whatever point he was making with wild hand gestures.

Grady watched him, enraptured, nodding along as though he was in a trance.

Holly placed her tea goblet on the glass side table with a little too much force and stood up. "I have to go."

"Good luck," Shelly said, waving from her chair without getting up. "Godspeed."

Shelly's words had a hint of amusement to them, though Holly knew the woman wouldn't find it a bit funny if her own kids were being influenced by a man who blew his nose by pressing his finger against one nostril and sending whatever was in his other nasal cavity spraying into the air for all to share.

Holly's shoes slapped down the concrete sidewalk even as she did her best not to look like she was hurrying.

Neither Rob nor Grady seemed to notice her coming up the driveway. When Holly cleared her throat just as Rob clenched his fist and reared his arm back, as though about to hit someone, they both jumped.

Rob dropped his arm quickly, his body relaxing back onto the concrete step unnaturally fast. In the entire week he'd been staying with them, the man hadn't shown an ounce of shame about anything. So if he didn't want Holly to know what he'd been saying to Grady, it couldn't be good.

Grady blinked up at his mom like he'd just walked out of a dark movie theatre, his eyes adjusting to the real world around him.

"What are you two talking about?" she asked, her voice bordering on maniacally pleasant.

Neither of them answered.

"Where's Dad and Alice?" Holly tried again.

"In the backyard finding caterpillars." Grady's shirt was still dirty, even though Pete had promised he'd take care of it. A small bit of dried blood remained smeared under his nose.

"Why don't we go finish cleaning you up?" Holly ruffled his hair and waved her hand, ushering him up the stairs and into the house.

Rob smiled at Holly as she passed, but didn't make a move to follow them inside or say anything.

Holly was fine with that. As far as she was concerned, he could stay on the porch all night.

No one would catch her complaining.

Pete took the weekend off work.

Holly didn't know if it was because of the laundry room conversation they'd had or because of the whole Grady debacle. Either way, her husband apparently felt like he needed to spend more time with his family.

On Saturday, they all went to the park—Cousin Rob included—and flew kites.

"They aren't going to get the kite to fly," Alice remarked sourly, shaking her head and stretching her leg out across the picnic table bench.

Alice didn't like how much attention Grady had gotten over his bloody nose, so she played it up big time when she tripped over a protruding tree root while running and hurt her ankle.

"They got it to fly once already," Holly countered.

Alice looked at her mom, pale eyebrow raised. "Yeah—into a tree."

Holly didn't know when her seven-year-old had become so opinionated—or so feisty—but she had to bite back a laugh and feign hope for Grady and his superhero kite.

Rob had volunteered to climb the tree and get the kite down. He kicked off his shoes and socks and scaled the tree like he'd done it a thousand times before. Grady was in awe.

"Rob and I used to climb trees all the time when we were kids," Pete was telling Grady. "You know that big tree in the middle of downtown? The one with the park bench underneath it?"

Grady nodded, mouth hanging open.

"I scaled that one in my day." Pete puffed out his chest. "The old women at the hair salon across the street got nervous and called the sheriff on us."

"Can you climb this tree?" Grady asked, pointing up to where Rob was untangling the kite. The thin branch beneath him bent under his weight.

Holly laughed to herself when Pete changed the subject suddenly, pointing out a woodpecker two trees over.

Alice was right, though—they never did get the kite airborne again.

On Sunday, Holly used her mom's recipe to make lobster quiche.

Mae had given Holly a clothbound book of family recipes passed down over the years when she and Pete got married, but Holly rarely cooked from it. Mostly because what she made never turned out as well as anything her mom could make.

The lobster quiche, however, she had perfected.

It was Holly's favorite kind of meal—one that felt like a luxury, but was actually simple to make.

She used a store-bought crust (Mae Benson would never!) and loaded it with cooked lobster meat leftover from a seafood chowder two nights earlier. Then she poured in her egg mixture, mixed with Dijon mustard and heavy cream, and topped it all with chunks of cream cheese, fresh dill, and asparagus pieces.

"I don't like the green things," Alice said, tongue stuck between her teeth.

Grady nodded in agreement. "Asparagus is gross."

Holly didn't have it in her to care when the kids picked all of the green bits out and piled them on the edge of their plates. In every way that counted, the brunch was a crowd pleaser. Even Rob enjoyed it, though thankfully he did so silently.

By the time Monday came around, Holly felt good. Better than she had in a long while.

"Since Billy is out of office, I can push my meetings to phone calls and man the phone from here," Pete said as he shoved his wallet in his back pocket and clipped his work phone onto his belt. "Just in case."

After last week, Holly felt anything really was possible, but she shook her head.

"I'm determined to ride the wave of this good weekend and have a good week, too. Go to work. I'll be fine here."

"Look at you and your positive outlook." Pete pulled Holly close and kissed her, smiling as he backed away. "I'll try and be positive, too. Maybe Mr. Thomas took a computer class over the weekend and won't need to call me again to figure out why his email won't pull up."

Holly wagged a finger. "No, I'm with Mr. Thomas. It should be as simple as typing 'my email' and letting the robots figure out how to make the darn thing work."

Laughing, Pete dispatched to work. Robin Schmidt picked Grady and Alice up for day camp—it would be Holly's turn to drive the carpool in the afternoon—and thus, Holly found herself with a relatively free morning.

Then, miracle upon miracles, Rob seemed to be changing his tune, as well. For the first time since appearing on their doorstep, he actually left the house on his own and went to explore downtown.

Holly secretly wished the townspeople of Nantucket who would cross his path good luck, but she was grateful to have the house to herself for a few hours.

She spent the free morning listening to a guilty pleasure celebrity gossip podcast and organizing her closet. It was a long overdue task. Some of the clothes hanging up were from before Alice was born.

Holly made a pile of clothes and shoes and purses to throw away and another pile to donate. When she was finished, an hour and several pairs of regrettably too-small jeans later, she snuggled into the green plaid arm chair at the end of her bed to read a book and drink a cappuccino.

The life she imagined Shelly Frank lived.

Of course, not ten pages into her book, her phone rang.

Caller ID said it was from the Nantucket Nature and Wildlife Center front office. Holly's heart jumped into her throat as she answered.

"Hello?" She tried to keep her voice even, not letting herself drift into thoughts of a tree having fallen on Alice or Grady being bitten by a poisonous snake.

Were there poisonous snakes in Nantucket? Pete would know. He'd been a Boy Scout.

"Hello. Is this Holly Goodwin?"

"Speaking. Can I help you?" The woman on the other end of the line sounded calm enough, but maybe it was because she made these kinds of calls all the time. Maybe the sight of some other person's child being rolled away on a stretcher no longer phased her.

"Hi, Holly. This is Miranda Chen with the Nantucket Nature and Wildlife Day Camp. I'm calling to let you know your son, Grady, was in an altercation today. He is in the office now, but we need you and your husband, if you're able, to come in immediately."

Holly blinked, trying to process what she just heard. "An altercation? With another person?"

"With another camper, yes," she said. "Can you come in today and meet with the director?"

"Grady was in a fight?" Holly asked again, trying to get more clarification. "Is he okay?"

"He's fine, Ma'am. Your son was actually the aggressor. He hit another camper."

Aggressor.

The word sounded nasty. Violent. Nothing like her Grady.

"Can you come in today for a meeting?" Miranda asked again. "As soon as possible, preferably? The other boy's parents are already here."

"Yes. Yes, of course." Holly jumped up, the book she'd been reading sliding from her lap onto the floor. Her bookmark skittered under the dresser, kicking up a dust bunny in its wake.

But it didn't matter. Holly had a feeling she wouldn't remember anything she'd read before the phone call, anyway.

"We will be right there."

She texted Pete: **Meet me at the Nantucket Nature Center right now. Camp called and Grady is in trouble. We have to meet with the director ASAP.**

A minute later, Pete responded: **On my way.**

After all the cleaning, her hair was a mess of flyaways and her forehead was shiny from sweat, but there wasn't much Holly could do about either of those things without being late.

So she smoothed her hands through her ponytail and dabbed at her face with a blotting sheet before she pulled on her slip-on sneakers and jogged down the stairs. Leggings and a long chambray shirt would have to suffice.

Just as Holly opened the front door, keys in hand, Rob appeared on the doorstep looking much as he had the first time Holly had seen him. Only this time, instead of a suitcase, he held a large kite in the shape of an airplane in his hand.

When he saw Holly, Rob grinned and held up the kite. "I bought this for Grady. I saw it in a shop window. Thought we might have better luck with it than the cheap kite from the dollar store."

Holly couldn't even register what he was saying. The only thing she could think about was that Grady had hit someone.

He was an *aggressor*.

And whose fault was that?

"What did you say to Grady the other day?" Holly asked suddenly. "When you were sitting on the porch. When I walked up, you had your hand in the air like you were telling him to hit someone. What did you say?"

Rob dropped the kite, his brows knit together. "Nothing. He was just down in the dumps about being hit, so I was talking to him about what happened when I got jumped."

"You talked to him about your time in prison?"

"Yeah, so?" Rob tucked his chin in, taking a more defensive posture. "I just told him that if he acted like a victim, he'd continue to be a victim. The kid who hit him has been bullying him all summer."

"No, he hasn't." Holly shook her head. "He would have told me."

Rob shrugged. "Some kid picked on him cause he couldn't climb a rope or something dumb like that. And the notes you put in his lunchbox aren't helping his popularity, I guess."

Holly had found the note she put in Grady's lunch box shoved under the seat last week—*Have a great day, honey! Love u xoxo*. She'd assumed he'd dropped it, but was that a dumb thing to assume? Maybe it was. Maybe he'd taken it out on purpose so he wouldn't get made fun of.

She shook her head. One thing at a time.

"What did you say to him?" she asked again. "The exact words."

"I told him he needed to stand up for himself and let these punks know he wouldn't take their crap. If he never fought back, they'll just keep coming. That's how it works." Rob's eyes glazed over as he stared just over Holly's head, his mind somewhere else.

"He's at day camp, not a federal penitentiary!"

Holly's hands were fisted around her keys so hard she accidentally hit the alarm button. The car horn started blaring, and she fumbled around to turn it off, furious enough that her fingers shook.

"You should have come to me or Pete if Grady was confiding in you. You are not his parent or anyone he should trust. You're a stranger! You don't give my son advice, okay?"

Rob's jaw clenched hard. A vein in his neck bulged.

Holly didn't know what he was going to say. But she knew she didn't have time for it.

With a wave of her hand, she moved Rob aside and stormed past him, climbing in the car and driving away without looking to see where he was.

She didn't care either way. The only time Holly wanted to be informed of Rob's movements was when he decided to move out of her house.

Until then, she wanted to pretend he didn't exist.

21

MAE

114 HOWARD STREET

The day visible to Mae through the double-hung living room window was gray and forlorn. The usual blue skies were darker than they should be at this hour, fleecy clouds heavy with rain curtaining the sun.

A fact that only served to make time appear to be passing even slower. Mae kept thinking it must be early evening, at least, only to look up at the clock above the fireplace and remember she hadn't even eaten lunch yet.

Mae watched Dominic lick his finger and turn the page of his book slowly. In no hurry at all to rush from one page to the next.

Just as he'd been in no hurry to do anything at all the past two days.

Since they'd woken up Monday morning, Dominic hadn't done a thing beyond pour himself a cup of the Snickerdoodle-flavored coffee Rose preferred and drop down into the white fabric sofa in the living room with his book.

Three hours later, he hadn't moved.

Mae was going batty.

"This house is so noisy," she said, voice soft. A book sat in her lap, but she hadn't opened it yet. "It's funny that I must have gotten used to all of the creaking and banging while I lived here, but now it's unfamiliar."

"The inn makes a lot of noises, too," Dominic murmured, brow furrowed as he read. He picked up his coffee and took a sip.

It was the same cup he'd made hours earlier. It must be stone cold, but he didn't seem to mind or even to notice.

Mae could not possibly fathom how he was able to sit in such contentment, oblivious to her racing thoughts and drumming fingers only two cushions away.

"I can never tell whether a noise is the house or the guests."

Guests. Goodness, how she missed those.

People to tend to. To talk with. To occupy Mae's time and attention and care.

Dominic nodded and kept reading, his eyes scanning across the page at an unflappable pace.

At least if he's reading, he won't stumble upon one of my lifelong secrets, Mae thought, surprising even herself with the bitter edge in her head.

She wasn't really worried Dominic would go snooping and discover Christopher's mobile, especially since he seemed content to remain stationary.

And she was fairly certain she didn't have any other secrets lying around the old house.

Still, Mae couldn't push the thought from her mind that Dominic would learn about Christopher and be upset with her for keeping the secret.

He'd revealed the loss of his daughter to her early on in their relationship. It would have been a great time for Mae to confide in

Dominic, but she hadn't even confided in her own children yet. So she'd remained quiet.

Now, it felt too late.

Mae sagged back against the couch, her head resting on the cushion, and closed her eyes. She wished she could nap. She'd just never gotten the hang of it.

"I forgot Susanna would be at nursery," Mae said, opening her eyes. "Or daycare. Or preschool. I'm not exactly sure what they are calling it anymore. But I thought she'd be home all day."

"I love her, but I'm glad she's not," Dominic laughed. "After Saturday, I'm spent. My arm is still sore from playing bocce ball with Grady."

"From *losing* bocce ball with Grady," Mae reminded him with a tease on the edge of her voice.

He hummed and turned the page of his book. "I'll challenge him to a rematch next time they come over. And I won't take it easy on him."

"I'm sure they'd love to come over for dinner." Mae brightened at the thought. "Maybe tonight."

Dominic let out a long whistle. "Kind of last minute for our hosts. Maybe next weekend?"

Oh, right. Not her house. She shouldn't be inviting guests for dinner.

What would Mae do until next weekend?

Rose and Brent were at work, Susanna was at nursery, and Mae didn't feel it was appropriate to do any cleaning or organizing in someone else's home.

Even if it had been hers for decades before, Mae was a guest now.

Besides, Rose had only just started to become comfortable with Mae staying in the house. She didn't want to undo their progress by overstepping the woman's boundaries.

But she also couldn't spend another minute sitting still, her conversation with Brent replaying in her mind on a near-constant loop.

She needed stimulation. A change of pace.

Something.

Anything.

"Let's go out for lunch," Mae said, jumping up from her spot on the couch.

He jolted in his seat, startled by her outburst, and looked up at her as though he'd forgotten she was in the room.

Mae wasn't offended by it. She knew how drawn into a good book he could get. Unfortunately for him, she didn't have the same ability. She needed to seek out entertainment.

And he would be recruited into the shenanigans whether he liked it or not. Such was life with a hummingbird.

"Didn't we bring some things from the fridge at the Inn? Can't we just make something from that?"

Usually, cooking would be the perfect thing to keep Mae busy. But it wasn't enough now. Not when the only person she'd be making food for would be content to eat silently with a book held open in front of his face.

"I never get to go out for lunch. I'm always busy cleaning up after breakfast at the inn and seeing people off to their afternoon activities. This is a rare opportunity to see what downtown is like in the middle of the day. I, for one, would relish a field trip."

"You've lived here your whole life. Surely you've been downtown for lunch."

Just last week with Debra for a red wine on the waterfront deck of a new brewery, as a matter of fact. But Mae didn't see the point in reminding Dominic of that.

"Come on. One hour. I promise your book will not run off in your absence." Mae plucked the spine of the book gently from between Dominic's tight grip, moved his bookmark into place, and set it on the side table. "There is more than one way to relax. I think a date night —well, a date day, I suppose—could do you some good."

Dominic smirked as he lifted himself to standing. "I appreciate the way you're trying to reframe this outing as a favor to me. As if you aren't crawling out of your skin with boredom."

"You noticed and didn't say anything?" Mae swatted his arm playfully.

He shrugged. "I was going to soak up my down time as long as possible. I'm surprised you made it this long, honestly."

As it turned out, Dominic wasn't as oblivious as Mae had thought.

She'd have to remember that.

Downtown Nantucket

"Park here," Mae said, pointing to a curbside space in front of The Rust Bucket.

"You want to go to a bar for lunch?" Dominic asked, pulling into the space. "Before noon?"

She laughed. "No, I want to avoid driving through the summer crowds downtown. Driving through a throng of tourists is not a good time for anyone."

Dominic shuddered, expression pinched. "'Throng of people' is quite possibly my least favorite phrase in the English language."

"Oh, quit your fussing and come along."

The outer rim of downtown was frequented more by locals than tourists. On the narrow brick sidewalks, Mae and Dominic passed lawyers' offices, an orthodontist and an optometrist, and the imported carpet store with a five-figure price tag hanging from a beautiful red and gold rug in the window.

It was easy strolling at first. But as they neared the center of downtown, the crowds began to pick up. Mae could hear the hum of people talking and laughing and the soft sound of music playing through speakers.

"The Book Corner is open," Dominic said, pointing to a red brick building on the corner, large windows facing out at each cross street, stuffed with towering book displays. He picked up his pace slightly, hustling ahead of Mae. "I ordered something that should be in by now. I'll only be a minute."

"And I'll turn into a bird and fly down the road to find where we should eat," Mae teased, looping her arm through his and reining him back to her side. "If we're out of here in a minute, I'll eat my hat."

"That would save us money on lunch," Dominic said, sounding every bit serious, though there was a glimmer of mischief in his eyes.

Mae sighed. "Fine. Go. But I'm starting my watch!"

The book shop was large, but the space was broken down into three separate rooms, giving each one an intimate, homey feeling. Small coffee tables stacked with books for sale sat in the middle of rings of tall-backed arm chairs. Themed shelves lined the walls, festooned with little telltale knickknacks—hearts hovering over Romance, a rocket ship hurtling through Science Fiction.

Dominic walked into the store and marched straight to the front desk, ringing the bell for assistance.

Other patrons were milling around the store, with a few clustering around one section in particular. Above the shelf in question, a sign read: *"Set in Nantucket."*

The store owner, Mr. MacDonald, was in the midst of three customers, all middle-aged women with armloads of bags and souvenirs. He was directing them to one book in particular.

"This is the book you're looking for," Mr. MacDonald said, holding it up.

Mae recognized the cover immediately. And, just a few feet away as he waited for the clerk to return with his order, she saw Dominic did, too.

Probably because it was his name splashed across the cover.

"A film crew is on the island right now making the movie based on this book. The author lives here in town. If you're lucky, you might get an autograph."

Mr. MacDonald turned Dominic's book so the cover faced out and set it back on the shelf.

When he then glanced up and saw Dominic standing aghast at the counter, he grinned. "In fact, here is the author right now. What luck!"

Dominic glanced at Mae as if she could get him out of this. But short of faking a medical emergency, Mae couldn't think of anything.

Besides—Dominic was going to meet fans of his books. It seemed like a dream come true, no?

"Would you sign a copy for us?" a red-haired woman pleaded at once, holding out a book and a pen she'd dug from her purse. "We can't wait to read the book."

"Maybe you should read it before you ask me to sign it," Dominic said with a nervous laugh. "It might not be any good."

"They wouldn't make it into a movie if it wasn't good," a dark-haired woman with a beauty spot above her lip said.

Mae didn't like the way the women were looking at Dominic. She walked over and squeezed Dominic's arm. "Sign their books, honey."

Maybe she imagined it, but Mae thought she noticed the dark-haired woman's eyes narrow.

As soon as he finished signing the books, Dominic dodged their follow-up questions and hurried away. Outside, he let loose a sigh. "You don't think this movie will get too popular, do you?"

"I'm not sure. Would that be a bad thing?"

"I'm not sure," he echoed. "I'd like to be able to go to my favorite book shop without running into fans."

Mae looped her arm through Dominic's. "Again, would that really be a bad thing? Don't most authors want to be famous?"

"Not this author. Besides, they hadn't even read the book yet. They weren't really fans."

"They were at a bookstore, in case you didn't notice, darling. I'm sure they like to read. And as handsome as you are, your face is on the back of the book, not the front. I don't think you have to be worried about getting mobbed by paparazzi anytime soon."

Dominic grimaced. "Don't even joke about that. What a horrid concept. *Paparazzi*," he growled, lip curled like he wanted to spit on the cobblestones.

As they ambled north, the road widened, making room for cars to park along the edges of the road, though every space was filled now. The sidewalk widened, too.

People window shopped at the brick-front businesses and sat on park benches licking ice cream cones they'd picked up from one of the ten different sweets shops along Main Street.

Banners hung from the forest green lampposts advertising the weekend farmer's market. And even though the sky was gray, the day was warm enough that many restaurants still had tables and chairs set up on the sidewalks.

"Are you thinking we'll go to Little Bull?" Dominic asked. "We haven't been in a while."

"We went last week, silly. And Sara brought us food just a few days ago," Mae countered. "Besides, every time we go, Sara covers the bill and gives us her best table. I don't want to steal more business from her than I already do. Maybe a sandwich?"

"I could eat a sandwich."

"Brent told me Eddie's Sandwich Shop named a sandwich after you since you put them in your book. Come to think of it, the movie is going to film a scene there, too," Mae said.

Dominic groaned. "Maybe not sandwiches then. Also, maybe we should move? I hear Greece is lovely this time of year."

"Come on. Enjoy your fifteen minutes of fame, Dom." Mae shook his arm. "And I don't think the Sweet Island Inn would work as a business idea if it was no longer on the island."

They kept walking, each of them tossing out lunch ideas the other turned down.

Dominic balked at the street-style taco shop and clutched at his chest dramatically. "I still have heartburn from the tacos Rose made for dinner last night. The woman loves her spice."

"Pasta, then? There's a lobster macaroni-and-cheese at Antonio's that I love. And they always play romantic Italian music. That's as close as you'll get to traveling outside the island for a while, I'm afraid."

He mulled the idea over, pursing his lips. "I think we've reached an accord."

"Finally." Mae tugged him forward, her stomach rumbling.

But a block later, they were stopped.

A wooden barricade blocked the street. On the near side, a large crowd of people milled about, all craning their necks for a view of whatever was going on.

"Is there a parade today?" Mae wondered, looking around for a sign or banner to explain the gathering.

"It would be a short parade to stop right in the middle of Main Street." Dominic stretched onto his toes with no luck. "Should we turn around? Maybe look for something in the other direction?"

"Not after it took us fifteen minutes to agree on lobster mac-and-cheese," Mae groaned. "No, we brave the crowds and push on."

The barricade only blocked off the street. The sidewalk was still accessible, aside from the crowd of people standing in the way.

"Excuse me, excuse us," Mae said over and over as she pushed her way through down the sidewalk, Dominic trailing right behind her.

Then a hand reached out and wrapped around Mae's arm. She startled, but turned to see her friend Lola standing there, a grin on her face.

"Did you come to see the excitement?" Lola asked, tipping her head towards the road. "I would have thought you two would have a front row seat!"

Lola had a folding chair with her, a bottle of water, and her phone in her hand, the camera app open and ready.

"What excitement?" Mae asked. "What is this?"

Lola looked from Mae to Dominic, shocked they didn't know. "The movie! They are filming right now. 'Establishing shots' is what I've heard, though I can't see enough to know any different. I would have assumed you two would be the first to know since you're the big author," she said to Dominic.

Much to his horror, her voice was plenty loud enough to be heard over the hum of the crowd. Dominic seemed to shrink at her words.

"I had no idea," Mae said, turning to Dominic. "Did you know? Did anyone tell you about this?"

He shook his head, his shoulders lifting until they nearly covered his ears. It only got worse as the people nearby turned towards them to scrutinize Dominic.

"Is that him? Is that the guy?" came whisper after whisper.

Finally, someone spoke up. "You're the author?" an older woman demanded, a shawl pulled over her shoulders despite the warm day. "Of the book being made into the movie?"

Dominic started to shake his head, but Lola jumped in to answer for him. "He is! Dominic O'Kelley. The man himself."

The whispers grew, and Mae could tell the information was spreading. Slowly but surely.

Dominic wrapped his hand around Mae's elbow. "Come on. Let's turn around."

"Maybe I could get an autograph?" the woman said, turning to dig in her bag for what Mae assumed was a copy of Dominic's book.

Mae tried to tug him forward. "We're only a block from Antonio's. If we keep going—"

"Let's go back," Dominic said, his voice the equivalent of a signal flare flashing through the sky.

Mayday. Help. SOS.

Mae leaned forward. "You talked with Joey about the movie at the party. You were excited about it. Why is this different? I'm sure we could go behind the barricade if we found the director. Get out of this crowd so we could see the action."

"I know Joey," he said. "I don't know these people. I don't want to see the action. I want to go."

His cheeks were flushed, eyes wide, and Mae's heart tugged.

She nodded. "Okay."

Saying a quick goodbye to Lola, Mae turned around, keeping a hand on Dominic's back as he gave a wide berth to the old woman who had finally found her copy of the book.

He picked his way back through the crowd, moving quickly. He didn't slow down until they were far from the hum and excitement of the movie set.

"There's pizza right here," Dominic said, head still lowered. "We could get a box to go. Take it back to the house?"

The idea of making it all this way just to carry a pizza box back to the house made Mae want to throw a temper tantrum.

She wanted the excitement of the movie set. She wanted to see the cameras swiveling around, taking in the scenery of her island.

But she didn't want to see Dominic in obvious distress. No matter how little sense his discomfort made to her.

So she nodded. "Okay. Whatever you want."

Moving faster than he had in weeks, Dominic ordered a box of supreme pizza to go and carried it quietly back to the car.

On the drive, before they even made it back to Howard Street, the thoughts Mae had been running from began to return. As though her anxieties were prying little fingers, stretching out to poke her wherever she was.

For a minute, she'd left her worries behind. She'd been able to set aside the resurfaced pain of Christopher's loss. Been able to stop imagining what it would be like if she had five children instead of four.

Now, however, it was all back. Dominic could run from his problems, it seemed. But Mae couldn't run from hers.

She had to live with them.

22

HOLLY
NANTUCKET NATURE CENTER

Pete was sitting in his car in the front office parking lot when Holly arrived.

There were open spaces in front of the Nature Center building, but he parked under the cover of a large elm at the far corner of the lot. With the dreary day and the extra coverage of the tree, Holly almost hadn't seen him at all.

For a moment, she flashed back to meeting Pete in dark corners of the park when they were teenagers. They never did anything too scandalous—just talking and kissing until a security guard came patrolling through or another car pulled in nearby. Then, rebellious spirits quenched, Pete would squeal out of their secluded meeting location and drive Holly home.

That was exciting.

This was... less so.

True, her heart was still pounding like it did back then. But with bad nerves and nausea and a throat tight from anxiety.

When Holly pulled into the space next to him, Pete got out of his car and hopped into her passenger seat, pulling the door shut behind him.

"What's going on?" he asked, voice almost a whisper.

Holly frowned. "What are you doing?"

"I don't know!" He threw his hands up. "You sent me a vague text message. I didn't want to park in front of the doors and have someone from the office come out and ask me what I was doing. Because I don't know what I'm doing."

"Grady got in a fight." She turned off the car. "He hit the kid who hit him last week. The same kid who has been bullying him."

"Grady has been being bullied?"

"Oh, so he didn't tell you either? Wonderful." Holly rolled her eyes and climbed out of the car, too frustrated to stay seated. Pete got after her and she continued talking to him over the roof of the car. "I talked to your cousin on my way out the door, and apparently, Grady told him kids have been making fun of him."

Pete ran a hand through his short hair, sending some of the strands sticking up at odd angles. "He just told me it was a dumb fight. It didn't seem like a big deal."

"Well, according to Rob, Grady has been getting bullied. And like the stunning male role model he is, Rob told Grady to stand up for himself."

"That's not terrible advice."

Holly raised her brows and threw her arms out wide, gesturing to where they were standing. "We are about to walk into a meeting with the camp director and the other kid's parents because our son hit someone. Are you telling me this was a good idea?"

"No!" Pete smoothed down the hair he'd mussed before. "No, I'm not saying that. Only that, if Grady had come to me, I would have told him to stand up for himself. Not to fight!" he added hastily before Holly could say anything. "I wouldn't have suggested he fight anyone, but I would have suggested he let the other kids know he wasn't going to be bothered by their bullying anymore. It sounds like that's what Rob told Grady, and Grady took it the wrong way."

Part of Holly—a small part, but a part nonetheless—wanted to give Rob the benefit of the doubt the same way Pete could. But she'd seen Rob and Grady together on the front porch. She'd seen Rob's hand cocked back in a fist, demonstrating to Grady exactly what he should do.

She wanted to believe the best in Rob, but she no longer had that luxury. She knew who the bad influence in her son's life was.

But there was no time to explain it to Pete right now. Not when Grady was sitting inside by himself.

Even if he was in trouble—even if he was the *aggressor,* a word that still made her retch—Holly just wanted to pull her little boy close and kiss the top of his head.

"There's no sense arguing about this right now. We should go inside." Without another word, Holly turned on her heel and marched inside.

Pete jogged to catch up to her, and they walked through the front doors together.

The inside of the office smelled like damp wood and dirt. It was obviously a nature center front office, but Holly didn't understand why it had to smell like nature.

The woman behind the front desk—Miranda, according to her name plate—stood up. She had on tan pants with an olive green button-down tucked in. Her brown hair was pulled back in a tight ponytail. "Are you Grady's parents?"

"We are. Usually, that's a good thing. Today, not so much." Pete laughed nervously, and Miranda gave him a tight smile.

Holly wanted to swat him. She knew he was only teasing, but joking was the last thing she felt like doing. If Grady overheard that, he'd be crushed.

"Everyone is waiting for you in the conference room. Follow me."

Miranda's hiking boots looked new, like she'd never walked through dirt a day in her life. She either took very good care of them or her job didn't extend much beyond the front office.

They turned left down a hallway that looked more like a wood-paneled cave and then opened a door on the right. There were windows set into the wall, but only a faint bit of light peeked out between the wooden blinds. The mood was somber, downtrodden. Which felt appropriate, really.

"Here you are."

The first thing Holly saw was Grady sitting at a long conference table.

He had his hands folded in his lap, his head hanging low. The office chair he sat in seemed to swallow him up. He was barely tall enough to see over the table.

"Mr. and Mrs. Goodwin, hello."

A wide, squat man with thick gray scruff on his face and very little hair on his head stood up. He had the same tan pants and green shirt as Miranda, but his was covered in patches and badges.

"I'm Dennis Baker, the camp director. Thank you for coming on such short notice."

The man held out his hand for a shake, which Pete stepped forward to take. Holly, instead, hurried around the table to sit next to Grady.

She laid a hand on his shoulder and squeezed. Only then did Grady look up and meet her eyes. His were shiny with unshed tears. Cheeks red with shame.

There were no new cuts or bruises, Holly noticed. And no blood. Was that better or worse? Holly wasn't sure which just yet.

"You okay?" Holly whispered.

Grady's lip quivered and he nodded, casting his gaze right back to his lap.

"Mr. and Mrs. Goodwin, meet Mr. and Mrs. Monroe. And their son, Elijah," Mr. Baker said, dropping back down into his chair. It squealed under his sudden weight.

For the first time, Holly registered the people sitting on the other side of the table. She'd been so worried about Grady, she'd blown right past them.

Even sitting down, Holly could tell the man was tall. He had a full head of dark hair with gray at his temples. He wore a navy-blue pocket tee shirt and an expensive gold watch on his wrist. As she looked up, he lifted the hand wearing the watch into a curt wave.

His wife didn't budge. She studied Holly and Pete like they were specimens on display. And she didn't seem to like what she saw.

She had on a bright blue wrap dress with a thin string of pearls around her neck and a matching set in her ears. Unlike Holly's rat's nest of a ponytail, the other mom's hair was brushed and shaped into a perfect wave, complete with a gold bar clip above her right ear.

Her makeup, too, was perfect. Holly could tell she had a lot of it on, but everything from her coral pink lips to the gold shimmer on her eyes was red-carpet flawless. Whatever event she'd come from must have been important.

Mrs. Monroe nudged her husband's elbow, and he looked over at her and then understood all at once what she meant.

He turned to the camp director. "Could we move this along? I'm afraid we have to get back to set. We've waited long enough."

Holly wanted to point out that they must have gotten the phone call first. When Miranda had called Holly, she'd told her the other boy's parents were already there. Busy though they may be, the Monroes certainly couldn't blame their wait on her and Pete.

"Set?" Pete asked. "Are you two working with the movie?"

"You could say that," Mrs. Monroe said, pursing her lips in a cheerless smile.

"My wife is the co-star of the film, and I'm the casting director," Mr. Monroe explained.

It wasn't quite nepotism. But something about that struck Holly as distasteful.

Mrs. Monroe draped a delicate arm around her son's shoulders. Holly took in Elijah for the first time. He had an ice pack pressed to his cheek, but when he pulled it away for a second, Holly didn't see anything.

No scratches, no broken skin, no bruising. Definitely not a split lip and blood running down his nose.

Why did this require a parent meeting, but Grady's *actual* injuries hadn't?

"Of course," Mr. Baker said, folding his hands in front of his face. "As you both know, there was an incident last week between Grady and Elijah. A disagreement that got out of hand. We handled it internally and both boys assured us the problem would be resolved. However, today, we can all see the problem was not resolved. There was a fight. Both boys have admitted that Grady hit Elijah—haven't you, boys?"

Elijah nodded quickly. A second later, Grady nodded, too.

"What about the fight last week?" Holly asked, leaning forward. "The one where Grady came home with a bloody nose and a split lip?"

"Holly..." Pete said her name softly under his breath. A warning.

Holly ignored him. "I don't remember getting a phone call about that *disagreement.*" She just barely resisted the urge to use air quotes.

The camp director leaned back in his chair like he was taken aback by Holly's outburst. The man dealt with children all day—big fish in a baby pond. He wasn't used to anyone biting back.

"As I said, we believed we could handle the matter internally. It isn't uncommon for children to argue, so we have methods to deescalate and resolve conflicts. We had every reason to believe the issue had been dealt with," Mr. Baker said.

"Of course," Pete agreed. "We understand. Kids will be kids, right?" He smiled across the table at the Monroes.

But if Pete hoped to find allies over there, he was mistaken. They met him with matching icy stares.

"They are kids," Holly agreed. "Which is why I should have gotten a call to warn me Grady was attacked."

"*Attacked?*" Mrs. Monroe seethed under her breath. When Holly looked over, the actress rolled her eyes.

Holly felt her own eyes narrow to slits. She couldn't remember the last time she'd felt like this—buzzing with adrenaline and frustration. *"Mama Bear Mode,"* Pete always joked.

"What would you call it, Mrs. Monroe?" Holly pressed. "I'd call a bloody nose and split lip more than a 'disagreement.'"

"I'd call this more than a disagreement, too," the woman said, pointing to her son. The boy had lowered the ice pack, but he quickly lifted it back to his cheek when attention turned to him.

"Okay, fine," Holly conceded, biting her tongue about Elijah's lack of any visible injuries. "But why does my son get sent home bloodied with no explanation, but your son gets an all-hands meeting?"

Pete laid a hand on her shoulder. "It has been a tough week for us," he explained, trying to soften the blow of Holly's anger. "What my wife is trying to say is that we want to get to the bottom of this as much as anyone here."

"We're at the bottom of it," Mr. Monroe rumbled. "Your son hit our son. What more is there to discuss?"

Grady sunk down in his chair. There was no telling what was said before Holly and Pete arrived. What these people may have said to him or in front of him while he was alone and defenseless.

Holly should have been called immediately. She should have been in this room before anyone sat down.

This was all so wrong.

"After *your* son hit ours!" Holly barked back.

Pete held up his hands. "All we are saying is that, if we'd been notified last week, we could have worked to prevent what happened today."

"Well, you're being notified now," Mr. Monroe snarled.

Mrs. Monroe nodded along with her husband. "Yes. We're only going to be here for a couple weeks, and we want our son to be safe while we're here. If your son can't handle this environment, maybe you should keep him home."

Holly couldn't stand the way Elijah kept glancing over at Grady. He looked just like his parents. Maybe the smugness was genetic.

"And who told you Grady was being a bully?" she asked. "Was it your son? Because something tells me he might not be telling you the whole story."

"Are you calling Elijah a liar?" Mrs. Monroe asked, rising up in her chair.

"Parents, parents," Mr. Baker said, standing up and waving his arms. "This is getting out of hand. We called this meeting today so everyone could be informed of the problem and solutions could be made. There is no need to cast blame."

"Feels like plenty of blame has been cast already!" Holly slammed her hand on the table, her palm stinging.

Immediately, Pete grabbed her hand and squeezed. Outwardly, it looked like a comforting gesture, but Holly felt like she'd been put in cuffs.

"I think now that we all know what is going on, we can be sure this doesn't happen again in the future," Pete said, his mouth stretching into an unnatural smile as he looked around the table. "Tensions are high, but it's only because we all love our children. I see that as a good thing. It means we all want to resolve this issue."

In the entire span of their marriage, Holly had never been so fed up with Pete's sunshiny demeanor. She wanted to grab him by the shirt collar, shake him, and scream at the top of her lungs.

These people are selfish! They don't want solutions; they want retaliation! There is no silver lining, the glass is not half-full, and the only thing I want to do with lemons is throw them at this arrogant woman's face.

It took all her willpower to swallow all that down.

"Agreed, Mr. Goodwin," the camp director said, drumming his fist on the table like he was calling a court into recess. "I expect you will all speak to your boys about their behavior and we won't have this issue moving forward. If we do, harsher punishments will be doled out."

"The brochure mentioned a zero-tolerance policy for violence," Mr. Monroe added with a half-shrug.

The director lifted a finger in Mr. Monroe's direction like he'd made a fair point. "In the past, immediate expulsion from camp has occurred in serious enough situations. It all depends on the situation."

"Like if the child being hurt has movie star parents or not," Holly mumbled.

Pete hurried to cover Holly's remark, thanking everyone for coming and then scooting Grady out of his chair and usher him towards the door. He didn't so much as glance up at her. Like she was a landmine and she'd explode if even he looked at her wrong.

Outside, the sun had started to peek through the clouds. The sound of children yelling and laughing filtered through the trees, and Grady turned his head towards the noise. Like maybe he'd see his real friends if he looked hard enough.

It broke Holly's heart.

"It's all right, buddy," she said, smoothing a hand down the back of his neck and tucking the tag of his shirt into his collar. "We'll talk about this later, but I know this wasn't all your fault."

It was Elijah's fault.

It was Rob's fault.

And while she was assigning fault, Mr. and Mrs. Monroe could take some, too. Heck, she might heap a spoonful on Dominic's plate, just for getting the ball rolling on everything that led to this.

"Thanks," he mumbled, pulling ahead and kicking at a pebble with his shoe.

There was a snort behind her. Holly looked back to see the actress herself standing in the lot, arms crossed, staring at her.

"Excuse me?" Holly asked. "You have something to say?"

Mrs. Monroe smiled, though there was nothing nice about the expression. Her husband's face looked equally grim. "No. I only find it interesting that you're so quick to let your son off the hook."

"Come on, bud. Let's get in the car." Pete rushed Grady away and got him into the car. Holly heard the engine start behind her, and then Pete reappeared at her shoulder.

"I told him it wasn't all his fault," Holly clarified. "It takes two to tango."

Mrs. Monroe snorted again. "Grady doesn't have a scratch on him."

Pete stiffened. "Maybe we should all go. Cool off. Talk about this later."

"Yeah, I'll pass on a rain check," Holly said. She could feel her heart beating in her ears, blood rushing to her head.

"Agreed," Mrs. Monroe snorted. "In fact, I'm done with your whole family. Don't think I don't know who you are. This whole town can do nothing but talk about '*the Bensons*' and '*how wonderful they are.*'" She scoffed, clearly not convinced. "If this is how your family behaves, I want to limit my contact with your bunch as much as possible."

Mr. Monroe raised a finger in the air. An idea striking him. "Oh, but honey, there is a Benson on the cast. A boyfriend, anyway. The firefighter?"

Mrs. Monroe's smile sharpened. Holly could have sworn she saw her teeth glimmer.

"Joey, that's his name," Mr. Monroe continued. "He's probably the most excited cast member I have. It will be a shame to cut him loose."

Pete frowned, stepping forward. "I don't see what Joey has to do with any of this."

Holly knew exactly what Joey had to do with this. Vengeance.

These people were petty and spiteful, and they wanted to make Holly regret coming up against them by wielding what little power they had.

Unfortunately for Joey, that meant the end of his big break.

"One bad apple can ruin the bunch. Better to cut it out early," the man said with a shrug, as though there was nothing he could do about it. "Your friend is out of the movie, and if you aren't careful, your son will be out of this camp."

With that, they turned in unison and marched to their luxe SUV, disappearing behind the deeply tinted windows.

"Unbelievable," Pete breathed. He turned to Holly, expression open and confused. "What happened in there? Why did you lose your cool like that? That wasn't good for Grady to see."

"What *I* did wasn't good for him to see?" Holly sputtered. "You just stood there! Wouldn't even defend him. *Kids will be kids.* What was that?"

"Me trying to show them we aren't a bunch of crazy hotheads!"

"They're blaming Grady for everything. They had him sitting in that room. By himself. What kind of camp protocol is that? You're the lawyer. You should be angry he didn't have representation."

"It wasn't a trial, Holly."

"It felt like one!" she shouted. "They wanted us to sit there and agree that Grady is trouble. But that Elijah kid is the one who's trouble. Grady has never had issues like this before. Not until this camp. Not until…"

Rob.

Elijah would still be a bully if Rob hadn't come into town, but Holly's son wouldn't have been pulled into the mess. Grady would have kept his head down and endured, or he would have told an adult what was going on. He wouldn't have hit anyone.

Not unless someone told him to.

All of this, in one way or another, came back to Rob.

"I'm going to talk to Rob." Holly clutched her keys and stomped towards her car.

Pete grabbed her arm and used the momentum to sling himself around her, coming face-to-face with his wife. "No, you aren't. I will."

"Oh, now you want to talk to him?"

"That's not fair." Pete clenched his jaw in frustration, but there was hurt in his eyes. "I was trying to make peace. To build bridges."

"Well, maybe it's time to draw up our bridges. Maybe... maybe we need to build a moat, okay? Stop letting people into our castle."

"Enough, Hol," Pete snapped. "You can't blame everything on Rob. Especially when I'm the one you want to blame. This is all because I haven't been around, right? Is that what you're trying to say?"

"It's because you aren't listening," Holly countered.

"Because I'm so distracted with work," Pete finished for her sarcastically. "Because I'm too busy and I don't do enough with the kids and I'm never home. That's the real issue, yeah?"

"That isn't it!" Holly clenched her hands into fists at her side. How many times would they have this same argument? "I never said that."

"You didn't have to." Pete spun around and walked towards his car.

"You're making this about something it isn't," she called after him.

"I'll be home early tonight," he said, ignoring her and waving a hand over his shoulder. "But right now, I have to get back to work."

Pete got in his car and drove away without another look at Holly.

23

SARA

SARA'S APARTMENT

Mondays were Sara's day off.

She had a medical drama on in the background, her feet propped on a bright green hand-knitted pouf Holly had made her for her birthday two years earlier, and she was anxiously waiting to have a lukewarm honey vanilla latte in her hand.

Sara was more than capable of making her own piping hot lattes at home. But days off were tailor-made for paying too much money for delivery and enjoying her favorite drink thirty minutes past its prime.

At least she'd only have to walk two steps to her front door to accept the delivery rather than all the way to the kitchen.

In the middle of an emergency heart surgery playing out on the small screen—yet another life-or-death situation that only Dr. Swoony McHandsome could solve—the doorbell rang.

When Sara opened it, Chris stood on the other side of the threshold, breathing heavily and shaking his head. "Sorry, Sara. I got here as fast as I could, but there was a whole mess of people in the streets today."

"Oh yeah, the movie is filming downtown today. I heard about that."

Ordering from Two Birds Coffee had become Sara's day-off ritual. She and Chris, the delivery driver, had become close.

"With the cameras and the crowds and the folding chairs, it looked like something out of a movie." He screwed up his face, nose scrunched. "That sounds dumb, but you know what I mean. My car got stuck behind barricades. I had to ride the delivery bike."

He hitched a thumb over his shoulder, pointing to the fixed gear bike leaning against the weathered fence. The grass from Sara's patchy lawn tickled his tire spokes.

"You should have called and told me. I woulda come and picked it up." Sara retrieved the tall paper cup from his hand and took a sip.

Lukewarm, and the foam was a little thin. But still delicious.

"Are you kidding? Lauren would skin me if she knew I flaked on a delivery for our best customer."

"I don't order that many lattes, do I?" Sara asked, suddenly self-conscious.

"Well, sort of. But I just meant that you send so much business our way," he explained. "We constantly have people coming in for an espresso after a meal at Little Bull. Your word of mouth is huge."

Two Birds Coffee was one of the standard recommendations Sara gave out to tourists. What could she say? They made good coffee.

Plus, the ambience was to die for. Sara could understand why the film crew had decided to film right in front of the shop.

All of the businesses downtown had brick fronts with beautiful wooden window trim painted in bright, cheery colors. Two Birds had kept it classic with an ivory paint, but they had large string lights and colorful banners hanging in the windows. Inside, the original hardwood floors had been refinished in a rich, warm stain that made it feel like you were drinking coffee in a cozy hobbit hole.

When Sara wasn't having one of her epic lazy days, she'd sit at the bar that ran along the window and read a book with a cup of coffee and a croissant. It was a great place to people watch.

"...And Dominic recommended us to the film crew, and they go through an honestly unreal number of coffee carafes. We are forever in the debt of Clan Benson," Chris was saying, bowing awkwardly as his voice took on a strange Scottish lilt. "Anything else?"

He asked that as if he'd really bike the ten blocks to Two Birds and back if Sara asked for sweetener.

Even if Chris had his car, Sara would never. She was on the outer edge of Two Birds' delivery range as it was.

"Just the latte, thanks." She took another sip and held it aloft in a cheers as Chris took the front steps of her duplex two at a time and threw a weary leg back over his bike.

Dr. McHandsome had completed his surgery by the time Sara dropped back down onto the sofa. The patient was thanking him for saving her life, but he wouldn't accept her gratitude. He wasn't only Dr. McHandsome—he was also Dr. McHumble.

Joey hated Sara's doctor shows.

"Completely unrealistic!" he'd shout at the television, pointing out when doctors didn't scrub in correctly or when they started slicing open patients without wearing gloves. "Infection central. That guy will be dead of sepsis within a week."

"I thought you were a firefighter, not a surgeon."

"I'm more of a surgeon than these clowns," he'd mumble.

When Joey wasn't on shift at the firehouse, he'd lounge with Sara on Mondays. He'd tease her about spending ten dollars on coffee just to get it delivered, and she would train him in the ways of Ultimate Laziness.

Ultimate Laziness involved dipping Oreo cookies in jars of peanut butter and watching a marathon of a show you didn't even like because the remote was too far away.

Even though he complained, Sara knew he loved it.

Today, however, he was "on set."

Joey called at the crack of dawn that morning—breaking rule number one of Ultimate Laziness: sleep in as long as possible—to tell Sara the movie would be filming downtown.

"They are going to shoot some establishing shots, and they want extras on hand to walk down the street. Maybe you could come and make it in the movie, too? Your part wouldn't be mentioned in the end credits like mine, but still. Could be fun."

Joey had asked a producer and been informed his name would be next to **Firefighter #4** in the scroll at the end of the movie. Truly the stuff dreams were made of.

"Sorry, I'm feeling a little run down today," she'd lied.

"Nothing like the excitement of a set to perk you up."

She'd chuckled. "I'm sure you're right, but my under-eye bags aren't movie-worthy today. I'll make it to another day of filming. Promise."

Joey had been disappointed, but Sara couldn't take the movie talk anymore. It was all he seemed to care about.

She needed a break.

Honestly, she was slightly relieved he had something else going on. She didn't know if she could handle another lazy day filled with endless chatter about "learning his angles" and the "Hollywood diet" he'd put himself on.

Suddenly, he was too good for chocolate cookies dipped in peanut butter, and Sara was tired of feeling judged.

"The camera adds ten pounds. Everyone says that, but it's actually true."

"Good thing I won't be on camera," she'd say, shoving another cookie in her mouth.

No, it was best she was alone today.

Work had been tense ever since she confronted Casey about the theft. He still showed up and did his job, but that only made things worse.

Just Friday night, he'd served the cod dish to three different tables without the tomato-lime salsa. Usually, that would warrant a stern reminder to pay attention and check with the service line that food was ready to go before serving it.

But Sara had just patted him on the shoulder. "It could have happened to anyone," she'd said.

Jose had given her a strange look—a silent *what was that?* Sara couldn't blame him. She felt like her legs had been swept out from under her when it came to Casey.

And Joey was far too preoccupied with his own problems to listen to Sara's. Every time she tried to bring it up, he'd assure her she'd figure it all out and pivot back to talking about how he would never be able to balance the filming schedule with his much less important duties of, oh, fighting fires and saving lives.

A new episode was starting and the theme song was playing, showing various clips of Dr. McHandsome striding handsomely down long hospital hallways, when there was another knock at the door.

Before Sara could peel herself off the sofa to answer it, the door opened.

She yelped and threw up her hands to shield her face from an inevitably attack by the intruder. When nothing happened, she peeked behind her hands and saw Joey standing in the doorway.

"You scared me!" she gasped, clutching her chest.

For as much as she'd complained about him recently—mostly only in her own head, but still—Joey really was movie star handsome. He could have his own show that aired right after the medical drama. Firefighter McHandsome—or something like that; the title might need a little more work.

He had dark curly hair that turned to loose waves when he brushed it out after his shower. His eyes were a bright turquoise. And the dimples bracketing his white smile still made Sara a little weak in the knees.

It was no wonder the casting director had noticed him in the frozen food section. Who wouldn't?

Sara was so busy letting her heart rate slow to normal and taking stock of him that it took her a second to recognize the deep frown pulling his lips down. His dimples were lost in the expression.

"What's going on?" she asked, setting her coffee cup on the end table and standing up. Crumbs from the sour cream and cheddar chips she'd been eating tumbled to the floor. "I didn't think I'd see you today."

He slammed the door behind him. The framed picture of Sara and her family standing in front of Little Bull on Opening Night rattled against the wall.

"The casting director banned me from the set."

"*Banned* you?" she asked with a frown. "What does that mean?"

"Banned. Like, a ban. Thou shalt not pass, y'know?"

"What did you do?"

Joey's eyes widened like Sara was crazy. "Nothing! Nothing, obviously."

"Why would they ban you for doing nothing?"

He threw his arms up angrily, his finger catching the cord of her blinds on the way down. The left side of the blinds lifted up, all askew. He growled as he straightened them back out. "I have no idea. No one would answer my questions."

Sara chewed on her lip, not sure what to say. This didn't make any sense. "Are you sure your scene didn't just get cut from the movie?"

He dropped onto the end of the sofa, chucking a throw cushion into the chair in the corner as he sunk down. "I know the difference between being cut and getting escorted off the set, Sara."

But did he?

This was his first movie after all. Maybe they'd decided he wasn't right for the part and told him as much.

Even that wouldn't make much sense, though. How could a handsome firefighter not be right for the part of a handsome firefighter?

"I'm just saying maybe they decided not to film the scene you were in," Sara offered helpfully. "I think that happens in movies a lot."

"I was *banned,*" he snapped. "Forbidden from returning. Escorted from the barricaded area. It had nothing to do with the movie and everything to do with me." He folded his arms across his chest, his biceps bulging as his fingers dug into his arms. "And there was no explanation."

Sara could think of a possible explanation or two. Like, if Joey had been as persistent with his line of questioning and excitement about the movie with other people as he had been for her. People may have grown annoyed.

Sara loved him, and she was still frustrated.

The L-word sneaking into her thoughts surprised Sara, but she decided now was not the time to investigate that slip-up. Not when Joey looked so dejected.

"So you're out of the movie? And they didn't explain why?"

"That's what I've been saying," he snapped.

"Okay," she mumbled. "Just trying to understand."

There was a long pause. And then he added, "...first time for everything."

Joey said the words so softly Sara almost didn't know if she'd heard him right.

By the time she was confident he'd said what he'd said, it felt too late to say anything about it. The silence between them stretched into an uncomfortable bridge Sara didn't know how to cross.

Joey tipped his head back and pinched the bridge of his straight nose between his thumb and forefinger. "It's all over. Before it could even begin."

"It's not *all* over," she said, curling her legs underneath her and facing him. "At least it wasn't your full-time job. There are still plenty of fires to put out, I'm sure."

Sara hated seeing Joey so upset. Usually, he was cheerful, chipper. He laughed at her jokes and could match her wit for wit. They had a great time together.

Well, they'd *had* a great time together. Before the movie had consumed Joey's every thought.

The more Sara thought about it, the more she couldn't help but be slightly... relieved. Maybe things could go back to normal now. He would be her McHandsome firefighter again. Preferably sans-dreams-of-fame-and-fortune.

"Could you at least pretend to be upset for me?"

Sara jolted at the sound of Joey's voice and looked over to see him staring at her, forehead creased in frustration. "I am upset!"

He snorted. "Could have fooled me. You look one second away from doing a happy dance."

"I do not! I was just thinking."

"About what?" he asked, eyebrow arching in a challenge.

"About how much I hate seeing you sad." *About how relieved I am this movie thing can be over.*

He narrowed his eyes. "I know you weren't really sick this morning."

"I never said I was sick."

"You certainly implied it."

"It was barely seven AM when you called. Being awake that early on your day off is the same as being sick."

"Every time I bring the movie up, you tune me out," he said, sitting up. "You knew I was excited about it, and you didn't care."

Sara shook her head. "No. I did care. But that doesn't mean I have to spend my one day off trying to be a background extra in a movie I couldn't care less about."

"I spent my one day off checking all of the fire alarms at Little Bull." His jaw was set, and he stared at her, waiting to see if she could top him. "And I always listen to your work problems. I know all of your employees by name. I could probably make the salsa myself."

Sara barked out a sarcastic laugh. "Yeah, right. You haven't been listening to me for a week."

"One week." He rolled his eyes. "Sorry, I focused on myself and my dreams for one week! What drama did I miss? A lettuce shortage?"

"Don't do that," she warned. "Don't minimize. There was a robbery. An actual crime. It had nothing to do with lettuce."

"Did you call the police?"

"No! If you'd been listening, you'd know it's one of the waitstaff stealing from me. I don't know who and I don't have proof. But you couldn't stop talking about your movie."

Joey's eyes widened in surprise, but he was nowhere close to conceding this argument. That was another thing the two of them had in common: neither wanted to be the first to admit they were wrong.

"I keep talking about the movie because you keep ignoring me. You're treating it like a joke, but it's serious to me." His eyes looked even bluer when he was angry.

"It's all you wanted to talk about, Joey! I had other things on my mind. I got bored. Sue me."

"Sorry my dreams aren't interesting enough for you. Not all of us can be 'renowned restauranteurs.'" He said the final word with a fancy flourish of his fingers, his face pulled into a mocking posh expression.

Sara groaned. "Oh my God, enough with Gavin. That was eons ago. And he is the worst! What is your deal with him?"

"I don't have a deal with him."

Somehow, Sara's ex-boss and longtime crush turned nemesis had become a sticking point in Joey's mind. Ever since Joey looked up a picture of him online after Sara ranted about how Gavin was a scourge on the earth, he had been weird about it. Every so often, he'd throw Gavin in Sara's face as if she was still into him.

To Sara, it seemed like Joey might be the one who was into him. There was no other explanation for the hang-up.

"I'm sure you didn't get bored talking food with him," Joey mumbled, arms crossed over his chest. "I bet he could hold your attention."

Sara wanted to scream. This was ridiculous. "Gavin tried to cheat on his girlfriend with me and then called in a favor to get a food critic to write a terrible review of my restaurant. I mean, it wasn't boring, I guess. But it wasn't exactly a good time."

She scooted to the edge of the sofa and dropped her head in her hands, speaking through her fingers.

"What does any of this have to do with right now?" she said. "We're off-track."

"This movie could have been my shot to do something more with my life."

"More than save lives and fight fires?" she yelped.

"To be more than the youngest firefighter on a small island! To actually accomplish something. Make a name for myself. And you never even cared."

Joey was only a rookie when Sara had met him, but he'd stopped complaining about the other guys teasing him a long time ago. He'd been the lowest man on the totem pole for a while, but as far as Sara was aware, that wasn't a big deal.

Maybe she didn't quite have the full lay of the land after all.

"I thought being a firefighter was what you wanted! Sorry I didn't catch on that being a movie star was your lifelong dream."

"Stop doing that!" He shouted, teeth gritted. "Stop acting like my dreams don't mean as much as yours."

"This wasn't your dream," Sara said, pursing her lips. The frustration and annoyance she'd been feeling for the last week was bubbling just under the surface. "Firefighter #4 in a made-for-TV movie was not your dream."

"It could have been the start of one." He spun away from the couch, pacing across the chevron rug in the middle of the room.

"Were you planning to take off for L.A. to pursue acting?"

"I don't know. Maybe. Who knows?"

"I can't exactly pick up Little Bull and bring it with me," Sara said. "Sorry I assumed you'd want to stay here with me."

Joey spun and pointed at Sara. "That. That's what I'm talking about. Everything is about you."

"Everything is about me?"

"I'm always helping you out. Going out of my way to support you and help your business."

Sara rolled her eyes. "Sorry you had to check my fire alarms one time, Joey. Next time I'll call the station and have someone else sent over if it's such a big deal."

"I don't mind doing it." He fisted his hands at his sides, his jaw tight. "I don't mind. I just... You could return the favor occasionally. I've been helping you for a year, but you couldn't be supportive for a week."

Sara didn't want his words to land, but they did.

Joey had a point. As much as she hated to admit it.

"Little Bull is my career," she countered anyway, not ready to concede. "But you don't see me talking your ear off about my indoor herb garden."

"Oh, nice. Compare me being in a movie to your single pot of dead basil. Real nice, Sara."

She winced. He was right about that, too. It was a low blow.

She was doing the thing her family always accused her of. The thing her dad had always warned her about. Speaking without thinking. Leading with her emotions.

She needed to take a deep breath. She needed a few seconds to think.

"I don't even know why I came here." Joey spun towards the door. "I knew you didn't care, but I thought you'd at least pretend."

Sara was still on the inhale part of her deep breath, her lungs filled with air. She had to force it all out fast to call after Joey before he could leave. "I do care. I said I was sorry!"

Joey turned around, his hand wrapped around the door, his turquoise blue eyes pinning her to the spot. "No, Sara. You didn't."

Then he was gone.

24

HOLLY

LATER THAT EVENING—SARA'S APARTMENT

It was Monday, so Holly knew Sara would be at home.

Getting her little sister off the couch and out of the house on her day off was like getting Alice to eat her spinach or Grady to wash behind his ears.

In other words, impossible.

She knocked twice. Her knuckles were still touching the wood on the second knock when the door wrenched open.

Sara's hair was pulled up in the messiest of all messy buns. Large chunks of hair had fallen out and were hanging around her face. And she had on her decades-old Christmas flannel pajama pants, the ones with little elves printed all over them.

Her eyes were wide, expectant. And when she saw Holly, her body sagged—but whether with relief or disappointment, Holly couldn't tell.

"Hey, Holls." Sara shuffled back to the couch and flopped down in the middle of what looked like a hoarder's nest. There were fleece blankets, empty fruit snack packets, and three different half-filled cups of soda and juice.

"What on Earth happened here?" Holly shut the door behind her and perched on the very end of Sara's sofa. She was afraid of what she'd find if she let herself sink into the cushions.

"Fight," Sara said, eyes glazed over as she stared intently at the television. It was a commercial for a spray mop. "With Joey. He won't respond to my calls."

"What a coincidence. That's why I'm here, too."

Sara turned to her, one eyebrow raised. "You got in a fight with Joey?"

She rolled her eyes at her little sister. "No. Pete."

"That makes more sense. What about?"

Holly wanted to tell Sara all about it. Truthfully, she wanted to tell anyone who would listen all about it. She needed a purge.

But she could not have a serious conversation with her sister when she looked like this. It was gross. And distracting.

"I feel like I should call the Red Cross to come in here. This place is a disaster."

"Rude," Sara said. "It's my lazy day. And I'm sad."

Holly stood up and held her hands out to Sara, pulling her from the couch and shoving her towards her bedroom. "Fix your hair and put on real pants. We need ice cream."

"We can order some," Sara said even as she pulled the ponytail holder out of her hair.

Holly took another look at the couch and wrinkled her nose. "You need to get off of this couch and out of this house. And so do I. We are hitting the town."

Downtown Nantucket

"I'm not sure why I wasted so many hours of my life standing in lines outside of bars and clubs," Holly said, taking a bite of her salted caramel waffle cone. "Hitting the town like this is way more fun. And delicious."

"The weather is perfect," Sara agreed, slouching back in the red metal chair outside of Sundae Best Ice Cream Parlor.

The clouds from the afternoon had lifted, so a few stars were visible in the dark blue night sky even with the glow of the downtown lights. There was a light breeze, but nothing a borrowed sweatshirt from Sara's closet couldn't handle.

Young women teetered on high heels towards the bars and clubs that were now buzzing down the block. It reminded Holly why she was happy to be in her slip-on sneakers and mom jeans. Those girls were one unexpected sneeze away from an ankle sprain.

The clock tower above the old church chimed eight o'clock. Holly couldn't help it—her thoughts flitted toward home. Alice would be asleep already, and Grady would be heading to bed.

Pete had come home from work early like he'd said he would, pizza in hand. He made it clear, through his body language rather than his words, that Holly didn't need to be at the house if she didn't want to be.

And since Holly didn't yet know if she was looking for an apology or prepared to give one, she decided that was probably best.

Sara leaned back in her chair, licking the drips from her cookies-and-cream waffle cone. "What say you we avoid our problems for a few more minutes, huh?"

"Agreed," Holly said, taking a bite out of her cone. Pete thought Holly was crazy for using her teeth to eat ice cream, but it was the only way to keep her lips clean. "Have you seen Eliza since they left the hospital?"

"I delivered some more freezer meals on Saturday. They should be set on frozen lasagna and breakfast burritos for a month, at least."

"Where were you when I had Alice and Grady?" Holly asked with a sigh. "We spent so much money on takeout when the kids were born. Pete knew even less about cooking back then than he does now, and I was exhausted."

"Hey, Eliza requested the freezer meals," she said. "I wish I was thoughtful enough to think of it on my own, but I'm not. Our oldest sister is just a good planner."

"That she is."

They sat in silence for a few minutes, licking their cones and watching people walk down the sidewalks.

Holly sometimes found it strange that she lived in a vacation destination. She spent every day of her life in a place some people looked forward to visiting all year long. So many people were probably deeply jealous of her life. And yet most of the time, Holly felt like she took it for granted.

Sara sighed. "That was a nice thirty seconds of avoiding our problems. But now you have your serious face on."

"Sorry. I suck."

"No, I'm already out of things to talk about anyway," Sara said. "You first."

Holly shook her head. "No, you. I've been a bad big sister recently. I've only been to see Eliza once. Maybe letting you go first will make me feel better."

"Always happy to assuage your guilt." Sara's shoulders sagged forward. "It's dumb. Well, actually, that's sort of the problem. Apparently, I'm not very supportive. Or attentive. Or caring."

Holly's expression must have revealed more than she'd intended because Sara promptly threw a napkin at her.

She held up one hand in surrender. "Sorry! I mean, it's true those are not the first three qualities people associate with you, but I'm sure that's not what you mean."

"It kind of is, actually. Joey got that part in the movie, and I was so busy being annoyed with him that I never got excited for him. Now, he's out of the movie and it's too late."

Holly froze.

Joey.

She'd completely forgotten about the threat Mr. Monroe had made.

"Wow, I really am a terrible sister," she said, pressing her palm into her forehead. She peeked around her arm at Sara's confused expression. "I sort of got into it with the casting director and his wife, and they said they were going to cut Joey from the movie. To sever ties with our family or something weirdly villainous like that."

Sara's mouth fell open. "What happened?"

"There was a fight, and—"

"You *fought* them?!"

"No! Grady did." Holly shook her head and took a deep breath. "Grady fought their son. He was being bullied and, thanks to Pete's cousin Rob, he decided to take things into his own hands."

"Good for him." Sara threw a fist of solidarity into the air. "Not great for Joey, admittedly. But good for Grady."

"No! No, God, no. Not good for Grady, either. I don't want him getting in fights."

Sara wrinkled her nose. "Would you rather he get beat up?"

"I'd rather he talk to me about what's going on."

"That's a big ask for a ten-year-old. I'm thirty-one and still no good at it." Sara licked a drip from the side of her cone. "Is that your problem then? Grady got in a fight?"

"More or less. Mostly more," Holly admitted. "Also, Pete's cousin is staying with us and he's horrible. He's lazy and a slob and sets a bad example for the kids."

"Hey, careful. This is starting to feel like a personal attack."

For the first time all day, Holly laughed. "Today was your day off. You get a pass."

"Much obliged."

"But every day is a day off for Rob. He has no ambition. I'm starting to think he'll never leave my couch."

"Have Pete tell him to hit the road."

Holly scoffed. "Pete likes having Rob around. I think it reminds him of when they were kids."

Sara bobbed her head back and forth. "I mean, I kinda get that. Life was easier when we were kids. Much less to worry about."

"Unless your delinquent second cousin shows up and leads you astray." Holly took a too-large bite of her ice cream, giving herself an instant brain freeze.

As soon as she had enough control of her motor functions to unpinch her face and open her eyes, she saw Sara staring at her, an eyebrow arched all the way to her hairline.

"What?"

"You cannot seriously be worried about Grady being led astray by one bad influence."

"Sure I can. Why not?"

"Do you remember the Frederickson family?" A smirk spread across Sara's face, her eyebrows wagging as Holly tried to jog her memory. "They moved into the rental three houses down for the entire year I was in sixth grade."

"Oh, okay, yeah. I was in eighth," Holly said, beginning to recall some details. "Danny Frederickson was so cute."

"And so much trouble! He stole cigarettes out of his mom's purse."

Holly laughed. "He made me try one, and I threw up."

"Made you try one?" Sara's expression said that was not how she remembered it. "From what I recall, you *asked* for one."

Holly's smile died on her lips. "I most certainly did not."

"Yes, you did!" Sara was having way too much fun with this. She used her dripping ice cream cone like a pointer, jabbing it in Holly's direction so cookies and cream splattered across the table. "You wanted to impress him so badly that you smoked your first-ever cigarette. It was up in our treehouse. When Mom asked why you threw up, you told her I punched you in the stomach."

Holly winced. "Okay. I might remember this a little."

"Bygones and whatnot," Sara said, waving a hand to dismiss the long-gone offense. "All I'm saying is, kids are impressionable. But they're also... unimpressionable."

Holly raised a brow. "What?"

"As soon as Rob is gone, Grady will forget all about him. Don't worry so much."

"Easier said than done," Holly said, echoing Sara's words from earlier.

Suddenly, her younger sister's smile turned devious. "I think I have an idea for how we can both forget and relax. For tonight at least."

"Oh no. What?"

"When Mom was moving out of the Howard house, I saved your old stash of movies from the donation pile. Along with a VHS player."

"My monster movies," Holly said in astonished recognition. "I forgot about those."

"Care to get another waffle cone and relive our youth?" Sara asked, wagging her brows.

Holly couldn't think of anything more out of character for her than binging on ice cream and watching B-rated monster movies. Which is why she promptly agreed.

They went back to Sara's place. Holly vacuumed under Sara's couch cushions while Sara fought with the VHS player, cursing the tangle of cords.

"This is why we invented streaming. So no one would have to deal with AUX cables ever again," she huffed when she finally dropped down on the sofa. After a second, she stiffened. "Where did I put my ice cream? That's probably melted by now."

Holly held out a bowl, Sara's ice cream cone overturned inside of it so it looked like a plated dessert from a fancy restaurant. "I saved it for you."

In an uncharacteristically sweet move for Sara, she reached out and patted Holly's hand twice. "You're the best."

"So are you," Holly smiled.

Suddenly, the screen burst to life in a grainy flash of black and green goo. A shrill scream echoed through the speakers. They both yelped and then dissolved into giggles.

Holly still felt slightly nauseous when she woke up in the morning. She didn't know if it was because she'd had two waffle cones and eaten half a box of Oreos dipped in peanut butter or if it was because she'd spent the night on Sara's lumpy couch.

"This is a truly awful couch," she called as she folded up her blankets and left them on the arm of the sofa. "Are the cushions stuffed with doll heads?"

Sara rounded the corner from the hallway, looking much more put together than she had yesterday. Her hair was smoothed back into a low ponytail, and she had on a pair of the black cigarette pants she always wore at work with a high-necked button-down tucked in.

"No, because I'm not a serial killer. What made you even think of that?"

"It's the only thing I could come up with to explain why this couch could be so lumpy. I thought maybe the doll hair could be the incredibly thin layer of padding."

Sara looked frightened. "No more monster movies for you. They make you weird."

Even though it was almost a mile out of the way, Sara insisted they stop at Two Birds Coffee for a croissant and a latte before she took Holly home.

"To thank you for a fun sister night," Sara explained, sliding her card across the counter. "I needed it."

Holly had needed it, too. More than she'd realized.

So many people thought the life of a stay-at-home mom was tedious at best and pathetic at worst.

On one hand, Holly could understand that. She was even guilty of it herself. As much as she idolized Shelly Frank's "easy" job parenting teenagers, she knew it wasn't real.

Kids always came with challenges, no matter what age. Holly didn't even want to imagine what trouble Grady and Alice would get up to in the years to come.

She'd have to be sure to warn them of the dangers of cigarettes. And following cute boys into treehouses.

But warning or no warning, some of this was inevitable, Grady was bound to get into his first fight at some point. It was a rite of passage. And if there was anyone in the world to punch—well, all things considered, the smug son of arrogant movie stars might've been a decent pick.

It'd be okay in the end. It always was.

Sometimes, you just had to say screw it, dip an Oreo into peanut butter, and remind yourself of that little fact.

Or have a sister to do the reminding for you.

So when Sara parked in front of Holly's house, Holly pulled her sister into a long hug.

Sara was squirming almost instantly. "This is getting mushy. No more sister days for another year, at least," she joked, trying to push Holly off. "It's too emotional."

Holly ignored her and kissed her cheek. "I love you."

"I love you, too," Sara muttered, shaking her head as she drove away from Holly's house.

Nothing had really changed in the Goodwin residence. Rob was still inside, Grady was still locked in a feud with the Monroe child, and Pete was still angry with her.

But Holly felt lighter.

She'd forgotten to take her keys with her last night, so she walked around the side of the house to hunt down the ceramic frog with the spare inside.

When she bent to pick up the moss-covered frog, she heard voices and stopped.

"...Hitting someone should never be about hurting them," Pete was saying. "I mean, if you do it right, it probably will hurt. But that shouldn't be your goal. It's a last resort. A way to disarm someone and protect yourself. Not something you do just because you're angry."

Holly crept to the corner of the house and peeked around the side. Pete and Grady were standing in the shade of the elm tree. Morning light slatted across the yard, golden and warm. Pete's dark hair had hints of red in it and Grady's was still mussed from where he'd slept on it last night.

"So I should only hit someone when I'm *not* angry?" Grady asked, cocking his head to the side.

Pete had his arms up in a boxing position, his feet spread in a wide stance. Grady was mirroring him, a small shadow of definition across his thigh and calf where he flexed.

Holly couldn't remember when Grady had grown into some actual muscle. It wasn't much, but it was more than the adorably dimpled spaghetti legs she'd remembered.

"Well," Pete said, dropping his arms and twisting his mouth to the side in thought, "I'm guessing you'll be angry if you have to hit someone. But that shouldn't be the *reason* you hit them. You should hit them because there is no other choice but to defend yourself. Does that make sense?"

"That's not what Rob said."

Holly's chest tightened. What had "Uncle Rob" said now?

"What did Rob say?" Pete asked.

"He said to hit people so they'd know not to mess with me. He said it was the law of the jungle. Or something."

Pete took two steps forward and knelt in front of Grady, grabbing his hand. "Standing up for yourself can be a good thing. I don't want anyone to pick on you, and I don't expect you to sit by and let it happen. But there are other ways to show people they shouldn't mess with you. We don't live in a jungle, do we?"

Grady shook his head.

"Right. We live in a community. And part of being in a community is learning how to get along with people."

"What if people don't want to get along with me?" Grady asked, his voice wobbling a bit at the end.

Holly wanted to run across the yard and curl him against her chest. But she knew she shouldn't interrupt. Pete was handling this situation perfectly.

"Then they aren't any kind of people I want to know, anyway," Pete said, ruffling their son's hair. "Because you're awesome. If they don't like you, it means they have bad taste."

Holly could feel emotion prickling the backs of her eyes. She spun around and walked to the front of the house before it could turn into full-on tears.

Pete loved their kids just as much as she did. It would serve them both well if she took a step back and let him lead the way from time to time.

Holly slid the key into the front door, but before she could turn it, the door opened.

Once again, she and Rob were standing on opposite sides of the threshold, looking at one another.

"Hi," she said, feeling slightly more sheepish than she had the last time they'd spoken.

"Hey." He shrugged his greeting because his hands were full.

Full of luggage.

His luggage.

Holly frowned. "Are you going somewhere?"

"Time to move on," he said, looking over her shoulder, eyes unfocused in the distance like he was a cowboy setting out on the Western Trail. "I've overstayed my welcome."

"No," Holly said on instinct, shaking her head, "that's not true. You don't have to—"

Rob chuckled. "You're nice, but you're a bad liar. I've overstayed and then some."

Okay, he was right. Holly couldn't deny it. She wanted Rob to leave. But that didn't mean she didn't feel bad about how they were leaving things.

Even if she didn't like Rob, Pete did. That meant something to her.

"Where will you go next?"

"I've been making calls and sending out emails all week, searching for a job on the mainland. Another buddy of mine—from prison," he added in a harsh whisper like it was a secret, "is working at a barber shop in downtown Boston. The owner is actually looking to hire felons. He's hoping to rehabilitate some of us, I guess. Either way, it's a good-paying gig, and I cut inmates' hair when I was locked up. I got pretty good at it."

"You've been applying for jobs?" All the times Holly had seen Rob sitting on the couch, scrolling through the new phone he'd just bought or surfing the internet on Pete's laptop, she'd assumed he was wasting time.

"Constantly," he said, his shoulders sagging. "Nobody is trying to hire someone with my track record. It's a tough market. So I have to jump on this while I can."

"Of course. That's great." Holly reached out and touched Rob's bare shoulder. He had on a tank top and the entire interaction was beyond awkward. "Congratulations."

Rob gave her a wide smile that actually reminded Holly of Pete. The two of them were just cousins—second or once-removed, she still hadn't figured out—but they had the same slightly turned-in upper lip.

"Listen," he said, dropping his luggage and leaning in, voice low, "I'm sorry if I got Grady in hot water. He's a sweet kid. I didn't want anyone messing with him."

"Neither do I. We can agree on that."

"When Petey and I were kids, I walloped too many kids to count for making fun of him." Rob clenched his jaw like the thought of it still made him angry. "He and Grady are so much alike. It was instinct. And I screwed things up."

For the countless time that morning, Holly's heart clenched. The last week had done a number on her, and she felt on the verge of tears at the smallest things. Like Rob defending Pete.

Holly could picture it. She'd loved Pete immediately when she'd met him, but he was always a little off-beat. A unique soul, someone who was easy for others to pick on. Kind of like Grady.

Rob's advice, while terrible, had come from a good place. A loving place.

"You didn't screw everything up," she said. "Grady will be just fine. Believe me."

A cab pulled up along the curb, and Rob grabbed his bags. "That'll be my ride. I already told the boys bye, but give Grady an extra hug for me. And Alice, too."

"I will," Holly said. "Do you need anything for the road? A snack or a drink?"

Rob chuckled like the thought was funny. "I'll be fine. Thanks for everything, though."

As she watched Rob climb into his cab, Holly realized he hadn't been with them all that long. Ten days wasn't so much in the grand scheme of things. Just a blip.

A blip she wasn't keen to re-live anytime soon, of course.

Holly watched Rob clamber in the cab and slip away. Then, sighing, she walked through the house to the back door.

In the yard, Pete was letting Grady box against his palms and Alice was soaring on her swing set, feet bare, hair flying behind her.

The kids ran over and gave Holly a hug as soon as they saw her, squeezing her like she'd been gone for a week instead of one night.

"Where were you?" Alice asked, clutching Holly's leg.

She patted her hair and looked at Pete as she answered. "I went to Aunt Sara's. The two of us needed a sister's night."

"That's nice," Pete murmured.

"Necessary, too." Holly looked at her husband meaningfully.

"I'm sorry I didn't listen to you about—" Pete started.

"I shouldn't have made you feel like—" Holly said.

They both stopped and laughed. Then Holly grabbed Pete's hand. "You're a great dad. A wonderful partner. A hard worker. I'm sorry if I ever made you feel like you weren't."

"You're a great mom. A wonderful partner. A hard worker." Pete wrinkled his nose. "I'm recycling your compliments, but I really mean them. I'm sorry I didn't listen to you about Rob. He can be... messy."

Holly waved her hand. "It's fine. I get it. He was trying to be nice. He just missed the mark."

"He is known for that," Pete laughed. "He has good intentions."

He pulled Holly against his side and kissed her temple. She curled her face against his chest. "I'm sorry," he said again.

"Me, too."

Maybe sometime soon they'd unpack the last ten days. But it didn't need to happen today.

For now, Grady was chasing a squealing Alice through the yard, a grasshopper clutched in his hand. The sun was shining. Her husband was holding her close.

And they were okay.

They were all okay.

25

SARA

LITTLE BULL RESTAURANT

Sara came in the back door of Little Bull and flipped on the lights.

The stainless-steel worktops shimmered, still clean and lemony from the night before. Knives hung from the magnetic strip along the wall in order from biggest to smallest. All of the mixing bowls, pots, and utensils were stacked neatly in their shelves.

Part of being a chef was coming in and mucking up a kitchen, not being afraid to get your hands, apron, and the walls dirty. But Sara also loved the way it felt when everything was in its place.

It was one reason why she liked to come in and open up so early. It gave her time to enjoy the view before the sink was full of soaking dishes and the counters were streaked after countless wipe downs during meal prep.

The other reason was that she didn't have anything waiting for her at home.

Joey hadn't texted her since he'd stormed out the day before. Sara hadn't texted him, either, but texting had never been her thing. Even more than in real life, she managed to put her foot in her mouth via text. It was better for her if the person she was talking to could hear her intonations and see her facial expressions. They tended to get less angry that way.

Sara turned on the radio she'd mounted into the wall. Usually, it was too loud to hear anything over the shouts of the service line, but when she was alone, she liked to dance around.

It was still set to the R&B station Jose liked, but Sara decided to keep it there. A little rhythm and blues could do her soul well.

The chef's special was usually decided on Sunday night, but Sara had been distracted. She'd planned to figure it out Monday, but then Joey and Holly and monster movies had all come demanding her attention one after the next. Sara had been swamped doing nothing and stressing out about it.

She was standing in front of the pantry, swaying along with a song about everlasting love, when she heard a click.

It sounded like the back door latching closed.

Sara paused, waiting to hear someone on her staff call out her name or announce themselves, but when no one did, she stepped out of the pantry and poked her head around the door.

The kitchen was still empty and glittering. Not a sign of anyone.

"Hello?"

She cringed as soon as she said it. The girl in the horror movie she watched with Holly last night had done the exact same thing, calling out after a weird noise in an empty building. And look how that ended for her.

So she shrugged it off and went back into the pantry.

Her produce supplier would be coming just before lunch, which was good because the potato supply was looking scarce. She also left

Annica a note on the whiteboard to make her apple Sharlotka cake before the last of the Granny Smiths turned.

What else needed doing?

Sara was bent over the pantry's lower shelves, taking stock of Little Bull's available fruits, when her phone rang.

She yelped and stood up so quickly she smacked her head on the shelf just above her. A can of tomato paste clunked off and rolled across the floor.

Her phone was still on the counter next to the door, so Sara stumbled out of the pantry, rubbing the back of her head.

The wave of disappointment when she saw Jose's name on the screen made her realize how much she'd hoped it would be Joey.

"What's going on?" she asked in way of a greeting.

"What are you doing at the restaurant so early?"

Sara spun around, scanning the room for any sign of Jose or a camera. "How do you know that?"

"I just drove by. The light is on."

She relaxed slightly, relieved to know she wasn't being watched. No more horror movies for a while, she decided. "I'm working."

"It's three hours before lunch opening. No one needs to be working yet."

"I'm trying to decide on the chef special."

"I thought I was doing the special this week?"

"Oh!" She suddenly remembered telling Jose on Thursday night that the special was all his. His salmon wrapped in flaky pastry and covered in a white wine sauce had been so good Sara felt like she was hallucinating after a single bite.

"It's okay if you changed your mind," he said quickly. "Or if you weren't serious."

"I was serious! Your salmon wellington was delicious."

"Thanks, but if you don't want to serve it, I get it. No hard feelings."

"Jose, I want to serve it," Sara said, enunciating each syllable clearly. Jose hadn't come to Little Bull with a ton of restaurant experience, but he was a natural talent and he learned quickly.

"This week?" he asked, still hesitant.

"This week! Starting tonight," Sara said. "I've just been out of it this weekend. I completely forgot. But yes, you are doing the chef's special this week."

"I can postpone until next week if you want," he offered. "I still want you to try the cream sauce one more time. I adjusted the ratio of cream to white wine, and I think it's good but—"

"It's great," Sara said, cutting him off. "It was great last week and I'm sure it's even better now. I'm writing 'Jose's Salmon Wellington' on the special's board as we speak."

He sighed. "Thanks, Sara."

"Thank you," she said. "You just saved me the trouble of throwing something together."

"It probably would have been better than what I'm—"

"No! It will be great."

He chuckled. "Your specials always do so well. It's a lot to live up to."

"You'll do amazing. The people will demand it become a menu item, I'm sure," Sara said.

Truly, Sara wouldn't mind adding a menu item she hadn't come up with. She loved the idea of promoting other chefs in her kitchen. Of letting Nantucket know she had a talented team working alongside her.

"Is the pastry already done? Is there anything you need me to prep?" she asked.

"Nope. I took care of everything last night."

Just in case he was wrong, she pulled open the refrigerator and saw the pastry sheets stacked in plastic wrap and ready to go.

"Oh, okay. Great."

Sara tried to hide her disappointment. Idle hands were doing her no favors at the moment.

At least she could still run the cash-out to the bank. That would give her something to do.

As if he could read her mind, Jose continued, "I also cashed out the register and took the cash to the bank. I know you said to leave the envelope in your desk drawer, but I wanted to try out the new auto-teller robot. It worked super well."

Scratch that. Jose had done everything.

"I'll check the bank statement and make sure that robot didn't steal our money," she joked.

"I already texted Patrick this morning and he said the accounts looked normal. Go home and sleep in," Jose said. "That's what I'd be doing right now, but we ran out of diapers at home. I actually just pulled in the drive, and I can hear the baby crying from outside. I've gotta go."

Jose hung up without a formal goodbye, which Sara didn't mind. Jose was her right-hand man. They were comfortable with one another.

Though right now, she wished he was a little less dependable. She could use the distraction of getting lost in dinner prep.

She opened and closed cabinets for a few minutes and contemplated trying her hand at a fun new dessert. But Annica was too good at her job for Sara to even pretend she could out-bake her pastry chef.

So, with nothing to do in the kitchen—and really, more as a way to keep herself from calling Joey than anything else—Sara left her phone on the counter and took off out the back door to go for a walk.

Almost immediately, this proved to be a bad idea.

The morning was beautiful. The air was crisp and humid. Dew stuck to the grass and glimmered in the soft morning sunlight. But Sara's head was stuffed with too many thoughts. Troublesome, inconvenient thoughts.

Could Joey have been right about everything?

Did Sara ignore him? Did she take his dreams less seriously than her own?

And did that stem from her not taking him seriously, or from jealousy?

If Joey had been right about his "big break," he might've taken off and left Sara behind. Nantucket wasn't exactly known for its acting scene, after all.

Maybe Sara hadn't supported him because she was afraid she'd have to let him go.

The cobblestone sidewalks of downtown were still empty. The shop windows were dark, signs flipped to closed. Most of them wouldn't open until mid-morning when more tourists were out and about.

There were no people to watch or any retail therapy to distract Sara from the pulsing reality that she hadn't been a very good partner.

Her walk took her north down Main Street, past Two Birds Coffee with a wave to Chris through the front window, and back around the block where the business district gave way to residential.

Sirens wailed nearby, no doubt coming from the shoreline. Downtown was close enough to the water and the marina that sirens were common ambience. Beachgoers cut their feet on rocks or stepped on lion's mane jellyfish and then called the emergency line in a panic.

She passed kids kicking soccer balls in the front yard. She passed wives kissing husbands and mothers kissing children as everybody dispersed out into the world to enjoy the day.

A few of the locals gave her odd looks as she meandered down the road, and it took her a second to realize that the furrowed brows were aimed at her chef's jacket. She probably should have taken it off before she left the kitchen, but Sara forgot she was wearing it more times than not.

These days, it felt like a second skin.

"Why'd you stop catering?" Sara had asked her mom one day when she was a little girl.

She was watching her mother break down a whole chicken on a large wooden chopping block. There was nothing prim or proper about the way Mom snapped bones and cut tendons. It was hard, physical work, all done with a razor-sharp knife.

Sara was in awe.

"Because I wanted to be a mom," she had said. "Daycare was expensive. Catering had long hours. And weekends were always hectic."

"But you love to cook."

"I love you more." She'd winked at Sara over the splayed open chicken carcass in front of her.

Turned out that Sara loved cooking just like her mom did. And through culinary school, through terrible jobs at terrible restaurants, through Gavin Crawford and all the headache he'd brought into her world, she'd kept on doing it.

Kept on chopping tendons. Kept on snapping bones.

And what'd her mom do the whole time? Supported her, of course. Mae Benson was nothing if not supportive—even when it came to her headstrong youngest daughter.

Why couldn't Sara do that for Joey?

It wasn't so hard. She could've just listened. She could've forgone her peanut-butter-dipped Oreos and gone to see him in action instead. She could've told him he could do whatever he wanted, and if that was fighting fires, then that was all well and good, but if he wanted to act instead, then he should and he could and he would.

No matter what he chose, she'd keep right on loving him.

There it was again—the L-word. It felt a little easier to think this time around.

The exercise didn't do as much to clear Sara's head as she'd hoped, but it did kill an hour. And she did feel slightly better.

That didn't last long. As she rounded the corner back onto Main Street, Sara saw the fire trucks.

They were parked in front of Little Bull.

When Sara looked up and saw dark smoke spiraling up from the rooftops, bruising the sky, she broke into a sprint. And when she got to the edge of the gathering crowd, she kept right on running. Straight into the mayhem.

Two large canvas hoses lay across the ground, feeding into the open front door of Little Bull. A few firemen in soot-covered gear drank bottled water on the sidewalk.

"What's going on?" she asked, breathless.

One of the men looked over at her and then picked up a radio. "Owner has been located outside the building."

Sara didn't recognize the man, but he clearly recognized her. Sara looked around for Joey's mop of bedraggled hair, but didn't see him.

"Is there anyone else inside?" he asked her.

Sara shook her head. "No. What happened?"

The man with the thick mustache who had radioed in to announce where Sara was looked up at the building. "A fire. In the kitchen."

Sara stared at him, waiting for more information. But it didn't seem like he had anything else to say.

"What started it? I was just in there. I didn't have the ovens on or anything. I wasn't even cooking anything."

"Coulda been anything," the man said with a shrug. "You'll get the report when we're done."

"I was alone inside. I've been gone for less than an hour. When did this start?"

"You'll get the report when the scene is secure," he repeated.

"When will that be?" Sara looked down at her wrist even though she wasn't wearing a watch. "I'm supposed to open in two hours."

The man lowered his water bottle and turned to Sara slowly. "Sorry, hon. That's not going to happen. Not today."

"When?"

"Not for a while, I'd guess." He shrugged again. Sara's heart squeezed.

"How long is 'a while'?"

He took another long drink of water. "However long it takes for repairs. A couple weeks?"

Without another word, Sara turned and ran through the front door, the fireman shouting after her.

He had to be wrong. There had to have been some mistake. Sara had just seen Little Bull and it was fine, it was good, it was great. Jose's special was ready to go and Annica was going to make apple Sharlotka.

Sure enough, the front of house looked untouched. For a second, Sara convinced herself the firemen had made a mistake.

Then she noted the thick haze in the air and the smell of smoke. She threw an arm over her mouth and coughed.

Sara had helped her mom after the inn fire last year, and they'd had to scrub, wash, and sanitize every nook, and cranny in the entire house. All this time later and Mom still found the occasional soot smudge they'd missed.

It would take weeks for this smell to clear out of here.

She pressed forward, moving towards the swinging double doors into the kitchen.

The circular port holes were dirty, impossible to see through. And just as Sara was gathering the energy to push the door open, it swung towards her.

She lurched back to avoid being hit in the face with the door, and instead found her face pressed firmly into the front of a fireman's suit.

"Sara?"

She recognized Joey's voice and looked up. She couldn't see much beyond his eyes. They were a bright blue, the whites around rimmed in red.

"What are you doing here?" Joey started pushing Sara towards the front door.

"Wait. I want to see!" she argued.

Joey kept a firm grip on her arm. "No, you don't. Not right now."

"Is it bad?" she asked.

Joey hesitated long enough Sara didn't think he was going to answer.

When he did, his voice was gentle. "It's not good."

Twenty minutes later, the firemen on the sidewalk were still ripping into one another about whose fault it was that Sara had raced past them and into a smoldering building. And Sara had the preliminary report in her hands.

Electrical ground fault, they were blaming. Sneaky little bugger.

"The fire seems to have started in the wall behind the refrigerator," the mustachioed fireman said. He'd given Sara his name at some point, but she couldn't remember it. "We'll know more in the coming days. In the meantime, you'll need to close down for repairs and clean-up."

Joey held her hand as the news was delivered. The drama between them didn't seem to matter in that moment. Sara was just glad to have him there.

"Luckily," the man continued, "no one was hurt. That's what is important. You and your employee made it out safely."

Sara frowned. What employee? There hadn't been anyone else in the restaurant with her.

But she was too overwhelmed and exhausted to follow up. It was probably just a slip. Nothing to worry about.

"We'll take you on a *guided* walkthrough of the restaurant here in the next half hour," the man said. "Guided. One more time: that's a *guided* walk."

"Right," Sara murmured. "Guided."

Grimacing, the man stomped away.

"Sorry I ran into a burning building," Sara said to Joey once he was gone.

"Not your best move," he admitted.

"And sorry I embarrassed you in front of your friends."

Joey smiled. "It's okay."

He was forgiving her so easily. Somehow, that only made everything worse.

Sara groaned. "Today has been a terrible day."

Joey smoothed a hand over Sara's back, rubbing his palm in small circles that did little to ease the tension. "Does that mean I should wait to tell you the other bad news? Or would you rather hear it all right now?"

Sara waved him on. "Lay it on me."

"Are you sure? I don't want to overwhelm you when—"

"Tell me," she said. "Is the building beyond being saved? Will I have to scrap everything?"

"No, no," he said. "Nothing like that. It just that... I was the first person inside the building and—"

"You were?"

He nodded. "I heard the call come in, and I freaked out. I called you three times on our way over, but you didn't answer."

"I left my phone inside," she said, hitching a thumb over her shoulder.

Joey leaned sideways and pulled Sara's phone out of his back pocket. "I know. I found it on the counter."

"Thanks." Sure enough, she had three missed calls from Joey. She'd been waiting for him to call all night and when he finally did, she'd missed it.

"No problem. But anyway," he said, "I was looking for you, and I went to your office, but there was a shelf blocking the door."

"A shelf?"

"One of the steel shelves fell off the wall and lodged against the door. It wouldn't open."

"My shelves fell down?" Sara pressed her palms against her temples and rubbed. "Of course they did. There's a fire. I don't know why I keep assuming there won't be much damage. How bad is it?" She thinks about the question and shakes her head. "Actually, don't tell me. I'll see for myself soon enough."

Then she frowned. "Was that the bad news?"

"Afraid not."

Sara took a deep breath, trying to ready herself for whatever Joey was going to say.

"I moved the shelf out of the way, and as soon as I did, the door hurled open and someone fell at my feet."

Sara gasped. "Who was it? Are they okay?"

Joey laid a hand on her shoulder and squeezed. "I thought it was you at first, but it was a younger kid. He said his name was Casey."

"Casey was inside?" Sara frowned. "He doesn't have a key. And he is on waitstaff. He doesn't need to show up until we open for service. Why would he have been in there?"

"Isn't he the employee you've been having the issue with?" Joey asked, not waiting for Sara to answer. "He's fine. And I don't think he set the fire, but I guess we'll find out. But yeah, he was in your office."

"That doesn't make any sense," Sara said, shaking her head. "I was alone in the kitchen."

As she spoke, she remembered the noise she'd heard in the pantry.

The sound of the back door latch clicking closed.

Had Casey come in and gone to her office without her knowing? It was certainly possible.

But why?

"I went into the office to make sure you weren't in there and your desk drawers were open," Joey continued. "It looked like he'd been rifling through your stuff."

Realization hit Sara all at once. "Casey was looking for the cash-out from last night. I always have Jose leave it in my desk on Monday nights when I'm off."

Joey straightened, his hand tensing on her back. "Do we need to pat him down? No way is he walking out of here with your money."

"No, Jose took the money to the bank for me last night. But Casey wouldn't have known that."

Her conversation with Casey that day in her office, when he'd been so defensive and offended by her accusation, made Sara feel nauseous.

He was lying right to her face. And he had the audacity to make her feel bad for even accusing him.

Not to mention he'd been inside the restaurant with her. Bold enough to steal while she was literally in the room next door.

Joey relaxed. "Well, he's still giving his statement in the back if you want to confront him. But if you don't want to, it can wait. Today has been a lot already."

Sara slid from the bench and stood up, shaking out her limbs. "No, I want to do this now. I need to."

"You sure?"

"Extremely."

He nodded. "I'll come with you."

"Thanks, Joey." Sara smiled as best she could, losing herself for a moment in the sweetness of Joey's expression.

He was worried about her. Sara was worried about herself, too. But it felt nice to know he cared.

"...But I think I should do this alone."

"Are you sure?"

Guilt twisted Sara's stomach. "I do want you there with me during the walkthrough. If you can stay?"

"Of course I can. Anything you need," he said. No hint of bitterness in his voice, even though Sara felt like he had every right to be bitter.

Maybe it wasn't the best time, but Sara couldn't hold it in another second to add, "I'm sorry, by the way. About not being supportive. Of you. With the movie."

So maybe her delivery needed some work. But the sentiment was there.

Joey's mouth opened and closed, probably surprised by the sudden shift in the conversation. "We can talk about this later, Sara."

She shook her head. "No, I want to do that now, too. I could have died in there. I mean, probably not. I'm sure I would have made it out."

"You would have." Joey's voice was tense, eyes narrowed. "I would have made sure of it."

"But still," she continued, "I don't want to fight anymore. Because I was wrong. I should have been more supportive."

Joey took a deep breath. "I always thought I'd celebrate the day I heard you say, 'I was wrong.' This is a little more bittersweet than I expected, though, because I was wrong, too."

"About what?"

"About Casey. You were right about him. And I wasn't listening."

Sara waved her hand. "I trusted him when he told me he didn't do it. That's on me."

"Your instinct was right, though. And if I'd been listening, we could have talked about it. You probably would have figured out he was lying to you."

"It's fine," Sara said, laying a hand on Joey's hand. "This was my apology, after all. You're kind of stealing my thunder."

Joey laughed. "Fine. Then you go deal with Casey before he gets sent home, and when you come back, it'll be my turn to apologize."

Just like Joey said, Casey was standing in the alley behind Little Bull. He had a foil blanket over his shoulders even though the morning was giving way to warmer weather. When he looked up and saw Sara walking towards him, his eyes widened.

He looked like a rabbit, waiting to see if it was in danger and needed to run or if it could carry on with its business.

All at once, he decided which route to take and rushed towards Sara, arms outstretched. "I'm so glad you are okay!"

Sara didn't say anything. Casey kept talking, too nervous to stop.

"I saw your car in the back. I wanted to come in and talk to you. About last week. I wanted you to know it's all water under the bridge. I forgive you. But you weren't inside. So, I was waiting in your office, and the fire alarms went off. It was just so—"

"Fake," Sara finished for him, stepping outside the range of his hug and crossing her arms. "Don't lie to me, Casey. I know what you were doing."

He frowned. "What do you mean?"

"It means you weren't going to find me hiding in my top desk drawer," she said.

Casey blinked. "I don't understand—"

"But my desk is where you expected to find the cash-outs from last night. Right?"

Casey's cheeks went pink. "I don't know what you're talking about. I saw the fire and came in to help, and—"

Sara held up a finger. "I thought you came in to apologize."

"I did!"

"Then when did you see the fire exactly?"

Casey threw up his hands. "I don't know. It's a blur. I went to your office to talk to you and—"

"Which was it, Casey? Were you already inside to try and talk with me when the fire started or did you see the fire and come to rescue me?"

His mouth tightened. Sara knew she had him.

"And what did you expect to find in my desk drawers?"

Casey stepped away from her. "This is unbelievable."

"It really, really is."

"I don't have to take this." Casey dropped the foil blanket on the bumper of the truck and stood tall. "I know the kind of person I am."

"I see the kind of person you are, too," Sara said. "You're a liar and a thief. And as of this moment, unemployed. You're fired."

"You don't have any proof!" he sputtered. "I can fight this. I will—"

"Just leave." Sara was too tired to waste any more breath on someone she couldn't trust. "I'm not pressing charges, so count yourself lucky."

With that, she turned on her heel and marched back around the building.

God, that felt good.

By the time she got back to where Joey was waiting for her on the sidewalk, all Sara could do was press her forehead against his chest and take deep breaths. He smelled like smoke and soot, but he also smelled like him. Woodsy and spicy. Comforting.

"I'm sorry," he said, smoothing a hand down her hip.

"For that ridiculous conversation I just had or something else?"

"Both," Joey said.

"So am I," she repeated. "For everything."

"Hey. This is my apology now, remember?"

Sara chuckled weakly. "Sorry."

Joey clicked his tongue. "You just can't help yourself, can you?"

"Sor—" She caught herself, laughed, and zipped her lips closed with her fingers. "Okay. Your turn. Go."

Joey took a deep breath. "I didn't listen to you, and you were right. That kid was stealing from you. I'm sorry."

"He was in the restaurant with me." Sara shivered. "He snuck in while I was in the pantry. I heard him, but I didn't know it was him."

"Maybe now you'll listen to me and start locking the back door when you're inside alone."

Sara pulled away and looked up at Joey. "I thought this was your apology. Why am I getting a lecture?"

He kissed the top of her head. "Because I love you, Sara Benson. And I want you to be safe."

Sara leaned away from him, eyes misty. "I love you, too."

He smiled, his movie star dimples making an appearance. "I promise to listen to you more."

"And I promise to support you more," Sara agreed. "I think it's amazing I'm dating a guy who literally saves people's lives for his job, so I never imagined that maybe you'd have other dreams."

"I like being a firefighter, but—"

"People can have more than one dream," Sara said.

Joey nodded.

"And whatever your dreams are, I promise to pay attention to them from now on."

Joey smiled. "Thanks. But I can also admit I may have ever so slightly, *perhaps*, gone overboard with the movie."

"You were excited."

"Yeah," he agreed. "But I may have been a little annoying."

"A lot annoying," the firefighter with the mustache said as he passed by right at that moment.

"A lot annoying," Joey amended, kicking a rock at the man's heels. "I'm sorry."

"It's okay. No more apologies necessary," Sara said. "I did like the promises, though."

"You have more promises?"

Sara nodded. "I promise to never watch the McFirefighter show they are making as a spin-off to the medical drama in front of you. I'll still watch it, obviously. But not when you're around."

Joey groaned. "I hate that I even know that exists. It's going to get everything wrong."

Sara laughed. "Exactly. I'll never speak of it again."

"Deal," he said, rubbing his chin as he thought. "Okay, and I promise to hand-deliver lattes to you whenever I can on your days off. That way you don't blow your life savings on delivery fees."

"I think I'm single handedly paying Chris' rent at this point," Sara sighed.

Joey squeezed Sara's waist, pulling her even closer. "I promise to love you as long as you'll let me."

Sara's throat suddenly constricted, and she decided to blame it on smoke inhalation. "It was my turn to make a promise."

"Okay, so make one."

"No way. Yours was better," she said.

Then he kissed her again, or maybe she kissed him—she wasn't quite sure. It didn't really matter much. All she knew as that at some point, they were kissing, and then they weren't.

Then Joey was standing at her side and taking her hand in his. "You ready to see the damage?"

Sara tightened her grip on his fingers.

She didn't think she'd ever be ready to see Little Bull in ruins, even partial ruins.

But with Joey by her side, she was as ready as she'd ever be.

"Let's go."

26

BRENT

EVENING—THE SWEET ISLAND INN

It was evening in Nantucket, fireflies blinking in and out of bushes, the sky slowly filling with stars.

But it looked like high noon at the Sweet Island Inn.

The lights the film crew brought were incredibly high-powered. Brent only had to catch them in his peripherals for his vision to be blurred and spotty for the next few blinks.

"Don't look at those lights," he warned Susanna.

She was playing with a stuffed rabbit, swinging it by the ears as she spun in circles in the grass. The second he cautioned her, she stopped and whirled around in search, eyes wide. "Which lights?"

"Now you've done it," Rose laughed. "She's going to go blind because you told her *not* to look at the lights."

"I meant, I'm ordering you to look right at the lights, Suz," Brent hurriedly corrected. "Look right at them and nowhere else."

Susanna didn't get the joke. When she couldn't figure it out, she ran over and collapsed next to where Holly and Alice were sitting on a picnic blanket in the grass.

"Good save," Rose said, wrapping her arm through Brent's.

"One of these days, I'll be as wise as you."

"I've had more practice being a parent. You'll catch up just fine." She tugged on his arm, trying to pull him down onto the blanket she'd packed. "Actually—"

Before Brent could sit down, he saw a little blonde head run across the gravel driveway. His sister, Eliza, wasn't far behind. "Watch out! Winter," she called out. "Be careful on the rocks."

Her newest daughter—and Brent's newest niece—was swaddled, safe and snug, in a floral wrap carrier around Eliza's chest.

"Oh, Eliza is here. I've barely seen her since Summer was born," Brent said, squeezing Rose's fingers. "Is it okay if I—?"

Rose waved him off with a smile. "Of course. I'll be here watching the action."

He could hear the sarcasm in her voice. Dominic and Mom had invited everyone out to see the first shots of the movie being filmed on location at the Sweet Island Inn. But so far, the cast and crew had been inside the entire time. There wasn't much to see. Even some of the lookie-loos from town had left when the excitement didn't pick up.

Brent didn't mind, though. He enjoyed it just being the family.

Dominic seemed to enjoy that, too. Right when everyone had first arrived, someone came up and asked Dominic for his autograph. He'd looked like he wanted to evaporate on the spot.

He'd smiled and signed the book, but then he and Mom had moved further away from the inn, out of sight. Brent could still see them hiding in the shade of the tulip trees.

Eliza was struggling to pull a blanket from her tote bag. Brent jogged over to help. He fanned the blanket out to lay it in the grass and Winter ran under it, squealing with delight as the blanket fell over her head.

"Thanks for the help, I guess?" Eliza smiled and shrugged. "Even if I can't sit, at least Winter is content."

"Content until my arms get sore," Brent laughed. He flicked the blanket up, wind catching under it, and let it drift slowly back over Winter's head. "Where's Oliver?"

Eliza groaned and pressed a hand to her forehead. "Trying to clean our car seat cover out with wet wipes. Don't ask."

Brent wrinkled his nose. "Gross."

"Yes. Babies are gross," Eliza agreed. "But wonderful, too. And exhausting. And cute. And loud."

"You're really selling me on this whole baby thing. Where do I sign up?"

Thankfully, before Brent's arms could get too tired, Winter saw Alice and Susanna running out to where Mae and Dominic were sitting. She toddled along after them.

Eliza opened her mouth to say something, but Brent shook his head. "She'll be fine. Mom'll watch her. That's what grandmas are for."

"That's what Mom always says. But sometimes I think she's lying. I mean, I'd get sick of all of those kids crawling all over me all the time." Eliza winced. "Is that a bad thing to admit?"

Brent held Eliza's hand for support as she dropped down onto the blanket, her other hand clutching Summer, who was snoozing against her chest.

He sat down next to her, legs stretched out into the grass. "I don't think it's bad. Honestly, I'm the same way. Holly has always been the maternal one in the family. No offense to you," he said, gesturing to Eliza and Summer.

"None taken. You're right. Holly was always like a second mom to us."

"I didn't think I liked kids at all until I met Susanna. Well, and Grady. And Alice. And Winter and Summer," Brent added quickly. "But you know what I mean."

Eliza laughed. "I know what you mean. It's different when it's your own kid."

Brent took care of Susanna every day. He helped cook her food and change her clothes. He gave her baths and read her stories before bed. But it was still strange to hear someone say she was "his kid."

"She is my kid, huh?" he said, mostly rhetorically. "It's still weird that she like... belongs to me."

"As much as any kid belongs to their parents," Eliza said. "Or vice versa."

Brent frowned. "What does that mean?"

Eliza looked down at Summer and smiled. "Kids are people, too. They belong to themselves as much as they belong to us. We take care of them and clean up after them, but they still have their own thoughts and feelings."

Brent nodded, and Eliza continued almost like she was talking more to herself than to him. "They pick favorite books without telling us and find new favorite foods. And one day, they grow up and leave, and they hardly belong to us at all anymore."

"Whoa," Brent said, holding up both hands, palms out. "That got unexpectedly deep."

"Sorry. I haven't had normal adult conversation in a couple weeks. I think I've forgotten how," she admitted.

"Well, you've got me worried now," Brent said. "Should I be requesting college brochures for Susanna?"

Eliza laughed. "Sorry to send you into an existential spiral."

"It's okay. I was due for one."

But truthfully, the same thought—maybe in a few less words—had been on Brent's mind all week.

Mom had always belonged to Brent, in a strange way.

He knew she put on her blinker two blocks before she turned. He knew she used a binder clip to get the very last drops out of every toothpaste bottle. He swore he'd be able to pick her cooking out of a line up ten times out of ten without fail.

And he had never wondered if there was more to her.

Now, he knew for a fact that there was.

As much as Mae Benson was his mom, she was her own person, too. With thoughts and a life beyond the bounds Brent knew.

It shouldn't be a surprise to him that Susanna would be that way.

And so would everyone else, for that matter.

He looked around the lawn at all of his family.

Sara and Joey were sitting in the back of Joey's truck with beers in their hands. Sara's white shirt was smudged with soot at the collar from that morning's fire at Little Bull.

Pete was bent over a book, helping Grady follow the instructions to fold a piece of printer paper into an airplane. Holly reclined behind them, watching the proceedings with a smile.

Oliver was coming up the gravel driveway with his sleeves rolled up. Winter, Alice, and Susanna nipped at his heel. Whenever they got close, he spun around and growled at them like a monster, sending the three girls squealing and scurrying away.

Mom and Dominic, now grandkid free, were walking hand-in-hand through the trees, making their way to the beach.

And then there was Rose.

She had her legs stretched out in front of her, ankles crossed. Here hands were folded over her stomach and she was leaning back against the cooler full of sandwiches and sodas and fruit Brent had brought from work. None of the clients he'd taken out on the boat had eaten much, so he had plenty of leftovers to get rid of.

Brent knew Rose better than anyone, but even he had no idea what she was thinking at that moment. Her lips were pulled up into a soft smile as she watched an actor cross in front of the Sweet Island Inn's open front window. The camera was positioned just outside to catch the action.

His entire family sat sprawled in front of him, and Brent had to accept that, as much as he loved all of them, none of them belonged to him.

He would never truly *know* any of them. Not fully. Not completely. Not every corner of every shelf in their brains.

But that didn't change how much he loved them.

Oliver walked to the edge of the blanket and sighed, sagging his shoulders. "I did my best, but you'll want to throw the car seat cover in the laundry when we get home. Or in the trash. Shoot, maybe burn the whole car."

"I'll try the laundry first," Eliza laughed. She waved Oliver on. "Come on, sit down. You've earned it."

Brent hopped up quickly. "Here, have my spot. I need to get back to my lady, anyway."

He waved to his sister and Oliver and made his way back over to Rose. She looked over as he approached and grinned, unable to help herself.

"Did you miss me or something?" Brent asked, sitting down and reaching into the cooler for a soda.

Rose curled into his side. "Always. Especially when I have something to tell you."

"Uh-oh." Brent was mostly teasing, but his heart rate did pick up slightly. "What is it?"

Someone from the movie set came out onto the front porch and waved their arms, directing everyone to quiet down for a minute.

"Quiet on set!" Sara hissed, holding her finger in front of her lips and narrowing her eyes at everyone.

Oliver wrangled the kids, and Rose dropped her voice but continued. "Things have been kind of weird this week. With your mom and Dominic staying with us. And you and your mom having a whole... *thing.*"

"I'm sorry about that," Brent interrupted. "I wanted to tell you, but—"

"No, it isn't that. It's okay that you don't tell me. Really."

"Really? Because if it does bother you, I'll tell you. I trust you not to tell anyone. It's just that it's my mom's story and—"

Rose interrupted him again, laying a hand over his heart. "I mean it. This isn't about you and your mom, okay? I'm not upset about that."

"Then what is it about?"

Now, the nerves Brent had joked about before were even less of a joke. His stomach was twisted in knots.

Rose sighed and sat up, crossing her legs and folding her hands in her lap. "Well, the night you came back from the beach, we talked."

"We did," Brent agreed.

"And I told you that people could keep secrets from each other. Even people who loved each other."

"You did," Brent said again. He felt silly echoing her, but it helped him keep track of what Rose was saying.

And he had a feeling he would really want to keep track of what she was saying.

Her expression was suddenly deadly serious. She pulled her lower lip into her mouth, chewing on it between her words.

"And I've been keeping a secret from you."

"You have...?" The two words came out half as a statement, half as a question.

Brent's mind immediately spun into a dozen different possibilities.

Was Rose sick?

Was she leaving him?

Had she lost her job?

Was something wrong with Susanna?

Rose must have seen the panic in his eyes, because she leaned forward and grabbed his hand, holding it between her own. "Relax, crazy. It's a good secret."

"A good secret?" Brent took a deep breath and closed his eyes. "You coulda led with that. You scared me."

"Sorry," she laughed, folding her fingers between his. "I wasn't trying to."

Brent opened his eyes and urged her on. "Okay. Let's hear it. What's the secret?"

Rose pressed her pink lips together, suppressing a smile, and then dragged his hand towards her. Closer and closer—until it was resting over her stomach.

Then, she stared up at him. Blinking. Waiting.

"What?" he asked, the early stages of realization dawning over him. He looked down at his hand on her stomach.

At Rose's hand pressed over his.

At his and hers, hers and his, back and forth until he wasn't sure where one ended and the other began.

"Is this your way of telling me...?"

Her fingers were shaking. She nodded. "Brent, I'm pregnant."

Immediately, the smile she'd been trying to bite down beamed out of her. Even brighter than the daylight lights the film crew had set up.

"Are you serious?"

"Very," she said. "I've been to the doctor to confirm it and everything."

When Brent stared at her, eyes wide, wordless, Rose took over speaking.

"We weren't planning this," she stammered. "So, I wanted to make sure I was positively positive before I told you. No sense scaring you for nothing."

"Scaring me?" he repeated.

Was he scared?

Yes. Yes, he was. That was easy to tell straight away.

But he was also thrilled. Beyond thrilled—ecstatic.

"This is incredible news," he said. "The best surprise I've ever had."

"Really?" Rose's eyes were misty and she was blinking to beat back the tears. "Because I know we didn't really talk about this. And you were just saying you have catching up to do as a dad. But you're so great with Susanna. She loves you. And I know you'll be a great father. So I'm just saying—"

Brent leaned forward and kissed Rose, cutting her anxious ramble short. He could feel her smiling against his lips.

"I'm excited. I swear. And only a little bit nervous."

"I think that's normal," she whispered. "I am, too."

He kissed her again because it seemed like the only right thing to do.

"Do you want to tell everyone? When we can talk above a whisper again, of course," she said when they broke apart, eyeing the crew member who was still standing on the porch, making sure everyone stayed quiet. "Your whole family is here, so it would be a good time."

Brent looked around at his family again.

Sara and Joey had moseyed on over to see Eliza and Oliver. Sara was holding Summer while Joey and Oliver stood under a nearby tree, each holding a beer.

Holly was playing a game of Silent Tag with the kids in the back corner of the lawn furthest from the filming area.

When Brent looked back to Rose, he shook his head. "No. Let's wait."

"You want to?" she asked. "It's completely up to you. I'm fine either way."

He nodded, even more sure. "I'm positive. We'll all be together plenty of times. We can tell them later. For now, let's keep it our little secret."

"All clear!" the crew member on the porch called.

Immediately, the yard burst into noise. The little girls screamed like they'd been holding in the noise for a lifetime. Even Sara immediately coughed into her elbow a few times, waking up Summer, who promptly began to cry.

It was instant chaos. Brent couldn't help but laugh.

Rose grinned and looked down at her stomach where Brent's hand was still resting. She rubbed her thumb over the back of his hand.

"Yeah," she murmured happily. "Our little secret."

From the bottom of my heart, thank you for reading NO SECRET LIKE NANTUCKET! I hope that you enjoyed another summer in Nantucket with the Benson family.

Be sure to check out the next installment of their saga, NO FOREVER LIKE NANTUCKET. **Click here to check it out!**

JOIN MY MAILING LIST!

Click the link below to join my mailing list and receive updates, freebies, release announcements, and more!

JOIN HERE:

https://sendfox.com/lp/19y8p3

ALSO BY GRACE PALMER

Sweet Island Inn

No Home Like Nantucket (Book 1)

No Beach Like Nantucket (Book 2)

No Wedding Like Nantucket (Book 3)

No Love Like Nantucket (Book 4)

No Secret Like Nantucket (Book 5)

No Forever Like Nantucket (Book 6)

No Summer Like Nantucket (Book 7) (coming soon!)

Willow Beach Inn

Just South of Paradise (Book 1)

Just South of Perfect (Book 2)

Just South of Sunrise (Book 3)

Just South of Christmas (Book 4)

Made in the USA
Las Vegas, NV
10 July 2021